Sea Of Grass

Kate Sweeney

SEA OF GRASS
© 2010 BY KATE SWEENEY

ISBN 13: 978-1-935216-15-5

First Printing: 2010

This Trade Paperback Is Published By
Intaglio Publications
Walker, LA USA
WWW.INTAGLIOPUB.COM

CREDITS

EXECUTIVE EDITOR: TARA YOUNG
COVER DESIGN BY TIGER GRAPHICS

ACKNOWLEDGMENTS

As always, many thanks to my editor, Tara Young, who does a wonderful job.

And to my beta readers on *Sea of Grass*, Maureen and Jule, whom I trust implicitly.

To my partner in crime at Intaglio, Sheri Payton. She is loyal, steadfast, and a little odd. We work well together.

Prologue

Professor Rawlins stood by the open window and gazed at the blue California sky. Far from Montana, he thought as he chomped on a piece of grass. He turned back into the empty classroom and smiled. There was Lenore standing in the doorway. She brushed the silver hair from her forehead and adjusted the wicker basket she held on her arm.

"What in the world are you doing here?" he asked his wife.

Lenore shook her head, walked into the classroom, and placed the basket on his desk. "I knew you wouldn't stop to eat." She plucked the thick blade of grass out of his mouth and kissed him soundly on the lips. "Working day and night on that grass seed." She shook her head. "Why, I don't know. Your father's ranch has a wonderful pasture for the cattle."

"I know, but it won't last forever. It's the twentieth century, Nore, and I'm trying to figure a way for Dad to keep the ranch."

Lenore pushed him into his chair and placed a napkin in his lap. "It's 1935 and cattle ranching may soon be a thing of the past, Jeremiah. You Rawlinses will have to face that one day."

"I know that, you know that, but try telling it to my father. I'm not the rancher, he is."

"As well we both know. He's a stubborn one," Lenore said and opened the thermos. "Hot soup."

"I didn't think I was hungry." He rubbed his hands together when Lenore produced the cold fried chicken. "I don't have another class for an hour."

"Good, this will give you time to eat." She filled his plate, then hers. "I don't think the agriculture department of Cal will mind if I join you."

Jeremiah waved her off as he ate his chicken leg. "I've got tenure. I've been here for nearly twenty years, and my papers have brought enough notoriety to this college. I think they can handle me having lunch with my wife."

After a few minutes of eating and talking of their children, Lenore asked, "So tell me. How is your research coming?"

Jeremiah wiped his mouth with the napkin and shrugged. "I think I've done it. That blade of grass you took was the product of all my work."

Lenore raised an eyebrow. "How did it taste?"

He laughed. "Like grass. It reminded me of the ranch and my childhood." He gazed out the window once again, thinking of Montana and the Double R Ranch.

"Sweetie, I know you miss the ranch, but you make a better professor than a rancher."

He looked back at his wife and grudgingly agreed. "My brothers and even my sister are better at it."

Lenore stood and walked over to Jeremiah, who looked up and smiled. She cupped his weathered face and kissed him. "Your work here is just as important as working on the ranch. You'll find a way to save the land and the ranch, Professor Rawlins." She looked on his desk and saw a thick leather-bound notebook. "What is this?" She picked it up and leafed through it.

"I was working on my memoirs, you know, the family and the ranch. Someday, my son or a grandchild might find it useful." He kissed his wife and pulled her onto his lap. They both looked out at the sky. "Maybe they'll love the Bitterroots and the land as we have…"

Lenore looked into his eyes. "And the sea of grass you worked hard to protect for them."

Chapter 1

Professor Rawlins pushed the window open and took a deep breath of California air. Gazing at the clear blue sky, she thought how much it was like Montana, just not as open. She missed it, missed the Bitterroot Mountains, missed the ranch, and missed her father.

"Professor Rawlins?"

She turned to see her assistant. "I've told you before, Bill, call me Tess."

"Sorry, Tess. I got the results from our tests. They look good. I think between you and Dr. Spellman, you're on your way."

"I hope so." She took the folder out of his hand. "Has Dr. Spellman seen it?"

"Not yet. I wanted you to see them first."

They turned around when someone knocked on the classroom door. Tess grinned and Bill grunted, which Tess heard.

Melanie Davis stood in the doorway. She grinned and ignored Bill, who looked as though he couldn't care less. He took the folder out of Tess's hand. "I'll just take this to Dr. Spellman." He looked at Melanie. "Nice to see you, Melanie."

"That's Professor Davis to you," she said, not looking at him as he passed. "Close the door, Bill."

He did with what Tess knew was with a little more force than necessary.

"You need a new assistant," Melanie said, walking toward Tess.

"The ag department would be lost without him, Mel."

Mel rolled her eyes. "I can find six people who could do his job."

Tess shook her head. "Thank you, but I'll take care of my department, you take care of…" She stopped and grinned. "What department was that again?"

Mel narrowed her eyes. "Communications."

"Ah yes, the media," Tess said, laughing at the irritated look on her lover's face. She pulled Mel into her arms. "Don't pout."

Mel reached up and slid her fingertips against Tess's lips. "You like my pout."

"True," Tess said and kissed her fingers.

"And why don't you let your hair grow longer as I asked? You have such wonderful thick blond hair, and I want to run my fingers through it."

"I don't like my hair long."

"I do," Mel whispered in her ear.

Tess shivered when she felt Mel's fingers rake through her hair. She stepped back with a nervous laugh. "Okay, that's enough of that. I don't want to lose my tenure." She backed away to her desk. When Mel followed, Tess put her hand up. "Close enough, youngster."

Mel stopped and folded her arms across her chest. "Youngster? You're not old, Tess."

"Older than you."

"I'm thirty-four. You look older because you spent too much time in the sun on that dude ranch or whatever you call it."

"It's not a dude ranch, it's a cattle ranch," Tess said. "And it's been in my family since the 1880s. So have some respect, woman, you city slicker from Los Angeles."

Mel struck a thoughtful pose. "Yes, I am and I like it that way."

Tess heard the challenging tone in Mel's voice; it had been this way since they met. Mel was a city mouse—Tess a country mouse. Although since her brother's death two years earlier, Tess had stayed at UC-Berkeley after the school year was over. She told herself she was needed for the research the agriculture department was doing, but if she were honest, it was too difficult to go back to Montana and the ranch. She felt guilty leaving her father to cope with the day-to-day business for the last two years. Though she

4

loved the ranch, there were times she wished her father would sell it.

"Hey."

Broken from her reverie, Tess looked up to see Mel smiling slightly. "You were miles away."

Tess leaned against her desk and let out a sigh. "I was thinking about the ranch and my father." She could practically feel Mel's body tense.

"You're not thinking of canceling our summer trip, are you?"

"No, no," Tess said quickly.

"Because you need a break and God knows so do I."

Tess raised an eyebrow. Melanie was a first-year professor, fresh out of grad school. She taught communications and had an average two classes per semester. "I know, don't worry."

"Good," Mel said in a low voice. "I'm looking forward to a month in Hawaii doing nothing but making love to you."

"I—" The cell phone buzzing in her pocket stopped her. Tess looked at the caller ID and frowned. "It's Maria," she said, almost to herself. Mel wasn't listening; she groaned as she walked away from Tess, who flipped the phone open. "Hey, Maria."

"Hello, Tess."

Tess instantly heard the serious tone. "What's wrong?"

There was a moment's hesitation in her voice. "It's your father. It's nothing major."

Tess sat at her desk. "Is he all right?"

"You know I would never speak of this. Your father is a proud man."

"Please tell me." Tess could feel her heart pounding in her chest. "And don't use your Cherokee intuition." Tess heard the soft laugh and smiled.

"He's doing too much on the ranch. There's much going on here, and he doesn't want to worry you."

"What's going on?"

"I will tell you one name and you will understand…"

"Telford," Tess said in disgust.

"Yes."

5

"He's still after Dad to sell the north pasture. The fat fucker," Tess mumbled, but she heard the soft laugh. "Sorry."

"It's okay. We all feel the same." Again Tess heard the hesitation. "I'm afraid for his heart. He needs you. It has been a hard winter. It will be spring soon and there's much to do."

"What about Chuck? He's still foreman…"

"He needs you. He missed you at Christmas."

Both listened to the silence until Maria spoke. "You've been away too long."

Tess heard the truth and closed her eyes. She had been away from Montana, the ranch, and her father on and off for five years now. And since her brother's death, nothing seemed to matter much.

"Tess?"

"I'm here, Maria. Look, I can get Professor Pruitt to take over till the end of the year. I'll get things in order and be home in a week."

"Thank you."

"It's okay. Please take care of him. And don't let Telford anywhere near him."

"I won't. Goodbye, my child."

"Goodbye, Maria."

She closed the phone and smiled when she heard "my child." It was what Maria always called her. Tess's mother died when she a teenager, and it was Maria, the cook at the ranch, who took Tess and Stephen under her wing. Maria Hightower was a kind, wise woman of Cherokee descent who boasted of her lineage to a great chief. Tess suddenly realized how much she missed all of them.

"So Hawaii is out?"

Tess had forgotten Mel was there and winced. "Uh, yeah. I'm sorry, Mel. It's my father. He's doing too much on the ranch and Maria is afraid. I don't blame her."

Mel did not hide her disappointment. "We've had this vacation planned for three months. We're locked in."

"You can still go." Tess looked her in the eye. "I'm going home for the spring and summer. I should have been there for Christmas."

"And now you're going to feel guilty about that."

"Please don't start the psychoanalysis."

Mel straightened her back and glared at Tess, who raised an eyebrow. "Don't give me that withering glare. I'm sorry this has changed our plans, but I'm sure you will still go to Hawaii."

"Yes, I will. I need a vacation and I'm going to take it."

She marched past Tess, who mumbled, "Yes, it's taxing teaching How To Be An Anchorwoman 101. Don't forget the lip gloss." She cringed when she heard the door slam.

Alone in her classroom, Tess walked over to the window and gazed once again at the blue cloudless California sky. Smiling, she remembered her childhood on the ranch. She remembered her family and warm summer days.

"Dad, will ya tell Tess to get off me?" Steve complained from the ground. Tess was sitting on him, laughing as she had him pinned.

Just then, their mother came out with the laundry. "Elizabeth Anne!" she scolded, and Tess winced.

"You're in trouble now," Steve whispered and Tess glared down at him. "Now get off me, ya heifer." He tried to buck her off.

"Tess, get off your brother and be a lady, for chrissakes," her father called from the stable. "Both of you, quit your clowning. Steve, clean the stable and, Tess, get the hay from the barn," he ordered, and both youngsters grumbled as Tess stood and offered her hand to her little brother. "Idiot children, you get that from your mother's side of the family."

Steve took the offering, then pulled her down and pinned her to the ground. Tess laughed as he narrowed his eyes at her. "You know now what has to be done, don't you, Elizabeth Anne?" he said, and Tess laughed, trying to buck him off.

"Don't you dare, Steve! Mom!" Tess called out while laughing.

Jed looked over to see Emily, his wife, hanging the clothes on the line and yanking the clothespin out of her mouth. "You asked for that, missy... Don't start something you can't finish," she reminded her.

"Thanks!" Tess called out, then looked up at Steve.

"Beg me…"

"No!"

"Say it," he warned and gathered the spit in his mouth. Tess's eyes widened.

Jed chuckled from the stable door.

"Don't you dare! Dad!" Tess called helplessly.

Jed shook his head. "You're on your own, Tess."

"Jed Rawlins! You're as bad as they are!" Emily exclaimed.

"Say it." Steve leaned over her.

Tess laughed and tried to wriggle out. "Okay, okay!" She hated herself for not being stronger. Steve sported an evil brotherly grin and waited. She felt him slack off for just a second, which was all she needed. "Ha!" she yelled and bucked him off.

"Darn it!" he said as Tess flipped him over and took off toward the stable.

"Elizabeth Anne!" Emily yelled, and Tess stopped dead in her tracks with Steve nearly knocking her over. "Both of you, stop the horseplay and get that stable cleaned," she said seriously as she lifted the heavy basket.

Steve ran up and gently took it from her. "Sorry, Mom. Let me get that."

Tess rolled her eyes and mimicked Steve. She turned to see her father standing in the doorway

Jed raised an eyebrow and handed her the pitchfork, then jerked his thumb toward the stable. Tess grumbled as she took the pitchfork.

She had a great childhood and a good relationship with Steve, who was more suited for life on the ranch. Oh, Tess loved it; she knew that. How could anyone be under that big Montana sky and not love it? But as she grew older, Tess wanted something more. Tess loved to hear her great-uncle talk about teaching. She was just a child, and Jeremiah was an old man but so soft-spoken and kind. She fell in love with the idea of traveling and becoming a teacher. So when the time came, off to school she went and never looked back.

Suddenly, a pang of regret rippled through her. Tess angrily rubbed her forehead, trying to dismiss the guilt she still harbored. Maybe going home was what she needed.

Chapter 2

Tess took Maria's advice and took the train from Missoula to her hometown of Silverhill. When Tess saw the old engine and three cars, she smiled and shook her head. Maria was a sentimental Cherokee. As she boarded the train, she heard someone call her name.

"Rick?" she asked. "My God, how long has it been?"

Rick Cumberland grinned; he jumped down from the engine car and wrapped his arms around her. "Holy moly, Tess. I haven't seen you in at least six years if not more." He held her at arm's length. "Still a looker, for an, um, older woman."

Tess laughed and playfully pushed him away. "You're still an idiot, and you're losing your hair."

Rick laughed along. "So you're back. For good?"

Tess shrugged and explained her conversation with Maria. Rick's smile faded as he listened. "Telford's trying to pick up all the land he can get his money-grubbing hands on, and your dad is one of the last holdouts. The other ranchers are worried. You know how hard it is keeping a ranch going."

"I know. It's been a struggle since Dad took it over in the fifties."

"Yep. And almost sixty years later, it's still the same." He then nudged her shoulder. "You'd better come up with something from all that fancy college learnin'."

Tess glared playfully as he laughed. "So what's the deal with the old train?" She pulled her coat around her. It was mid-March, and though spring was just around the corner, it was still cold. She remembered the brutality of a Montana winter.

"It was the city council's idea to bring some tourists in. It runs from Missoula all the way to Wyoming and Yellowstone. Ya know, see the Old West. I'm the engineer."

"Gotcha. It's not a bad idea." She looked around and nodded.

"I can see the wheels turning under that blond hair," Rick said. "C'mon, get on board. I'll stop by the ranch later and see ya."

Tess kissed his check, then boarded the train.

"Hey," he called as he walked back to the engine. "I'm still not married."

Tess laughed and called back, "I'm still gay."

Rick let out a laugh and waved as he boarded the engine car.

Tess settled back by a window seat; there were plenty to choose from. Winter was still in the air, and patches of snow dotted the landscape. Tess figured the only passengers were probably on their way to Jackson Hole to ski for the last time before spring. Her body swayed with the rhythmic *clickity-clack* of the train. She chuckled to herself, feeling as though she were transported back in time to the Old West. Maybe the council had a good idea to revive this train. Rick thought so.

She smiled again thinking of Rick. He was Stephen's good friend. They all grew up together, and although Stephen was the youngest, he fit right in. It was probably because he was an old soul. That's what her mother would say. Stephen took to riding, roping, and ranching at a very early age. Her parents were glad to see it. Tess did, as well, but it was Stephen who was the golden child in this aspect. The survival of the Double R was strictly in Stephen's capable hands. It was fine with Tess; this afforded her a chance to go to college with no regrets.

She gazed out the window and watched the last snow of winter covering the grassland whisk by. Underneath that snow was what her father, Jed Rawlins, and the other ranchers fought so hard for. Tess wondered if she could ever feel that for something—or someone.

Maybe she was destined to be single. She put her head back and let out a thoughtful sigh. Perhaps she was too old. Everyone seemed so young at Cal. Hell, she thought, I'm only forty-nine.

Mel's face flashed through her mind. Mel was thirty-four, but a very young thirty-four. "Or maybe I'm just an old forty-nine," Tess whispered.

This might be a good spring and summer for her; maybe she could do some soul-searching and help her father. God, I haven't been on a horse in six years, she thought, let alone try roping a calf again. "Good God. I may do more harm than good."

Two hours later, the train pulled into Silverhill. Tess couldn't help but grin when she saw the old depot just outside of town. She got off the train with the few passengers who were oohing and ahhing over the quaint western town. As they gathered their skis, Tess was curious.

"Excuse me," she said to one. "Are you staying in Silverhill?"

The woman nodded. "Yes, we saw it when we booked our ski trip. So we thought we would stay over, then take the train down to Jackson Hole for a last ski for the year. Are you on vacation?"

"No, I live here. I was just curious."

The couple nodded and scurried off the train. Tess followed and grinned when she saw the Jeep. How that thing still ran, she would never know. And there stood Chuck Edwards with his big grin and his old cowboy hat pulled down over his brow, protecting him from the wind. He looked the same, but as she neared, she saw how he had aged when he took off his hat. His hair now was more salt than pepper and his face more weathered.

"My God, Tess!" He put his hat back on and threw his arms around her waist and lifted her off the ground, though Tess heard his deep groan. "You haven't changed at all."

"Put me down before you rupture something, Chuck. I've put on a few pounds sitting in a classroom."

He obeyed and stepped back, then kissed her on the cheek. "You look just fine, Tess. C'mon, let's get out of this wind."

As they drove through town, Tess eagerly looked out the window. "It's still the same."

"Nothing changes around here, you should know that by now," he said, watching the road. "I was glad when Maria told me you were coming back."

"How's Dad?" she asked, watching his face. She could always tell when Chuck was lying. He'd frown and bite at his bottom lip.

"He's okay," he said as he chewed his lip.

"Liar. Tell me the truth."

Chuck glanced at her and grinned. "Still the same smartass. Like your mother."

"Yes, I am. Now tell me."

Chuck took a deep breath and let it out slowly, as if preparing Tess, who felt a sick feeling deep in her stomach as she waited.

"He's doing too much, and he's getting on. He's too old for the day to day, but you know how stubborn he is. And now with Telford breathing down his neck."

"That fat fucker," Tess said angrily and blushed when Chuck laughed.

"Watch that, you know how your dad hates it when you curse. Doesn't matter if you're an old professor."

"Shut up. Has he been to the doctor?"

"You know him. Maria had to threaten him with a frying pan. But Doc came out to have a look. He told him to take it easy and get some help on the ranch."

Tess looked at Chuck again. "Why is he doing too much?"

Chuck shifted uncomfortably behind the wheel. "We lost a few hands. Telford got them all convinced they'd be out of a job if they stuck around. And you know how hard these winters are. Money talks."

"So who do we have left?"

"Me, Stan, and Luke," he said. "And you."

Tess gave him an incredulous look. "Me?"

"Well, yeah."

"Listen to me. I haven't been on a horse in years. I haven't had anything to do with the ranch in almost six years. I'll help out with the finances and see what…"

"It don't matter how long it's been."

Tess rubbed her temples and groaned. The idea of riding the range and taking care of the cattle was absurd. Her ass was killing her already just at the thought of it.

Chuck seemed to sense her irritability and laughed. He reached over and patted her knee. "You'll be fine." He squeezed her knee a few times. "Hmm, you may need to firm up those thighs after all."

Tess shot him an angry glare as he smiled sheepishly. They both broke into a fit of laughter. "My thighs are the least of our problems."

Chuck pulled onto the property. The long road leading to the range went on for miles. Tess felt that anxious, pulling sensation in her stomach when she saw the fence and the gate leading to her home. She looked up to see "Double R Ranch" etched in the log timbers that framed the wooden gate.

"I'm glad you're home, Tess."

"Me too."

As Chuck pulled up to the house, he honked the horn a few times. In a moment, her father walked onto the front porch. He was smiling and waving.

"God, Chuck...." Tess whispered.

"I know. Don't let him see that concerned look on your face."

Tess nodded and smiled as she waved. Jed Rawlins ambled down the porch steps as Tess jumped out and hugged him fiercely around the neck. "Dad, it's so good to see you."

"Oh, Tess, it's good to see you, sweetie. I've missed you."

Tess pulled back and wiped the tears from her cheeks, seeing her father do the same.

"C'mon, let's get out of this weather. Maria made stew and—"

"Biscuits." Tess licked her lips. "I can taste them already."

"Remember those thighs," Chuck whispered in her ear as he passed.

Tess was about to retaliate when she saw Maria standing at the front door. "Wipe your boots, Chuck." She then opened her arms; Tess quickly mounted the steps and wrapped her arms around Maria. "Oh, child, it's so good to see you. I've missed you."

"So have I, Maria."

"You've lost weight," Maria said.

Tess stuck her tongue out at Chuck, who laughed and struggled out of his heavy coat.

Jed put his arm around her and kissed her check. "I'm starved.

Now let's eat and you can tell us all about California and you being a big important professor."

They sat around the kitchen table as Maria served the meal. "Nothing has changed." Tess looked around the kitchen. It was the same as when she was a child.

The kitchen was quite large, and in those days, the ranch hands used to eat at this table while Tess and her family ate in the dining room. Emily would make the meals for all of them.

When Tess was a child, she remembered how her mother was constantly at the stove cooking for ten ranch hands and the family. How she did that, Tess never knew, and she did it with no complaining. She seemed to love to cook for so many people, three meals a day. Or perhaps it was just the way of life, and you did what you had to do because Tess knew her mother loved the ranch as much as her father did.

"Tess?"

Tess looked up to see her father grinning. "You didn't hear a word I said."

"Oh, sorry, Dad. I was just thinking about Mom. What did you say?" She took another mouthful of stew and moaned happily.

"I said I was so happy when Maria said you called and you were coming home for your summer." He reached over and took another biscuit off the plate.

Tess glanced at Maria and Chuck, seeing their pleading looks. "I've been away too long. It was time I came home for a while."

"So you'll stay on?" he asked. Tess heard the hopeful tone. "I mean till your classes start again in the fall?"

Tess reached over and took his hand. "Yes, Dad."

"Well, the weather is clearing," Chuck said and drank his coffee. "Tomorrow you can take a ride and see the herd. We'll need to move the fences day after tomorrow."

Tess nodded and took another biscuit. "You're still bale feeding?"

Chuck and Jed exchanged happy glances. "What else?" Jed asked.

"I don't know. We might try swath grazing. How was the summer hay? Are you still getting it from Bob? We really should

15

have our own hay."

"Bob has been very good to us. And buying the hay from him is no hardship."

"I understand, but we have to think of the future."

Jed leaned over and placed his hand on Tess's forearm. "If surviving means putting another rancher and friend out of business, then we're no better than Warren Telford."

"Okay, we'll think of something."

"Well, I'm stuffed," Chuck announced as he patted his stomach.

"Me too," Tess said. "Maria, you still make the lightest biscuits in Montana."

"That's only because you've spent so much time in California."

Jed laughed, then regarded Tess. "I'm so proud of you."

Tess cocked her head. "Why?"

"Because you followed your heart. Just like Uncle Jeremiah did. And your mother would be just as proud of you knowing you went to the same university."

Tess saw the tears well in his eyes. She stood and kissed the top of his head. "I'm going to change and go out to the stable. Do you think Stella remembers me?"

Jed grunted. "That ole horse won't let anyone else near her. Give me a minute. I'll go with you."

"It's so cold, Jed," Maria said.

"I'm fine. No fussing." Jed walked out of the kitchen. "Your room is all set for you, Tess."

Tess walked down the hall to her room. As with everything else, nothing had changed. The huge four-poster bed still looked inviting; she suddenly realized how exhausted she was. She opened the closet and grinned when she saw her old black cowboy hat hanging on the peg and her deerskin winter coat. "God, I hope the damned thing fits."

She was glad she at least had a good pair of boots, broken in just right, though she spied the old comfortable-looking pair on the floor of the closet. She reverently took the hat and placed it on her head, then took it off and worked the brim until it was just right. "Yep, nothing has changed." She looked at her reflection in the mirror, then slipped into the deerskin coat. "Thank God. A little snug and one more of Maria's biscuits…" she whispered and walked out.

"I've never seen the moon this bright." Tess sighed as she led the mare into the stable.

Jed lifted a pile of loose hay with the pitchfork and tossed it into the stall with a grunt. "You've said that about every moon since you were a little girl," he reminded her.

She pulled a childish face. "Well, it's true," she countered as she examined the mare. Tess gave her a playful slap on her rump. "You're in good shape, Stella." When she slapped at her flank, the horse gave a loud snort and slowly loped into the stall. "Good girl, sleep tight. I missed you, too."

Tess blew into her cupped hands to warm them as she looked around for her father. She walked out of the stable and noticed him leaning against the fence post gazing at the moon.

She cuddled her deerskin coat around her, walked up next to him, and looked up into the night sky, as well.

"Hmm, you just might be right, Tess. It is a handsome moon tonight."

Tess noticed the touch of melancholy in his voice. She put her arm around him, took off her old beat-up cowboy hat, and laid her head on his strong shoulder.

"I'm so glad you're here."

"You said that already. Now how are the cattle?"

"All settled. This has been a mild winter. I don't think we lost too many."

"We'll be fine," she assured him with a hearty hug. "And if we aren't, I've got a few irons in the fire. We'll make it one way or the other."

Jed Rawlins glanced at her. "You are a beauty. You've got the golden hair and piercing blue eyes like your mother. You're a fine catch."

Tess snorted and leaned against the fence post. They stood in comfortable silence for a moment or two before Jed spoke.

17

"You're the next heir to the Rawlins dynasty passed down from my grandfather to my father and to me. This will all be yours someday. I hope there's…"

Tess kissed his cheek to quiet him. "You're an old softy, Jed Rawlins," she countered happily. "We will make it. They won't take the Double R from us, not while I have a breath in me."

He nodded. "I know you'd prefer teaching about the land, but I'm sure you'll fight to your last breath and so will I."

"I hope it won't come to that." Tess turned to face him.

"You and me both."

"Does Telford know I'm home?"

"Sweetie, I'm sure he does."

"Well, maybe tomorrow I'll take a drive into town."

"You still love to poke the tiger in the cage, don't ya?" he asked as they made their way back to the house.

"What? I'm home and I want to see the town. What's wrong with that?"

"And just happen to run into Warren Telford?"

Tess shrugged. "It's a small town."

"And it's going to get smaller."

Chapter 3

"So she's back," Telford said. He sat behind his big desk, puffing on his cigar. "I wonder why."

"I have no idea, but you'll never get them to sell, Mr. Telford," Ed Chambers said as he took off his hat and slapped it on his thigh. "Tess Rawlins will die first."

Telford snorted. "Don't tease, Ed, they'll sell. Once the others see the Double R go under, they'll all follow suit, you watch."

Ed shook his head. "I don't know, Mr. Telford. I've worked for you for many years, and in all that time, the Rawlins family has never wavered. There's no love lost between Jed Rawlins and you, I know that. He'll never sell, and Tess will never allow it, but I hope you're right."

"I'm right. I'm always right where money is concerned."

A woman poked her head in the office, interrupting them. "Mr. Collins is on line two for you, Mr. Telford."

The old man grinned and nodded as he picked up the phone, putting it on speaker. "Go ahead, Collins. Ed's here. What have you got?"

"Sorry, there's nothing on Tess or Jed Rawlins. They're squeaky clean. If you want this land, you'll have to find another way. Well, you've known him all your life. Jed was in the Army for four years. He married Emily Richardson, who died from cancer. They had two children. The youngest, Stephen, died two years ago, an apparent accident—thrown from a horse."

Ed glanced at Telford, who was just gazing out the window, puffing on his cigar like a steam engine.

"Tess graduated from University of California, Berkley, with two degrees—agriculture and business. Got her PhD. She's the brains behind this, even though she's been in California for the most part. She came back yesterday, as you know."

Ed shook his head. "She's the brawn, as well. She's as strong as a fricking ox."

Telford grunted. "That was years ago. We all grow older. Even Tess Rawlins. She has to be close to fifty, and she's a woman not a man. As much as she'd like to think she is," he added with disgust.

"She'll probably take over the day to day on the ranch and the finances. And if we're not careful, she'll make the Double R once again the wealthiest ranch in this part of Montana."

"Shit," he muttered.

"Shit is right. We both know Tess Rawlins. She was as tough as the boys were. Wouldn't take shit from anybody. When her brother died—" He stopped abruptly when Telford shot him a venomous glare.

"She's been a thorn in my side since she learned to speak."

"What do you want me to do, Mr. Telford? It's your money," Collins said.

"Keep digging. Everybody has something to hide, Collins— even the sacred Rawlinses," he spat and angrily disconnected the line.

Ed winced at the vehemence.

"Those fucking Rawlinses..." Telford snarled, then took a deep breath. "Keep your eyes open, Ed. I want that land!"

Ed nodded and walked out.

Warren Telford narrowed his eyes as he looked out of his big second-floor office window. Through the blinds, he saw her—her tall figure confidently walking out of Tom's feed store. She wore her old black cowboy hat pulled low over her eyes. Though she looked like she put on a few pounds, her Levi's hugged her hips nicely, he thought. All that time in the classroom. He wished Tess Rawlins had stayed in California.

He watched Tess in deep conversation as she spoke to Tom, who nodded in agreement. After shaking hands as if sealing a bargain, she slapped Tom on the back and slid into the old Jeep. Telford nearly growled at the Double R Ranch stenciled on the back.

Women, he thought angrily. It started with the grandmother, who saved the ranch during World War II and Korea, selling their beef to the government at a ridiculous low price. Eleanor Roosevelt was to blame. She got them all fired up—going to college, starting their own businesses, getting in the way.

"God, I hate that family," he hissed as he watched the big station wagon drive through town.

Telford remembered all the stories about how the Rawlins family kept the ranchers in the area safe from foreclosure for decades. It's still the same. They all love the damned Rawlinses, he thought. Tom and the others didn't buy their supplies from the big stores in Helena or Missoula. Single-handedly, the Rawlinses kept Emerson's Feed and Grain in Silverhill in business. He couldn't keep up with their orders. Now Tom was buying from the smaller stores, getting distributor pricing and passing the savings along to the Double R Ranch.

That was the old man's idea. Tess Rawlins kept it up until she left for college. Now she's back. Damn that woman, he thought angrily. Bob Hastings followed. His small farm supplied the Rawlinses with winter hay, and he now bought from Tom. Telford had to be careful. The other small ranchers from Three Forks and the surrounding area would catch on, as well, then what would happen to his plans for the plush resorts he was going to build on all that land?

God, I hate that family, he thought again, and slammed the blinds closed.

As Tess pulled through the entrance of the Double R, she smiled as she looked around at the landscape. Settled at the foot of the Bitterroot Mountains, Silverhill, Montana, was a nice quiet town.

Since most of the men went off to war in 1941 and a good many had not come back, it had seen some changes. Some farms went under back in the 1930s with the Depression, which Warren Telford's family gobbled up, the money-grubbing bastards, she thought angrily. Roosevelt and his New Deal helped some back then. She vaguely remembered her mother and father retelling family stories of how the Rawlins clan would sit in the kitchen listening to the radio and Roosevelt's Fireside Chats.

With the war ending, the economy came back. Then Korea happened, and her family struggled all over again to keep the ranch going. With the war over, Silverhill boomed along with everything else in the fifties. Those ranchers and farmers who stuck it out through two wars were starting to thrive once again. The Double R was one of them. And now, though cattle ranching was truly a way of life that was nearly extinct, the Rawlins family was still trying to hang on, and every member did his or her part.

As a young woman, Tess felt the responsibility and was torn between staying on the ranch and going to college. She didn't want to leave for college, but she knew the world was changing and she needed to change with it or straggle behind. She smiled openly, remembering her mother's words on her graduation day from high school—

"Elizabeth Rawlins, you are a smart young woman. Don't depend on anyone for your happiness. Go out in the world and find your life and your love. This world is changing, women are no longer doing what my generation has done. Find your own way—your own life. Then you'll be ready for someone…Promise me, Elizabeth. You'll never be ready for someone if you're not sure of yourself and your life."

Her mother died soon after Tess started college. She was going to come home and take care of Jed and Stephen, but her mother's words drummed in her brain. So she stayed and learned about the soil, about the land; she learned how to keep the Double R for her father just as her great-uncle had done. When she graduated, she knew she had kept her promise to her mother. She was ready…

Tess shut off the engine and got out of the Jeep. It was a bright clear morning. The snow was nearly gone off the grassland as the sun took hold, spreading its warmth across the pasture. Tess smiled, knowing in a few short weeks the brown pasture would be a bright, plush green. She pushed the heavy wooden gate open and walked toward the pasture. She crouched down and plucked a few blades. Tess remembered her father and her grandfather doing the same thing she was doing now, and she remembered them saying the same thing. "This is fine for the cattle. They'll grow strong and we'll get a handsome price for them in the fall." They were right then, but now? An anxious feeling hit the pit of her stomach at the thought of losing this ranch and the idea she could do nothing to stop it.

Her mother's words flashed through her mind—*"Be sure of yourself and your life..."*

Tess reverently held the brown grass between her fingers. "Be sure of myself, huh?" She looked around the sloping pasture. With the Bitterroots as a backdrop, it made for a majestic scene. The only thing Tess was sure of in her forty-nine years was she was a lesbian with a PhD in agriculture and failed relationships. She walked back and leaned against the fence post, chewing on the piece of grass.

She closed her eyes remembering her college experiences. Joan Danvers was her first. At the tender age of nineteen, Tess got her first taste of love...well, sex. It was remarkable. It beat kissing Billy behind the bleachers at the homecoming game. Hell, it beat anything young Tess had ever experienced.

It lasted through sophomore year, and Tess's heart broke when Joan graduated and left without a word. "What an idiot I was, acting like a love-struck fool, chasing her car." Tess laughed aloud as she shook her head.

An older and wiser Tess got over the pain quickly. Rhonda Monroe was her next "love" during her senior year. Tess actually thought Rhonnie might be the one. She had a chance to continue her education and get her master's, which she took. Rhonnie had other plans, however.

Rhonnie was a nice caring young woman who truly loved Tess but loved her work more. The research took Rhonnie to Europe and Asia. They kept in contact for a year, then as with most things, life got in the way, and the letters grew more infrequent. The last Tess heard, Rhonnie was happily living in Germany with a woman.

Over the years, there had been a few women, and finally Tess met Melanie. Tess was intrigued and captivated by Mel, who was fifteen years her junior. Though it was an enjoyable relationship with Mel, Tess knew not to make it more than it was—enjoyable and sexually satisfying, nothing more.

Tess laughed. "Oh, Mom. Ready for someone?" She tossed the blade of grass down and stretched, letting out a loud groan. "I sincerely doubt it."

Off in the distance, she saw her father. "Riding out on a cold morning like this," she said, shaking her head.

As he rode up to Tess, she looked up and waved. "What are you doing out here?" she asked as she stood.

Her father pulled the horse to a halt a few feet from her. Leaning on the pommel, he gave her a stern look. "I'll ask you the same thing. You're daydreaming again," he said with a mock glare. "Just like you did as a young girl."

Tess took off her hat and ran her arm across her brow. "I know. I stopped to take a look at the land and I got sidetracked," she said with a sheepish grin. "What are you doing out here?"

Jed sat tall in his saddle to stretch his back and looked around. "Doing the same thing, I guess. Telford called again this morning. God, he wants this land."

Tess grunted rudely. "Who gives a fu—?"

"Tess! You have a foul mouth, young woman." He sighed and his daughter grunted again.

"He's an asshole, Dad. He'll do anything to get the Double R. He's just angry because I got the better of him with Tom a few years ago." She laughed again. "Remember how red in the face he got when Tom told him we were buying exclusively from him?"

In spite of himself, Jed laughed along. "He almost blew a gasket. Thank God for your degree in business from that fancy college of yours."

"It was worth all the years of studying marketing and business just to see the look on his face. He wanted Tom's store, as well. The money-grubbing old fu…"

"Ah, ah, how in the hell are you ever gonna get married with a mouth like that?"

Tess heard the serious tone behind the laughter. She glared up at him. "I'm not getting married," she gently reminded him.

Jed took a long patient breath. Tess gave him a stern "don't start this again" look, and he let out a sigh of resignation.

"I want a grandson."

Tess gave him an incredulous look. "A grandson? Dad," Tess started. Her father groaned and hid his face in his hand. "I know I've been gone for a while, but did we forget one teeny tiny fact?"

Jed groaned more deeply and did not respond.

Tess hid her grin. "Dad?"

"What?"

She laughed openly then and walked up to his horse. Reaching up, she tugged at his arm until he looked down at her. "I love you, and you know I'd do anything for you."

Jed beamed. "Rick Cunningham is still single."

"It's Cumberland, and I'm still a lesbian."

Jed grimaced and shut his eyes. "Still? I thought maybe you'd have come to your senses." He opened his eyes and chuckled. "No, huh?"

"No." Tess smirked and put her hands on her hips. "You'll have to adopt."

She was pleasantly surprised when her father let out a hearty laugh. "So much like your mother. Just as sarcastic and independent as she was." He stopped and frowned for a moment. "Come to think of it, you're just like my mother. It's in the Rawlins women's blood, I suppose. God help us all."

"Yes, it's a curse. C'mon, get down from there. You look tired. Take the car home. I'll ride Daphne."

"You remember how?"

Tess glared as he slid off the mare and stretched his back. She gave him a stern look. "How long were you riding this morning?"

"Oh, hush. I'm fine. I can't stay off a horse for too long. You know that," he said seriously. "I remember the days when I'd ride the range all day and into the night." Jed looked around and smiled. "I was happiest out here in the open with my brothers and your granddad. Being in the house sometimes makes me feel closed in and restless."

Tess said nothing as she took the reins from him. She watched him stretch his back; he looked so tired.

"I remembered how your mother and I would ride together at sunset and watch the moon as it swept across the grassland. Just as my mother and father did and his before."

They stood in silence for a moment almost, Tess thought, out of respect. Finally, Jed reached over and kissed Tess on the cheek.

"That's what I want for you, sweetie. Someday to have someone—"

"To ride into the sunset with?" Tess grinned innocently.

"Yes. Even if it's another woman and I don't get a grandson. I love you."

Tears leapt to her eyes. "Thanks, Dad." She sniffed loudly as she mounted the horse, ignoring the deep groan. "I love you, too. Now get back to the house."

"Yes, ma'am." He mumbled back, "Just as bossy as your mother."

Chapter 4

Tess rode Daphne as hard as the old mare would allow or perhaps as much as Tess could stand. She felt her thighs burning and her ass aching after only a few minutes. She enviously watched her father drive down the road leading back to the warm house and immediately thought of Chuck's idea of her helping out with the cattle.

"He's insane," she said, deciding to take the shortcut across the grassland to the house. Haven't been on a horse like this in years and he wants me to herd cattle, she thought, trying to ignore her sore ass and how her insides were being jostled around.

On the way, she slowed as she came near the old family house. It still looked in pristine condition, considering no one had lived in it for years.

Her great-grandfather Ned Rawlins married Lucy Rogers from nearby Missoula in the late 1880s. That's where they got the name for the ranch, Double R—Rawlins and Rogers. Together, Ned and Lucy built the six-bedroom mansion in 1887. There were seven children born in that house; five survived. Her great-uncle Jeremiah was the last of five children who, as they grew, helped work this land. Tess's uncles and aunts each lived in that house even after they married. Jeremiah was the only one who left. Jeremiah wanted to be a teacher, so he left for California, met his wife, and stayed on at the university, the same university—University of California at Berkley.

Still deep in thought, Tess slowed the old mare and trotted to the road leading to the big house that was now abandoned. The log house was enormous with a wraparound porch that gave it a wide-open look. Tess remembered playing on the front porch with her brother and cousins as her grandparents laughed and rocked on the porch swing. Times were lean in the sixties, and the Rawlins family pooled their resources and their love; they dug in, holding on to the land and the Double R Ranch.

Tess jumped off Daphne and tied her loosely to the front porch rail. She walked up onto the old wooden porch, amazed that the flooring stood the test of time and the Montana winters. The sound of her cowboy boots against the wooden planking echoed along the lonely porch. As she turned around, she leaned against the railing and looked out at the Bitterroot Mountains.

The sprawling pasture in the foreground wonderfully landscaped the majestic mountains in the distance. My God, she thought, this is heaven. Somebody, anybody, everybody should be enjoying this scenery, she thought as she rode back to the house.

She was starving, her mouth watering for one of Maria's biscuits, when she heard Chuck's voice booming from the kitchen.

"Quit? You can't, Maria!" Chuck exclaimed as Tess walked into the kitchen. Maria nodded sadly as she dried her hands on the towel.

"What's all the barking about, Chuck?" Tess asked, looking from Maria to Chuck.

Chuck ran his fingers through his hair and groaned. He pointed at Maria. "She's quitting!" he squeaked out.

Tess was smiling, however, upon hearing the word, she frowned deeply. "What?"

"I must go home, Tess. I just got word. My cousin has left to help with his family. There will be no one left, so I must go."

"Shit, Maria. Of course you have to go."

"Thank you. As I said, there's no one left now but me. I leave in a week. I'm sorry," she said. Tess took off her hat and tossed it on the long table. "Take that off the table, young lady," she said just as softly.

Tess frowned and grabbed the hat, hanging it on the back of the chair. "What are we supposed to do without you?" Tess asked. In an exasperated gesture, she ruffled her short blond hair. "I just get home and you're leaving?"

"Don't whine. I have a friend who knows a young widowed woman who is a cook in Helena. She needs the job and is very good. She'll do fine until I return in the summer."

"So you're not quitting really?" Tess asked.

Maria gestured to the smiling and much relieved Chuck. "If he would stop crying like a baby, I was trying to tell him," Maria scolded Chuck, who turned red and chuckled nervously.

"So this woman, is she as good as you?" Tess grumbled childishly. "God, Maria, you're family. What is Dad going to say?"

Maria winced. "I-I haven't told him yet."

"Are you insane? You're leaving in a week and you haven't told him? Oh, God, he'll flip!"

"Flip? I don't understand flip…"

Tess rolled her eyes. "He'll be angry, very angry."

"You tell him for me," she said and grinned.

Tess gaped at Maria, then shook her head rapidly. Chuck threw up his hands and dashed out the door, unnoticed by both women.

"No, no, no," Tess argued. "I am not telling Dad."

"Tell me what?" Jed said from the kitchen door. Both women froze. Jed slowly walked into the kitchen, his fingers looped in the pockets of his vest. "Tell me what, ladies?"

Maria sighed and stood tall. "Jed, I must go back to New Mexico. My family needs me now. I'll return in the summer."

Jed blinked a few times. "Leave the ranch? What are we supposed to do?"

Tess tried to slip away.

"I have told Tess—come back here, child," she said, glaring at Tess, who stopped dead in her tracks, "that a friend of mine has someone who is looking for a job. She's a good cook, works in Helena, and is a widow. She has a young son, but he can work around the ranch. It will only be for the spring and midsummer. It will go by quickly. Then I'll be back to take care of you… both," she amended and looked away from Jed.

Father and daughter let out an unhappy resigned sigh. "When you go, I'll drive you to the train station," Jed said firmly.

Maria shook her head. "I'll take the bus."

"You will not. You'll fly home. No arguing."

Maria was looking at the floor. "I'm an employee, Jed."

"You're more than an employee here. I've told you that for years now," he added softly.

Maria looked up with teary brown eyes. It was then that Tess noticed how attractive this woman was. She was slim and average height with deep silky brown hair with a few strands of silver running through it. Her high regal cheekbones were her predominant feature.

"I'll take the train to Helena…" she said stubbornly.

Jed let out an exasperating sigh. "Are all you women so stubborn?"

"Yes," Tess and Maria said at the same time.

"Fine. But you'll fly home from Helena," Jed said, wagging a finger in Maria's direction. She nodded and grinned.

"Well, it's all set," Tess said sarcastically. "This will be wonderful. Maria will go home to New Mexico. Dad will be miserable until August. I'll have to break in a new cook. Boy, she'd better be able to make biscuits like you do."

Maria gave her a stern look. "You just behave yourself and do not get in her way and be nice."

Tess grumbled. "I'm nice."

"I mean be a lady, not the ruffian, ill-mannered tomboy you still are," she said severely. Jed chuckled and avoided the scathing look from Tess. "It wouldn't hurt you to wear a dress."

Tess laughed out loud as did Jed. "A dress? Maria, I'm forty-nine. I haven't worn a dress since—" She stopped and thought about it. So did Jed.

"I think you were three," he said, and Tess nodded in agreement.

Maria rolled her eyes and waved her hands in defeat. She mumbled in her native Cherokee all the way out the door.

It turned very warm, for which Tess was grateful. She sat outside the bus station in Silverhill. The new cook, Claire Redmond, was due on the ten forty from Helena. She had a good twenty minutes, so she stretched out her jean-clad legs and crossed them.

Pulling the worn cowboy hat down over her eyes, she yawned and shifted in her seat; her ass was killing her when she thought of the riding she had to do with Chuck. As the morning sun warmed her, she wondered just how young this Mrs. Redmond's son was and if he knew how to ride; she smiled at the prospect.

"Excuse me?"

Tess heard the soft voice and smiled. "Hmm, not now. I'm so comfortable." Tess sighed, then heard the laughter.

Her head shot up as she sat erect. Pushing her hat back on her head, she looked up into the sun, then took off her cowboy hat to shield her eyes.

A woman stood there, her head cocked. "Miss Rawlins?" she asked tentatively.

Tess immediately jumped up. "Yes. I'm sorry. I'm Tess Rawlins. Mrs. Redmond?"

"Yes, sorry to wake you," she said and smiled slightly.

Tess gave a nervous chuckle. She looked at this woman who was about three inches shorter. With her long brown hair pulled back, it gave Tess a good look at the smiling face. The woman's skin was fair and her cheeks flushed. Her eyes were a deep dark blue. She was an attractive woman—an attractive widow, she reminded herself.

Tess looked over to see a teenage boy standing nearby.

"Hey," Tess said, and the boy, who looked to be fifteen or so, smiled as Tess stuck out her hand. "I'm Tess."

"Jack Redmond," he said. His deep brown eyes watched her warily.

"Well, let's get going. Do you have luggage?" she asked, and Mrs. Redmond nodded and pointed at three weary-looking pieces of luggage standing by the curb.

"Great. Jack, give me a hand?" Tess looked over at the young man, who nodded and followed her.

Once the luggage was set in the back of the old wagon, Tess slammed the door and slid in. She glanced at the woman sitting next to her. She wore a heavy coat and wool slacks. Tess couldn't tell her age, but she looked young, but then everyone was looking young to Tess.

31

"So, Mrs. Redmond, I hope you won't mind cooking for us. There were supposed to be seven ranch hands, but we lost a few during the winter. I'm working on hiring a couple for the spring and summer." Tess put the car in gear. She eyed Jack in the backseat.

The woman chuckled. "I've been cooking for more than that for the past year or so. I won't let you down, Miss Rawlins."

"I'm sure you won't. I appreciate you moving like this on such short notice. Do you have any family that you're leaving behind?" she asked casually, then turned bright red. "Oh, shit, I'm sorry."

"No need, thank you," she said and looked out the window. "We have no other relatives to speak of."

Tess winced at her own stupidity but said nothing. She glanced in the backseat and noticed Jack eagerly looking out the window. "It's a long bus ride from Helena," Tess said, and Mrs. Redmond nodded as she looked around.

"It is beautiful and so open. My God, you can see forever," she said in amazement.

Tess grinned as she looked around, as well. "Yeah. They mean it when they say Big Sky country," she said, realizing she sounded proud of that. "We're almost there, another half hour."

As Tess neared the entrance, she pointed out a few things to her new cook. "This is Rawlins land as far as the eye can see."

Jack suddenly came alive and leaned in between them. "Wow, you own all this?" he asked with enthusiasm.

"Yep, wait till you see the cattle and the horses. Do you ride, Jack?" Tess asked and stole a glance in the rearview mirror.

"A little," he said sadly. "Not as much as I'd like."

Tess noticed his mother's face. A look of resignation flashed across the soft features. "Then I guess I'll have to get you on a horse. My father's an excellent teacher. I think he'd like having another man around the house," Tess said, and the boy's eyes lit up. She glanced at Mrs. Redmond, who gave her a smile of thanks.

"Speaking of the house, where will we be staying?" Mrs. Redmond asked.

"We only have one bedroom left. It was my brother's, but it's huge. We've already put a small bed in there for Jack. I didn't know he was older. Maybe he can bunk with the boys after we get you all settled." Tess saw the look of uncertainty on Mrs. Redmond's face. "Only if it's okay with your mom."

Jack gave his mother a pleading look. "We'll see," she said.

They pulled through the fenced gate that led to their property. Above the fence, the arched gateway read *Double R Ranch*. Jack looked up and grinned. Tess could see his eyes fill with anticipation of being on a real live ranch.

"You must love living here, Miss Rawlins," Mrs. Redmond said, still taking in the scenery.

"I've been gone for quite a while," Tess said with a shrug.

Mrs. Redmond looked at her then. "You have another home?"

"This will always be home. But I live in California. I'm a professor in the agriculture department at Berkeley."

"Really?"

Tess raised an eyebrow and glanced from the road to the near shocked look on Mrs. Redmond's face. She laughed. "That's what my students say, as well."

Mrs. Redmond laughed nervously. "I'm sorry, I didn't mean to sound so incredulous. What made you want to teach instead of ranching?"

"It was my great-uncle's fault. He made it sound so appealing. He developed the seed that's planted in the pastures. Uncle Jeremiah wanted to do his part to save this." Tess motioned out the window. "He said he was a better teacher than he was a rancher." She stopped, very aware of Mrs. Redmond's scrutiny. She glanced once again and saw the curious look.

"So you followed in his footsteps," Mrs. Redmond said.

Tess heard the softness in her voice and tightened her grip on the steering wheel. "Something like that, I guess. All I know is now I'm horribly out of shape for cattle ranching."

Tess wasn't sure if she was grateful or not when Mrs. Redmond laughed and drew her attention away from Tess and back to the sprawling landscape.

Jed met them at the front steps with a welcoming wave. He opened the car door for the woman. "Welcome, Mrs. Redmond. I can't tell you how much I appreciate you doing this on such short notice. Are you sure you can cook for—?" he blurted out.

Tess grimaced and turned bright red as she cleared her throat. "Um, Dad, Mrs. Redmond is more than qualified," she said, giving him the eye.

Her father winced apologetically. Mrs. Redmond laughed and shook his hand. "No offense meant, Mrs. Redmond."

"None taken, Mr. Rawlins. This is my son, Jack," she said proudly.

Jed's eyes lit up. He held out his hand and gave the strong hand a healthy shake. "It's a pleasure to meet you, son. Good strong handshake. Now let me show you to your room."

Tess and Jack picked up the luggage, Tess leaned into her father. "Good strong handshake?" she whispered with a grin and dragged the luggage down the long hallway.

"This is the best we can do, sorry," Jed said as he opened the bedroom door.

Mrs. Redmond peered in and blinked in amazement. Her son followed suit. The bedroom was enormous. To the right was a huge four-poster bed with a dresser on the opposite wall. Placed in the far corner was the smaller bed with a small dresser next to it. Next to the window was a nice size desk and chair.

"Mom, look, a fireplace!" Jack exclaimed as he walked into the hardwood-floored bedroom.

Sure enough, on the outside wall was a small brick fireplace with a cozy-looking chair in front of it.

"It gets pretty chilly at night in the spring, and it'll keep you nice and warm," Tess offered. Father and daughter were shocked to see tears brimming in Mrs. Redmond's eyes. "Hope it's okay," she added, exchanging a worried look with her father.

"It's more that okay, Miss Rawlins. It's more than I expected." She tried not to cry.

Jack saw it. He walked up to his mother and took her hand. "Don't cry, Mom. This is gonna be okay," he whispered, and she only nodded.

"We'll leave you to get settled in. Maria is in town. When she gets back, she'll familiarize you with the kitchen. Until then, take a rest. You both look tired," Tess said.

As they walked down the hall, Tess and Jed sported the same worried look.

"Did you see how grateful she looked?" Tess asked, and Jed nodded. "Shit, it's only a bedroom."

"I know and watch that foul mouth of yours. There's a youngster in this house now," he said fatherly.

Tess grinned and patted his shoulder. "Well, shit, Dad. You're right." She dashed out the kitchen door as Jed reached for her.

Tess spent the rest of the afternoon on the range with Chuck counting the herd. She sat in the saddle with book in hand while Chuck made the head count. He ticked off the calves as they stayed close to their mothers. "I thought we'd had more than this."

Tess glanced around the wide-open pasture. "You got the little ones tagged?"

"Yep. It wasn't easy, believe me, but between the four of us, we got 'em. Now they just need the brand."

"Maybe we lost more than we thought during the winter. It's been worse, but still…" she said thoughtfully.

"Tomorrow we'll start branding them. Then we'll fatten 'em up and head them down to Colorado. We'll get top dollar, look at them already."

The herd in this pasture lazily grazed on the grass as the two ranch hands dashed around chasing strays. "Tell them to let 'em roam, Chuck. They'll be fine. Why are they fussing over them?"

Chuck scratched his head. "Stan was in Silverhill and heard Ed yakking about how if he finds any strays he's keeping 'em."

"Damn him. If he sets one foot on Rawlins land," she threatened.

"Easy, Tess, he's looking for you to fly off the handle. That's why I didn't tell your dad. He'd be on his horse and at Telford's doorstep."

"I know. That's what that fat fuck wants," she hissed. "All these years. He has to know Dad won't sell this property."

35

Chuck laughed at her colorful language. "Better not talk like that in front of your father." He tried to sound stern.

"I know. He nearly caught me earlier." Tess laughed and closed the ledger, pulling her hat down over her eyes.

"We're gonna have to hire more hands."

Tess nodded as she watched the only two ranch hands left. "Any ideas?"

"Luke knows of a few drovers up from Texas. They're looking for work."

"Do you trust Luke?"

Chuck scratched his chin and shrugged. "We'll see. I'll have him bring them in tomorrow. How about you and me talk to them?"

"Me?" Tess asked. "What about Dad?"

"You and me need to talk a little more about your dad."

Tess reached over and grabbed his arm. "What about him?"

Chuck chewed at his bottom lip, then looked around. "You know I love your dad."

"I know. Hell, you've been here all your life and you've stuck by him when things really sucked. Now tell me what you're thinking."

"You just watch him, that's all I'm saying. He's getting a little forgetful."

Tess took off her hat and ran her fingers through her hair. "Shit, he's not that old."

Chuck smiled and patted her shoulder. "He's going on seventy."

Tess's head shot up at the realization. Good God, she thought, Chuck was right. "Okay, we'll have a look at the men tomorrow." She couldn't help the anger that was mounting. Maria was leaving. Her father was getting forgetful. She had to leave her teaching job. What else could happen?

"I'm going to ride back. Maria is getting Mrs. Redmond used to the kitchen. God, I hope she can cook." Tess clicked her teeth as she dug her heels into Stella and took off, scattering the cattle as she rode through the herd.

As she rode back, she noticed a calf away from the herd.

Riding closer, she heard it making a horribly mournful sound. It was standing with its front leg lifted slightly. Tess looked back to see Chuck too far to call him for help.

"Damned barbed wire," she hissed and slid off her horse. "Easy, sweetie," she cooed and saw the wire wrapped around the front leg. "Okay, now, I'm gonna try not to kill you. It's been a while for me, so don't go kicking me."

She took a pair of pliers out of her saddlebags and began snipping the spiny wire off the injured calf as much as she could. Then, with a deep painful groan, she lifted the calf in her arms. "God, for a baby, you're awfully heavy." Tess grunted as she hoisted the calf across Stella's back. Slipping her foot in the stirrup, she mounted the mare and held onto the moaning calf. "Oh, relax, you're getting a ride, for chrissakes," she said, wincing as the muscles in her thigh contracted. "God, no cramp now, please."

As she rode to the barn and corral, she noticed Jack looking at the horses. Jack saw her and his eyes widened as he ran up to her.

"Is that a cow?" he asked.

Tess dismounted and gave him a disturbed look. "No, son, it's a calf and she's got an owie," she said, and Jack laughed as he watched her gently take the annoyed calf off the horse and into the barn. "Get my father and tell him what's happened, okay?"

"Sure." Jack made a mad dash for the house.

Tess had the poor calf lying on the hay in a stall. With that, Jed, Jack, and Mrs. Redmond barged into the stable.

"What happened?" Mrs. Redmond asked in a panic. Jack was scared to death.

Tess looked up at Jed, who shrugged as if to say, "City folks."

"It's really okay. It happens all the time. The little ones stray too far and sometimes they get snagged in the barbed-wire fence." Tess took off her hat and rolled up the sleeves of her denim shirt.

Mrs. Redmond gently pulled at her son. "Jack, give Miss Rawlins room. Why don't you go back into the house?"

Tess saw the look of dejection on the boy's face. "If it's all right, I might need him to hold her head," she said, looking up at the woman.

Mrs. Redmond hesitated.

"Mom, she needs me," Jack pleaded.

"He can help," Jed assured.

Mrs. Redmond merely nodded. "Do exactly as Miss Rawlins tells you," she said in a nervous voice.

Tess winked at Jack. "Okay. Jack, kneel at her head and gently stroke her ear. Real gentle, that'll calm her when I have to cut this wire."

Jack did as she asked. Tess looked at Jed, who nodded and knelt beside the boy. "She looks small, but if she gets ornery, she may jump," he offered his assistance. Jack nodded and began stroking the calf's ear.

His mother stood there looking nervous. Tess looked up and smiled. "I could use a little help."

Mrs. Redmond blinked. "I don't think I'd be very good at this."

Tess gave her a frowning grin. "I'm not asking you to marry it, just hand me the stuff when I ask for it."

Tess laughed but quickly recovered when she saw the glare from Jed. "Sorry."

Mrs. Redmond narrowed her eyes in anger. "That's quite all right. I'm not the marrying kind anyway," she added dryly, and Tess laughed.

She knelt next to Tess and watched as Tess used the wire cutter to free the bleeding leg from the barbed wire. She handed her the antiseptic and poured it on the injured leg, causing the calf to let out another mournful grunt.

"Easy now," Tess cajoled as she took the rolled gauze from Mrs. Redmond, who surprisingly did not pass out.

"You're doing fine, Jack. Keep it up," Tess said, not looking up as she tied off the bandage. She then sat back on her heels admiring her handiwork.

"There, that ought to do it." She stood and stretched her back.

"Ya still got it, Tess," Jed said with a wink.

"It's been a while. I'm glad I didn't cause further damage," Tess said, rubbing the back of her leg.

"Are you all right?" Jed asked with a devilish grin. "Something achin' ya?"

Tess sneered in his direction but ignored him. Instead, she offered her hand to Mrs. Redmond, who took it and stood, as well.

Jack still sat there cradling the calf's head in his lap. He looked up at Tess. "Maybe I should stay with her for a little while. She probably misses her mom."

Jed grinned and ruffled his hair.

Tess nodded. "I think that would be a good idea. I think she likes you. You have a gift, Jack. Usually, calves don't like to be touched like that."

Jack looked down at the calf and stroked its head. "I think she needs me," he said almost to himself.

All three adults stood there watching as Jack took care of the injured animal. It was a touching scene for Tess, who felt the tears stinging her eyes, and as she looked at her father, she could see the old gray eyes watering. Mrs. Redmond sniffed.

"Okay, let Jack take care of...well, you'd better name her now, son," Jed said with a chuckle.

"What should I name her?" he asked and looked up.

Tess took off her hat and scratched the unruly blond hair. "Well, I found her in a clover patch..."

"Clover," Jack exclaimed, and the calf moaned as if angry that Jack stopped rubbing her head.

Mrs. Redmond shook her head. "Okay, Jack. Dinner will be ready in one hour. Make sure you wash your hands," she added with a grimace and walked out of the stable.

Tess and Jed watched the retreating figure. "It's a good thing she can cook," Tess mumbled out of the corner of her mouth.

"I guess we'll find out," Jed said.

By five o'clock on the dot, Stan, Luke, and Chuck came lumbering into the huge kitchen. Maria and Mrs. Redmond were manning the stove as the men sat in their usual places. Stan and Luke eyed the new cook.

Tess stood in the doorway and saw the look. She instantly bristled but said nothing. A few mumbles and chuckles ensued, and Tess cleared her throat and walked into the kitchen.

The chuckling stopped.

"Boys, this is Mrs. Redmond. She'll be taking over for Maria until the fall. You will respect her as you respect Maria," she said, looking at the culprits, who buried their heads in their coffee.

Mrs. Redmond whirled around and gave Tess a stern look but said nothing. Maria caught the look and continued with dinner.

"Have a good meal," Tess said, then walked out.

Mrs. Redmond watched the door swinging. "Maria, I'll be back in a minute." She dried her hands on the towel and walked out.

Tess was standing in the huge living room by the fireplace. "Miss Rawlins, can I have a word with you?"

Tess looked up and started to smile but saw the dark look. "Sure."

"I don't know what you meant in there, but please, I can take care of myself. I've been leered at before."

"Perhaps, but not by the men on this ranch," she countered evenly.

"I appreciate the gesture, but if I'm to work here, they have to know I can take care of myself."

"I'm sure you can. However, I will not have any leering or snickering going on."

"Any leering or snickering going on, I will take care of," she insisted as she put her hands on her hips.

For an instant, their gazes locked in a battle of wills. Tess ran a hand through her hair in an impatient gesture. She then took a deep breath. "It was not my intention to irritate you on your first day. I'm sure you can take care of yourself." She smiled slightly and offered her hand.

Mrs. Redmond took the offering and gave it a healthy pump. "Thank you. Dinner will be ready for you and your father after the men eat. That's usually what you do, correct?" she asked and smiled in return.

"Yes, ma'am, if I remember, that is correct," Tess said with a slight smirk.

Mrs. Redmond nodded and walked back into the kitchen.

Dinner was outstanding. Fried chicken, mashed potatoes, and

gravy, and to Tess's absolute delight, the biscuits were light and heavenly.

In the kitchen, Mrs. Redmond paced back and forth, biting her lip. Maria sat drinking her coffee.

"Claire, sit, you're make me dizzy."

"Do you think the chicken was cooked enough? God, I don't want to make them sick," she said and paced.

Maria shook her head. "You did not make the men sick. Now sit," she ordered, and with that, Jed and Tess came through the swinging door grinning.

"Wonderful. Maria, your excellent culinary skills are only preceded by your extreme good judgment," Tess said and bowed to Mrs. Redmond, who blushed horribly. Tess then spied the pie on the stove.

"God, don't tell me…"

"Pie," Jed said with a hint of question in his voice as he licked his lips.

Mrs. Redmond sported a superior grin and nodded. Father and daughter bowed in awe.

Chapter 5

Tess desperately tried not to limp up the back porch steps. Jack sat at the kitchen table drinking a glass of milk and eating a piece of pie. Tess's stomach growled at the sight. She heard the soft humming coming from Mrs. Redmond, who stood at the stove. The heavenly aroma made Tess groan openly.

"What's wrong? You hurt?" Jack asked as he shoved a forkful of pie into his mouth.

Mrs. Redmond turned around as Tess eased into the closest chair. "Nope. Just got a hitch in my git-along."

Jack laughed, nearly snorting milk through his nose.

"Jack!"

"Sorry, Mom."

"Would you like a cup of coffee, Miss Rawlins?" she asked, still glaring at her son, who spread his hands out in a helpless gesture.

"No, thank you. I think I'm going to go and soak this tired body of mine. I'll take a rain check, though. Whatever you're concocting at the stove smells heavenly."

Tess found herself smiling when she heard the laughter from Mrs. Redmond. As she gingerly walked toward the bathroom, she decided she liked the sound of it.

After the hot bath, which did nothing for her aching ass, Tess flopped down on her bed. That was the last thing she remembered.

She woke early to the heavenly smell of cinnamon and bacon. "Good Lord, I'm starved," she exclaimed as she hauled her naked body out of bed. She immediately shivered and hopped from one foot to the other. "Damn, it's freezing!" she grumbled as she jumped back into bed.

Tess finished a quick shower and stepped out of the deep tub. Shivering, she quickly dried off and dressed. Her stomach told her just how hungry she was as she made her way to the kitchen.

Mrs. Redmond was humming in the kitchen. Her dark hair was pulled back, and her hips swayed to some old song coming from the radio on the counter. Tess raised a curious eyebrow as she leaned against the doorjamb.

Tess grinned as she listened to the waltz rhythm; it had her swaying, as well. With that, Mrs. Redmond turned from the stove and stopped dead. She blushed from her head to her toes, and Tess's grin grew even wider.

"Good morning," Mrs. Redmond said. "It's early."

Tess walked into the kitchen. "I know, but the smell was heavenly. What are you making?" she asked excitedly as she looked beyond Mrs. Redmond.

"Cinnamon rolls, and no, you can't have one. I haven't iced them yet," she scolded as Tess reached for the hot rolls cooling on the rack.

Tess pulled a face and stepped back. "I'm your employer, Mrs. Redmond," Tess tried and got a smirk. "No go, huh?"

"No. Besides, you'll burn your mouth. Sit, I'll get your coffee."

Tess sat at the long table and smiled her thanks as Mrs. Redmond set the steaming cup in front of her. "What'll it be?" she asked over her shoulder.

"I'm so hungry, I don't care," Tess said happily as she blew at the steaming cup. "So tell me about yourself, Mrs. Redmond."

With her back to her, Tess thought she saw Mrs. Redmond stiffen momentarily. It was forgotten as she watched her drizzle the icing over the warm sticky rolls.

"There's not too much. I was born in Portland, Oregon. Married, had Jack, and my husband was killed in a car accident."

Tess frowned for a moment at the abrupt tone. "I'm sorry. I didn't mean to pry."

"No. I'm sorry. You weren't prying. It was just a painful time."

"I understand. And I'll never ask again if you would please let me have one of those." She motioned to the cinnamon rolls, newly iced.

"Deal. You can have one."

Tess grinned and licked her lips, grabbing a sticky roll off the rack. "Oh, my God!" Her exclamation was muffled by the mouthful of warm cinnamon, brown sugar, and the lightest dough she ever tasted, the topic completely forgotten as she concentrated on breakfast.

"Mrs. Redmond, that was the best breakfast I... Well, Maria has her work cut out for her when she gets back. Thank you," Tess said, wiping her mouth.

Mrs. Redmond eyed the cleaned plate. "You're welcome. And Maria's job is very safe. I have no problem moving on in August."

Both women were silent for a moment. Tess saw the faraway look as Mrs. Redmond drank her coffee. "Well, I'm grateful for you. It's amazing how quickly you and your son eased into the family routine. And it's only April, let's not talk about leaving," Tess said as she stood. "Would you tell my father I'll be back later in the day, maybe around suppertime? We're going up on the high ridge to do some branding, which I haven't done in almost six years, the poor calves. If you see a calf with a double R branded on its forehead, you'll know who did it."

Mrs. Redmond laughed again as she cleared the dishes. "Why do you still brand them? I mean, isn't there a more humane way of keeping track of them?"

"We ear tag the calves when they're born to match the tag on their mamas, so we can make sure we know which calf belongs to what cow if they get separated."

"Doesn't it hurt them? The branding, I mean."

"If I had to guess, I'd say yeah. Hell, if I were stuck with a red hot poker on my ass—" She stopped when Mrs. Redmond laughed; she laughed along. "You know what I mean. Anyway, I have to go into town later and see Tom about our order. I'll take a ride out to the south pasture on my way back. I should be back by supper," she said quickly, avoiding Mrs. Redmond, and slipped into her buckskin jacket.

Tess caught her staring at the fleece-lined coat. "You like it?" she asked and modeled it. "I snagged this buck, skinned it, and had it made."

"Really?" Claire said dryly as she leaned against the counter.

Tess saw the wary look and grinned. "I was online between classes, saw it in a catalog, and just had to have it?"

"That sounds more like it. Now what about lunch?"

Tess shrugged and put on her cowboy hat.

"I'm no expert, but that hat looks like it's seen better days."

Tess gave her a scathing look. "This is brand new, only five years old. Hell, it's just broken in, the way I like it. Don't you like it?" She took the cowboy hat off and dusted the brim, then replaced it on her head.

"Yes. You look great."

"I do?"

Mrs. Redmond quickly continued as she wiped off the countertop, "What about lunch?"

Tess hid her grin and slipped on the worn work gloves. "I'll get something on the way back. I'll be out saddling my horse, if I can remember how, if my father wakes up anytime soon." Tess smiled and walked out.

The sun was barely up as she walked into the stable. Clover was lying in the vacated stall on the bed of hay, licking her bandaged leg. "Good morning, Clover. Jack should be out to see you later."

After saddling Stella, Tess mounted the mare and trotted out of the stable. She pulled the reins when she heard Mrs. Redmond calling her name. She ran up with a bag in hand.

"Here, I have a feeling you'll get hungry. You can't go all day without eating." She handed the bag up to Tess.

"Thank you. You didn't have to do that. I'm sure I won't starve." She sniffed the bag. "Hmm, you gave me cinnamon rolls, thanks."

Mrs. Redmond ran her fingers through her long dark hair and grinned. "You're welcome. Don't fall off that horse. Have a good day, Miss Rawlins."

Tess pulled on the brim of her hat. "We'll have to do something about this 'Miss Rawlins' thing," she said with a smile and rode down the dusty trail away from the ranch.

When she was almost out of sight, she turned and waved. Mrs. Redmond grinned and waved back.

Tess met up with Chuck on the south pasture. He was standing there with several new men. "Well, here goes."

As she dismounted Stella, she glanced at Chuck, looking for some sign. He nodded with a wink; Tess hoped that was a good thing.

"This is Tess Rawlins, she and her father own the Double R," Chuck said. "This is Pedro Garcia, and his son, Manny. And this is Kyle Mathis from Texas."

Tess shook hands with Kyle first as they took off their hats. He looked to be about twenty-five; his hands were rugged and calloused, which was a good sign to Tess. When she took Pedro's hand, he only smiled and nodded.

"He doesn't speak much English, miss," Manny offered in perfect English.

"That's fine," Tess assured him. "As long as he can work the ranch with all of you, we'll be fine."

"Oh, yes, ma'am. We've worked in Texas since I was a boy."

Tess raised an eyebrow. "And how old are you?"

"I'm nearly eighteen."

"You speak very good English."

"I just graduated high school."

Tess grinned then. "Good for you. What about college?"

Manny frowned and shrugged. "We will see."

Tess understood and merely nodded. She then regarded Kyle. "And where have you worked, Mr. Mathis?"

"Texas, Arizona, and New Mexico. Been doing this all my life, as well."

"Why did you leave Texas?" Tess noticed his bright smile and a twinkle in his brown eyes. Oh, brother, she thought and glanced at Chuck, who hid his grin.

"The ranch was being sold. Besides, the ladies are more attractive in Montana," he said with a grin.

Tess looked him in the eye. "I couldn't agree more, Mr. Mathis. I'm partial to Montana women, as well."

The flirtatious grin quickly faded from Kyle's face. Chuck rolled his eyes and groaned. Manny snickered and his poor father didn't know what had just happened.

"I think we understand each other?" Tess asked Kyle.

"Yes, ma'am, we surely do." His face was as red as the bandanna he wore around his neck.

"Good. I'll leave you to Chuck. He'll show you the ropes, literally," Tess said with a smile. As she turned to mount Stella, Pedro quickly stood beside her.

"Gracias, señorita," he whispered and held out his hand.

"De nada," Tess said. "And that is the extent of my Spanish." She turned to Manny. "Please tell your father it is I who thank him for helping us."

Manny nodded and spoke to his father, who watched Tess. When he spoke to his son, Tess waited for the translation.

"My father said we will work hard to bring the cattle to market. This is a beautiful ranch with good pastures."

Tess nodded and looked around. "Like a sea of grass."

"Mar de hierba," Manny said to his father.

"Ah," Pedro said and smiled. "Sí." He bent down and plucked a few blades of the thick grass. "Mar de hierba. Bueno."

"Let's hope it's very bueno." Tess mounted Stella and pulled at the reins. "It sounds so romantic when they say it," she said to Chuck.

"Good morning, Mrs. Redmond," Jed called out from the doorway of the kitchen.

"Good morning."

"Everything go all right this morning?"

"Very well. All the men fed and on their way. Your daughter included."

"They'll be gone most of the day so you won't have to worry about lunch. However…"

"I know. Come six o'clock, there will be several hungry men ready for dinner."

Jack walked in sleepily behind him. Jed turned and laughed at the tousled dark brown hair and sleepy face. "Well, good morning, Jack."

"Hi, Mr. Rawlins." He yawned and slipped into a chair. His mother ruffled his head and put a glass of orange juice in front of both of them.

Jed watched the boy with interest. He reminded him of Stephen when he was a teenager. Steve was a quiet child, so unlike Tess, who was running any time her feet hit the ground. The tortoise and the hare, he thought.

"Mr. Rawlins?" Jack asked, breaking him from his reverie.

Jed blinked a couple of times and looked over at Jack. "I'm sorry. I was daydreaming, son," he said fondly.

"I was just asking if it was okay if I went to the stable to see Clover," Jack asked as he ate his cereal. Jed smiled tenderly at the youngster. His mother watched the quiet scene.

"Sure you can. I bet she misses you," Jed said with a smile.

"Thanks. I miss her, too. Is it dumb to miss a cow?" He looked up from his cereal.

So much like Steve, he thought. He shook his head. "No, it's not dumb at all."

"Good. Okay, I'm done. See ya," he said quickly and slid off his chair.

"Hold on, young man. Wash your hands," his mother said and pointed to the sink.

"But I'll just get them dirty in the stable," he grumbled but obeyed. He looked at Jed. "She has a thing about clean hands," he whispered.

Jed chuckled as he drank his coffee and leaned in. "It's a mom thing. Go on now, do as you're told," he said with a wink.

Jack ran to the sink, splashed water on his hands, dragged them through a towel, and dashed out the screen door. Both adults laughed at the retreating figure.

"He's a good boy, Mrs. Redmond. You can be proud of him. He reminds me of my son, Steve, when he was a young one."

"Tess mentioned having a brother. Does he live here, as well?" she asked as she cleaned the dishes. When Jed didn't answer right away, she looked back at the table. The look on his face made her heart ache.

He stared off and looked as if he may break down. He shook his head. "No, Mrs. Redmond. My son died in a riding accident a couple of years ago. He was thrown from his horse," he said, and Mrs. Redmond heard the incredulous undertone.

"Oh, God, I'm so sorry."

"Don't be, you had no way of knowing."

Mrs. Rawlins sank in a chair across from him, shaking her head. "Unbelievable," she whispered sadly.

"Yes, it was. He was an excellent rider just like Tess," he said and chuckled. "They were always competing, bringing out the best and the worst in each other."

"Sounds like they loved each other very much," Mrs. Redmond said. Jed nodded.

"They did." He sighed and looked around the kitchen. "There was an awful lot of love around here. I miss having children running around. When the kids were little, before my brothers and sister moved away, there'd be kids all over the place. Especially at my dad's house, where we grew up. Good Lord, we had a big family. Emily had a few miscarriages. We only had the two."

Mrs. Redmond brought the coffeepot over and filled his cup, and Jed nodded his thanks. She was about to ask him about his wife but figured she had passed away, and she didn't want to make another blunder.

Jed Rawlins stared out the kitchen door. "She had cancer. Took her quick. Hard to believe. Emily was a sturdy woman."

"I'm sorry, Mr. Rawlins," she said.

Jed drank his coffee. "Well, enough of this. I'm going to see where Jack is. Maybe I'll take a drive up to the ridge and see how Tess is faring with the branding. Would you like to come along? I'm sure Jack would love to see it."

Later in the day, Mrs. Redmond decided to take lunch to the men. Jed tried to explain it wasn't necessary, but she insisted. They drove the Jeep up the dusty road as far as it would take them.

"It's just up a ways," Jed said. "We can walk the rest."

Mrs. Redmond looked over the landscape as Jack and Jed hauled out the baskets full of lunch for the ranch hands. "It is magnificent here. I can see why you and Miss Rawlins love it."

The grassland stretched for miles on the sloping ridge with the cattle dotting the landscape. The men had fires going, heating the hot branding irons.

"Does it hurt them?" Jack asked as they walked up the ridge.

"Not really. They have tough hides. But we need to put our mark on them, son. They roam all over, and even though it's the twenty-first century, there are still cattle rustlers out there. This is our only way of proving the cattle belong to the Double R," he said, and the boy nodded in understanding.

Jack and his mother set up the baskets and thermoses. She looked up to see Tess riding close by. She barked her orders to a couple of men who nodded and took off, chasing down a few strays. She put her hand up to shield her eyes from the warm midday sun and watched as the two men roped and tied a calf, leading it to the branding fire.

They watched for a while until Jed let out a short whistle. Tess quickly turned their way and waved. She tossed the iron into the fire and motioned to the men.

Like bees to honey, they were at Mrs. Redmond's side in a heartbeat. Laughing, she passed out the sandwiches and coffee. Tess stood back and carefully watched Stan and Luke, the two culprits from dinner. Both men took off their hats as they took the sandwiches.

"Thank you, ma'am," they said solemnly.

"You're welcome," she said and leaned in. "Her bark is worse than her bite, correct?"

Both men blushed and chuckled nervously. "Nope. She bites hard."

The three laughed heartily; she saw Tess frown, knowing she was the subject of conversation. Tess glared at the two laughing men, who made a beeline for a shady spot.

"Something to eat, Miss Rawlins?"

"No, thanks. I just ate the cinnamon rolls. I will take the coffee, though." She took off her dusty hat. She wiped her forehead with her sleeve and looked up into the sun.

"Looks like we have a few new men." Jed motioned to the three new hires.

"Yes, Chuck found them. They'll do fine. One's a young man like Jack here," Tess said.

Jack's eyes lit up. "He's a cowboy?"

"Yep. Maybe we'll get you two together and Manny can help you. Whattaya say?"

"Sounds fine to me. I'd like to earn my keep here," Jack said.

"If it's okay with your mom, then it's all settled." Tess wiped her brow once again. "Warm for late April, huh, Dad?"

"Yep. How's the branding coming along?"

Tess took the offered cup of coffee. "Just fine. Chuck said we didn't lose as many as we suspected in the winter. We'll fatten 'em up."

"Planting that new grass seed on this pasture was a marvelous idea, Tess. I've never seen the pasture this green."

Tess nodded and looked around. "Uncle Jeremiah was right. It was his idea. The tractors did a good job of broadcasting it. It took a while, but it produced some fine grass and alfalfa. As Pedro says, 'mar de hierba.'"

"Sea of grass," Mrs. Redmond repeated.

Tess raised an eyebrow. "You speak Spanish?"

"Sí," she said with a grin.

"Bueno. You'll be our translator along with Manny. Things are coming together, Dad."

Mrs. Redmond watched Tess as she spoke with Jed. Tess was certainly not your average woman. Dressed in Levi's, leather chaps, and cowboy boots, in no way did Tess Rawlins look like a college professor. Glancing at the full curve of her hips and swell of her breasts, suddenly Mrs. Redmond's mouth went dry, and she took a deep breath and a long drink of lemonade.

Tess looked over at Jack, who was gazing at her horse tied to an oak tree. "Her name's Stella, and if it's okay with your mom, you can go over and say hi." Tess smiled at the look of hopefulness on the boy's face. His mother gave a worried look that Tess found too irresistible to pass up. "Unless you think Stella might eat Jack. I know she hasn't had her oats today."

"I'm just concerned. He's never been around this many animals."

Tess nodded in understanding. "Ah, okay, Jack, wash your hands first."

"That's not what I meant," Mrs. Redmond explained, then saw the lips twitching with amusement. "Fine. Jack, go ahead. Just be careful."

Tess laughed, looked into the basket, and plucked out an apple. Taking her pocketknife out, she cut the apple in half. "Here, she's hungry." She took the half and laid in it the palm of her hand.

The tall chestnut mare easily snapped it up. Jack watched carefully. "Stella, this is Jack. He's a friend, so watch your manners. His mother is a bit skittish and afraid you'll eat her son, so behave."

Jack snorted a laugh and tried not to look at his glaring mother.

Tess glanced at her and laughed. "Here, hold it in the palm of your hand and leave your hand flat."

Jack licked his lips and did as instructed. "Hi, Stella," he said, and the mare gobbled up the remainder of the apple. Tess cut another and Jack had the time of his life.

In moments, he was stroking the long neck of the gorgeous horse and kissing her nose.

"Aw, Jack." His mother winced and picked up a towel.

Tess rolled her eyes and grabbed at the towel. "Mrs. Redmond, let him be. He has a way with animals, can't you see that?"

She reluctantly looked at Jack and had to agree. The horse was perfectly content to receive the attention from Jack.

"He must get that from his daddy," Tess teased.

"Miss Rawlins…" she started in a terse voice.

"Tess…"

She blinked and opened her mouth, then shut it and laughed at the innocent look. "Tess, I just don't want him hurt," she said evenly.

"I don't, either. Do you honestly think I'd allow that, whatever your first name is?" she asked, grinning wildly. She took a healthy bite of an apple.

"Claire," she said.

Tess cocked her head. "That's a pretty name. I like it." She announced her approval with another crisp bite.

Claire shot her a look. "Thank you. Do I get to keep it?"

Jack laughed behind them as he petted Stella. Tess tossed the remainder of the apple to Jack. She took the pocketknife and closed it. "Here, use this, Jack," she suggested and tossed that, as well.

"Ahh!" Claire exclaimed in horror as she watched the knife fly through the air. Scaring the hell out of her son, Jack jumped back and the closed knife fell to the ground.

Tess rolled her eyes and picked it up. "Claire, holy cow. It's closed," she assured her. She opened it and cut the apple.

Claire turned red and fidgeted with the lunch baskets. "I-I'm sorry. I'm..."

"A city slicker," Tess offered with a teasing grin.

Claire closed her eyes and counted to ten. Jack laughed into the horse's neck.

"We'll have to do something about that," Tess said. "C'mon, we're going into town. I have to go to Tom's, then we're going shopping."

Tess mounted her horse with a stifled groan. "Jack, wanna ride back with me?"

Jack almost swallowed his tongue. He gave his mother a pleading look.

Claire hid her worried face. "Sure," she said, mustering all the courage she could find.

Tess saw the petrified face. "We'll ride slowly," she assured her. She looked around and found Chuck and called to him, "Chuck, let Jack borrow your horse. You can ride back with Dad."

They waited while Chuck rode over. Jack grinned as he mounted the black horse.

"Be careful," Claire pleaded.

"Mom, I'll be fine," Jack insisted, his embarrassment evident.

"We'll go slow," Tess said again.

Jack gave Claire a look of pure gratitude and delight that it nearly broke her heart.

"Oh, God," she mumbled to herself.

Jed put his arm around her shoulders. "Don't worry, Tess is an excellent horsewoman. He'll be fine. C'mon, I'll race ya back!" he yelled to Tess.

Claire saw the gleam in Tess's eye and nearly fainted. Tess laughed openly and slowly trotted across the grassland with Jack at her side. Claire whirled around at the older Rawlins.

"Sorry, Claire. Can I call you Claire, too?" Jed asked and backed up.

Chapter 6

Tess was tempted to take the old station wagon into town but opted for the more reliable Jeep. Claire sat in front and Jack in the back leaning in between them, filled with anticipation. She pulled in front of Tom's store. He was sweeping up in the front and turned when he saw them.

"Tess, hey," he said and shook her hand. Tess offered the introductions. "How's the order coming?"

Tom grinned. "Just about done. We'll deliver the last of the grain on Tuesday."

Tess nodded. "How much am I saving, Tom?" she asked with a wicked grin. Tom laughed evilly and glanced around.

"If you'd have gone to the big stores in Missoula and Helena, it'd cost you over four thousand dollars. With me getting those distributor prices, it's costing ya two thousand seven hundred fifty dollars."

Tess laughed and slapped him on the back. Claire and Jack exchanged glances as the two laughed heartily. "Are you making enough?"

Tom rolled his eyes. "I make more money being a distributor than I ever made on my own. God, Tess, that was a brilliant idea of yours, you college grad you. I'm so glad you're back," he said and they both laughed again. "Warren is fit to be tied," he said through their laughter.

"The old fu…" She stopped herself and cleared her throat as she glanced at her two companions. "The old geezer," she amended with a deep blush. "Tom, Claire is our new cook. She'll give you her order each week. She and I will come into town and pick it up, just like usual."

"Usual? You never came into town for that," Tom said seriously.

It wasn't possible for Tess Rawlins to blush deeper; she avoided the raised eyebrow from Claire. "I didn't? Well, it's been a long while."

Tom shrugged and turned his attention to Claire. "It's nice to meet you, Claire, and you, too, Jack. I look forward to working with you."

"Thanks, Tom. It'll take some getting used to," Claire said.

"Are you kidding?" Tess argued. "Tom, she makes the lightest biscuits, they melt in your mouth. This morning, she made these cinnamon rolls with icing."

Tom licked his lips and held up his hand. "Whoa! Enough. I'm starving. Will you be cooking at the party?" he asked, and Claire gave him a confused look. "The annual Double R barbecue."

Tess grimaced and winced. "I completely forgot. We still do that?" She caught Claire's look of confusion. "I'll explain later. Thanks, Tom."

They stopped outside Harry's department store. "It's not really a department store like in the city. However, Harry likes to think so. Humor him," she whispered into Claire's ear.

"Tess, what a surprise. I haven't seen you in years. Are you back for good? Got tired of the city life, huh?" Harry asked.

"Something like that. Harry, this is Claire Redmond and her son, Jack. Claire is working at the ranch, taking over for Maria until she gets back. We need some ranching clothes for the young man. The works," Tess said, and Harry rubbed his hands together.

In a short time, Jack stood there in his new Levi's, cowboy boots, and denim shirt. "Three pairs each, Harry. Except the boots, one pair should do it," Tess ordered as she perused the cowboy hats.

"Tess, I can't let you buy this," Claire said as she came to her side.

"Which hat do you think?" Tess asked, ignoring her. She picked up a black ten gallon and held it up to Jack. "Nah," she said with a frown.

"Tess..." Claire insisted.

"Here, try this one, kiddo." Tess handed him a tan Stetson

with gold braiding around the crown. Jack's eyes lit up as he tried on the hat and stood in front of the mirror.

It was then Tess turned to Claire. "Claire, he needs to fit in. You can pay me back. I'll take it out of your salary."

"Which we've never discussed," Claire reminded her.

"We haven't?"

"No."

"Don't worry. I'm going to pay you."

Claire put her hands on her hips. "I didn't think otherwise. My point, Miss Rawlins, is I don't want you to be paying for my son's clothes."

"I didn't mean to offend you. We'll discuss your salary when we get back. You're worth your weight in gold with your cinnamon rolls alone. How about five hundred a week, plus room and board?" She absently watched Jack and took the cowboy hat off his head.

Bending the brim to soften it, she handed it back to him. "Thanks..."

"Tess..."

"You're welcome," Tess said to Jack with a wink.

"Tess," Claire said again. Tess noticed the exasperated voice and hid her grin. "I want to be fair. That's too much money."

"I've never had an employee tell me that," she said and winked again at Jack. Tess looked back at Claire. "I'm the heir to the Rawlins dynasty. Stop arguing with an heiress," she said in a haughty tone that emitted a snorting laugh from Jack.

"If you continue to spend money like this, you'll have no dynasty left," Claire said, trying to make her understand.

"Okay. I understand your concern, and I appreciate you looking out for the future of the Double R," she said seriously. "Now let me make it up to you. You need a cowboy hat, as well, and a good pair of Levi's."

Claire ran her hand over her face. "Do you always get what you want?"

"I never thought about it." Tess struck a contemplative pose. "Pretty much, yeah."

Claire narrowed her eyes at the grinning woman and shook

her head. "Fine, I give up."

"Good, knew you'd see it my way," Tess said with a sly grin.

"Mom, you look great!" Jack exclaimed as he walked around Claire.

Tess was sitting in the chair waiting, twirling her hat as Claire changed. She glanced up and blinked several times, dropping the hat. Claire Redmond has hips, Tess thought stupidly.

The Levi's fit snug and the brown cowboy boots gave her just enough lift. Her white denim shirt tucked in accentuated her trim shape.

Harry came rushing over. "Here, this will go beautifully, Mrs. Redmond." He handed her the leather vest. Claire, who was blushing, slipped into it. "Perfect! Tess, what do you think?"

Tess, trying to find some moisture in her mouth, just gave a noncommittal shrug. "Looks all right," she said nonchalantly and leaned back into a hat rack. She avoided Claire as she and Harry picked up the wayward hats.

The trio walked down the sidewalk. Tess was giving Jack a lesson in walking cowboy style. Claire smiled and kept silent as Tess spouted her words of wisdom.

"It's been a while, but as I remember, you have to walk like you don't have a care in the world," she said and Jack listened intently. He took a deep breath and walked ahead of them.

"There you got it," she said. "Now you need to swagger just a little. Kinda like John Wayne."

"You're not serious," Claire said.

Tess laughed. "Of course I am. He has to walk the walk."

"I love John Wayne! I know what you mean," Jack said eagerly.

The imitation had both women screaming with laughter. Jack was in heaven. "Now you just wait a minute, missy," he drawled and swaggered closer. "What's s'golldarn funny?"

"Jack, stop! Please," Tess begged as she doubled over with laughter. She took her hat off and fanned herself. "God, I'm having a stroke."

Claire wiped her eyes. "Jack, you belong on stage. That's enough, let's not kill Miss Rawlins. She hasn't paid me yet."

A voice called out from behind them. "Well, Tess, you've come back. And who have we here?"

Tess immediately stopped laughing. "Telford, good afternoon."

Claire watched the exchange between them; she saw the dark look on Tess, which changed her appearance completely. Gone was the fun-loving nature. She glanced at the object of Tess's dark mood. He was average height, perhaps an inch or two shorter than Tess was. He was a rotund man who wore a gray suit and a bolo tie and a pair of shiny black cowboy boots. He took a long puff on his big cigar. He looked like a man on the verge of a heart attack.

"And who are you, young man?" he asked with a smile that didn't reach his eyes. Jack stepped closer to his mother.

"This is Mrs. Redmond and her son, Jack. This is Warren Telford," Tess made the introductions.

"Friends of the family?" he asked as he looked at Claire.

"No, Mrs. Redmond is an employee. She's taking over for Maria. It's always nice to see you, Telford." Tess took Claire by the elbow and led them down the street.

"You look a little tired, Tess. You can't run that ranch by yourself. Now that Stephen is gone," he added, and Tess froze.

Claire saw her entire body tense as Tess let out a low growl and started to turn around. Instinctively, Claire put a firm hand on her forearm. The muscles underneath her fingers flexed.

"It's getting late, Tess. I need to get back and start supper."

Tess looked into her eyes; Claire smiled when the angry look dissipated. The three walked away without another word or look back.

"Nice to see you, too, Tess. A pleasure, Mrs. Redmond," he called after them.

They drove through town in silence.

"Who was that man, Tess?" Jack asked, breaking the silence.

"Jack, it's none of our business," Claire said.

"It's all right. He's been after the Double R for as long as I can remember." Tess rubbed her face. Claire noticed the tired lines etched in her brow.

"He's huge," Jack said from the backseat.

"Jack!" Claire exclaimed, then gaped at Tess, who was laughing.

"Well, he is. He's an old…" Tess started.

"Enough, the both of you," Claire said.

Later that night, Tess sat at the large mahogany desk in the living room. The small light illuminated the area as she looked over the books. Sipping on brandy, she sighed heavily as she checked the figures.

"Are we still in business?" Jed asked from the doorway.

Tess looked up and grinned tiredly. "Yes, Dad. We're fine. Actually, we have more cattle than we originally anticipated."

"Then why are you up so late and why the glum look?" He sat on the edge of the desk.

She tossed down the pen and rubbed her eyes. "I saw Telford this afternoon when I was in town with Claire and Jack. He made a comment about Steve."

"What did he say?"

"Oh, nothing," she said quickly, seeing the anger in his eyes. "But that I even hear Steve's name on that fat fucker's lips," Tess hissed. "How could Steve have been thrown from his horse? I still can't believe it. Do you buy it at all?"

He took a deep sad breath. "No, I don't believe it. But Pat Hayward investigated and…"

"Shit, Dad. Telford had Pat in his back pocket for some reason. I don't trust him."

"Maybe there is something to what Tom said about the night Steve died. He said Steve was on his way home to tell me something. Damn it, I wish I knew what it was." Jed put a gentle hand on Tess's shoulder. "There was just nothing I could do. I tried getting the district attorney in Helena involved, but with Pat Hayward finding it an accident…" His voice trailed off.

Tess saw the tired look in his blue eyes.

"I'm so tired of thinking about it."

Tess remembered when she got the call about Stephen. She made it home just in time for the funeral. Warren Telford had the nerve to show his ugly face. He hated her family and Tess never quite understood why. Perhaps it was because her father was an honest man who owned most of the land in the county. Everyone respected Jed Rawlins, and no one seemed to care for Warren Telford. He was a money-grubbing old man who would steal from his mother if he could make a profit.

When a couple of other farms went under, instead of helping, Telford foreclosed without a moment's hesitation. Tess remembered her father and the other ranchers going to Telford, pleading with him to give the owners until the end of the planting season. Jed was furious when he came home that night. She and Stephen were sitting at the kitchen table doing homework. Her father came in swearing, and her mother tried to calm him down. Young Tess had never seen her father so angry. From then on, the name Warren Telford was synonymous with Satan.

"What makes him hate so much?"

Jed took a deep contemplative breath. "I don't know. Well, I know why he hates me."

"Why?" Tess asked and sat forward.

"He had his sights on your mother, and I think he just couldn't stand it when I married her."

"Yuck, he loved Ma?"

Jed laughed and nodded. "So remember, it could always be worse. You could have Telford as your father." He kissed her head. "Go to bed, Tess. Let's not worry about Telford."

Tess agreed as she reached up and kissed him. "I'm sorry I left," she whispered.

Jed kissed her once again. "You're here now, and that's all that matters. I miss your brother every day and your mother. I tried getting the district attorney in Helena involved. Did you know that?"

Tess saw the flash of confusion in his eyes. "Yes, Dad. You told me."

Jed nodded. "Well, I'm off to bed. G'night, Em."

Tess hesitated for a minute, close to tears. "G'night, Dad," she whispered. He ruffled her hair and walked away.

Tess took off her boots and let out a sigh of relief as she put her feet up on the desk and leaned back in the chair. She picked up the brandy and sipped it, not wanting to think of her father calling her Em. She shrugged it off. People do that all time, she thought. It doesn't mean his mind is slipping. Trying to think of something, anything else, her mind drifted back to the day she came home after her father called.

She had gone straight to the sheriff's office after she viewed Stephen's body, which Chuck had found after Stephen's horse wandered back to the ranch. His body was in the south pasture, his head crushed. The coroner determined that the horse threw him and kicked him in the head. Tess remembered the conversation clearly.

"What the fuck is this called, Pat? You've known Steve his whole life. When was he ever thrown from his horse?" Tess bellowed.

Jed gently pulled at her arm, but she angrily shrugged him off. "And what about his crushed head? I saw it. Did you see any sign of his horse kicking him in the head? Shit, Pat, what's going on?"

"I have to go by what the coroner said, Tess. It's like I told Jed, they determined it was an accident."

"I suppose that it means nothing that he had words with Telford that night or that Telford warned him to back off, in front of witnesses. I suppose that means shit, right?" Tess yelled, and Pat winced at her anger but said nothing. Tess wiped away the angry tears.

Jed agreed with Tess. "She's right, you know. Warren Telford killed my son as sure as you're standing here denying it."

Tess took a menacing step toward her old friend. She never wanted to hit someone so badly in her entire life, but she knew Pat was not entirely to blame.

"Go to hell, Sheriff Hayward," she said in a dead flat voice. Without another word, she turned on her heels and stormed out, slamming the door with such anger, it shattered the glass paneling.

Tess finished her brandy as she reminisced and put her head back. Tears filled her blue eyes while she watched the dying embers of the fire flickering across the log-beamed ceiling. With a sad, tired sigh, she closed her eyes.

Someone was shaking her.

"Tess," Claire whispered.

Tess blinked and opened her eyes and focused on the worried face. "Go to bed. You'll be stiff as a board tomorrow."

Tess sat up, shaking the sleep from her eyes. "God, I fell asleep. What time is it?" she asked through a yawn.

"Nearly midnight. C'mon."

Tess groaned and stretched. Claire noticed the ledger and bills on the desk. She said nothing as she turned out the light.

Standing in the glow of the fire, Tess looked down into Claire's blue eyes. "Why are you still up?"

Claire pulled the flannel robe closer and shrugged. "I couldn't sleep. I heard mumbling. You were talking in your sleep."

"Really? What did I say?" Tess asked with a small grin.

"You mentioned some man named Mel."

"Man...?" Tess chuckled. "Mel is short for Melanie. She's a, well, a colleague at the university."

"A colleague?"

Tess laughed again and scratched her neck. "A long story for another night. Go to bed. Thanks for waking me up. I would have been a pretzel by morning."

Claire laughed as they walked down the hall and stopped by her room; she handed Tess her cowboy boots. "Thanks again for today. Jack had a wonderful time. It was very generous of you."

"Did you have a good time?"

Claire smiled and nodded. "I had a very good time. I only hope you didn't destroy too many cowboy hats. Good night, Tess."

"Good night, Claire." Tess laughed and backed up as Claire walked into the room and closed the door.

"I can't believe I knocked over that rack," she said with a sigh and limped back to her room.

Chapter 7

Tess walked into the kitchen the next morning and heard Pedro talking in Spanish; she assumed he was talking to Manny and was shocked when she heard Claire's voice. The two of them were conversing, and of course, Tess had no clue what they were saying. She was vaguely aware this bothered her as she walked into the kitchen.

"Bonito tardes," she said with a grin.

Pedro and Claire stopped and exchanged quick glances, then started to laugh.

Tess immediately frowned and was acutely aware this bothered her. "What's so funny? Didn't I say good morning?"

Claire stopped laughing. "No. You said pretty afternoon."

Pedro hid his grin in his coffee cup. Tess grunted and sat opposite him at the table, mumbling a thank you to Claire when she set the hot coffee in front of her. After a moment, Tess shrugged. "It could be a pretty afternoon."

Claire laughed and explained to Pedro, who laughed along. He stood and picked up his hat. He nodded to Tess and Claire and walked out.

"Nice guy." Tess watched him through the screen door. "He'll do fine. So will his son."

"That's good," Claire said as she loaded the dishwasher.

"So where did you learn Spanish?" Tess asked as she drank her coffee and watched her. She noticed the hesitation in Claire's movements.

"High school, then from the people where I worked," Claire said. "Now what would you like for breakfast?"

"Nothing, thanks. I'll grab a cinnamon roll, though." She took two sticky rolls off the plate and headed out the door.

"You really should eat something more substantial."

Tess poked her head back in. "And gain ten more pounds," she said with a grin and a wink. "See ya."

She was still grinning when Jack led Stella out of the stable. "Good morning, Tess."

"Good morning, Jack. And how is Clover this morning?"

"Doing better. I saddled Stella for you."

"Thanks. You're doing a fine job around here."

Jack shrugged as he petted Stella. Tess watched as she slipped on her gloves; she saw the disappointment. "But you know, I really could use another man watching the herd."

She glanced at Jack, whose eyes widened. "I'm getting better at handling a horse. Your dad is really helping me, and well, maybe I can help...somehow."

Tess smiled when she heard the frustration in his voice.

"How old did you say you were?"

"Sixteen, seventeen in the fall."

She wanted to ask him about his father, but for some reason, it didn't seem appropriate at the time.

"Well, you are riding better," Tess said, scratching her chin.

Jack said nothing as he continued stroking Stella's neck.

"And you're sixteen, practically seventeen. If I decide to let you help with the herd, you might have to sleep in the bunkhouse with the other men."

"That would be okay," Jack said, nearly pouncing on her words.

Tess slapped him on the shoulder. "We'll check with your mom later. You keep up with the stable and the corral for today."

Jack's grin spread across his face. "Okay. Thanks, Tess."

Tess mounted Stella and pulled on the reins. "No, Jack, I thank you." She leaned down to him. "Between you and me, getting you out there will save my aching arse."

Claire sat on the back porch peeling potatoes in the shade of late afternoon. She watched Jack riding the filly around the confines of the corral and chuckled at the fierce look of concentration on his face. As Claire looked past him, she saw Tess riding toward the corral. When Tess slowly dismounted and flexed her back, Claire saw how tired and dirty she appeared. The vision of Tess in a classroom with book in hand and wearing something other than dusty blue jeans had her dropping the paring knife into the bowl. It was then she also noticed how fit Tess had become; maybe it was her imagination.

"Tess! I'm getting better," Jack exclaimed.

Claire was amazed and had to agree with her son; he took so easily to riding a horse.

Tess dismounted and tied Stella off to the post. "You're doing just fine, Jack. Maybe after supper we can take a ride out in the open and let that filly run," she said with a tired smile.

She walked over to the horse trough and took off her hat, then plunged her head into the water. Claire grimaced as she watched.

Tess lifted her head, shaking it like a dog. Jack dismounted his horse and took off his hat. Claire knew what was coming next.

"Man, it's hot," Tess exclaimed as she ran her fingers through her wet blond hair, then grabbed the towel hanging on the fence.

"No kidding," Jack said and took off his hat and dunked his head in.

Tess threw her head back and laughed, then saw his mother sitting on the porch. She poked Jack on the shoulder and he came up for air, his wet face looking up in confusion. Tess motioned to the porch.

Jack sported a sick smile. "Um, sorry, Mom," he called out as Tess threw him a towel.

Tess gave her a teasing smile. "Me too, Mom," she called out.

She unbuckled her chaps and flung them over the railing. She saw Jack eyeing the leather. "Go on, you're tall enough. They're about your size," she said, and Jack quickly pulled them off the fence. "You just buckle them like a belt, then they have a strap behind the leg. There you got it. You look like a real cowboy now," Tess said proudly and turned him around.

"Yeah? Why do you wear them? I see them in the movies, but I never really knew."

"For driving the herd and riding through the brush and thickets. They protect your legs." Tess watched as Jack walked around. "You can have them. I've got another pair. Once you get used to riding, I'll take you out to see the herd."

"Great! Thanks, Tess," he said sincerely.

"You're welcome. Now get back to practicing," she said as she walked up to the porch. "Good afternoon, Claire." She gingerly sat on the top step. "What's for supper?"

"Beef stew and biscuits."

Tess let out a sigh of relief as she leaned against the railing.

"Are you done for the day, Tess?"

"Yes, thank God."

Jack came bounding up, then stopped short and slowly swaggered up to them. Claire and Tess exchanged quick glances.

"Tess, can I take care of Stella for you?"

"Sure. You know where to put the saddle and where the brushes are. Give her a good brushing and let her cool off. I had her running this morning. Got a few strays stuck in the thicket on the north pasture."

"I'll take care of her for you," Jack assured her and led the chestnut mare to the stable.

"He's a good young man, Claire. You should be proud of him," Tess said as they watched him.

It was then Claire noticed blood on the collar of Tess's denim shirt. "What happened?"

Tess followed her look. "I don't know. What is it?" She strained to see her shirt. "God, it's not a bug, is it?"

"You're bleeding." Claire walked into the kitchen and came back with the first aid kit. "Sit still." She sat next to Tess on the step and gently pulled the collar of her shirt. "Geez, Tess. Where were you? In the thicket with the cows?"

Tess chuckled as Claire cleaned the deep scratch on the side of her neck. "Yes, I was. I had to get them out of there. Chuck was chasing down strays, and the boys were in the other pasture." She flinched as Claire dabbed the cut. "Stinging, stinging," she exclaimed and tried to pull away.

"It's supposed to. Sit still." Claire leaned in, gently blowing on the cut. Tess instantly shivered and Claire laughed.

"Now I know how Stella feels, trying to get a fly off her back."

"So I remind you of a fly on your back?"

Tess looked up into her eyes. "No, not really."

Claire said nothing for a moment. "There, keep it clean. That means no dunking your head in a horse trough."

Tess laughed and flexed her neck. "Yes, ma'am."

Claire smiled in spite of herself. She walked back inside and came back with a bottle of ice-cold beer.

Tess looked up and took the offering. "Join me. I don't drink alone." She waited until Claire came back out and sat next to her.

"Thanks for the first aid." Tess touched the top of their bottles.

"You're welcome."

After taking a long pull from the bottle, Tess turned and leaned her back against the porch railing to get a better view of Claire. "Want to learn how to ride a horse?"

Claire stopped with the bottle up to her lips. She glanced at Tess, who was sporting a challenging grin.

"No."

Tess laughed at the resolute tone. "Why not?"

"Because animals and I don't get along. When I was a child, my dog bit me. My cat scratched me and the bird we had actually flew out of the cage and out the window," she said seriously, and Tess let out a genuine laugh at the mental picture. "It's not funny. I don't have a way with animals like you and Jack."

Tess let it go as she drank her beer. "Ah, this tastes good. Where's Dad?" she asked casually.

"He said he was going into town. He seemed a little restless," Claire said and drank her beer. She glanced at Tess. "Can I ask you a question?"

"Of course you can," Tess said and closed her eyes.

"Why doesn't your father go out with you during the day?"

Tess opened her eyes and took a deep breath and a long pull on the icy beer. "Doctor's orders. A couple of years ago, Maria said he had a mild heart attack. He's got to take it easy."

"Was it because of your brother?" she asked, and when she saw the curious look from Tess, she went on. "Your father told me about your brother. I-I'm sorry," she finished in a quiet voice. Tess nodded and sighed.

"Thanks. Yes, it was shortly after that. Dad took it very hard as you can imagine, having a child die so young and being the heir. He had big plans for Steve, being the only son. It nearly killed him when Steve died. He was all alone. I was in California at the time. I came back for the funeral, but…"

"You had your life in California."

Tess looked out at the land in front of her. Claire took the unguarded moment and watched her. She had a strong, yet very feminine profile. The wind lightly blew her blond hair away from her face, and when Tess turned her head slightly, Claire nearly gasped when she realized how pretty Tess was. Tess continued to gaze at nothing in particular, and Claire was happy not to interrupt. She gazed, too, but at Tess.

After a moment or two, Claire couldn't help it. "What are you thinking?" she asked quietly as she picked at the label on the bottle.

Tess turned her gaze to Claire, who was shocked to see a tear well in her blue eyes. "Nothing, everything." She took a long drink from the bottle before continuing. "I do have a life in California. But I was wrong to stay away for so long. I can see that now. Dad's getting older, a little forgetful. I don't know if you see it."

"I do. He called Jack Stephen the other day. But that doesn't mean…" Her voice trailed off because she had no idea what to say next.

"I have to figure out what to do here," Tess said.

"What do you mean? About your father?"

"No, about the ranch." Tess put her head back and closed her eyes.

"You need to rest more." When Tess didn't respond, Claire grinned. "You're not getting any younger."

Tess's eyes flew open then. "What is that supposed to mean?"

"Oh, nothing."

"Hey, I can still take care of things. I'm not in a wheelchair yet. And I'm getting back to my fighting weight, so watch it."

"I can see that."

Tess raised an eyebrow then. "See what?"

"I can see you're getting back in shape. Riding all day will do that. You're looking fit."

"I am?"

Claire laughed and finished her beer. "Yes, and that's the last ego stroke you get. Now tell me about California."

"It was eye-opening."

"Really? How so?" Claire asked. "Trying to find yourself?"

"I suppose."

"And did you?"

"Oh, yes, I believe I did."

"Now you have to tell me. I'm intrigued."

Tess turned her gaze toward Claire. For a moment, she looked as though she was sizing Claire up for something. "I found out I was gay."

Claire blinked several times. "Really?"

"Really." Tess leaned back and smiled.

"So that's who Mel is?"

"That's who Mel was," Tess corrected her. She continued when Claire gave her a curious look. "We were planning a summer vacation to Hawaii before I got the call from Maria."

"And I take it she was not thrilled with the idea."

"In a word, no. In two words, definitely no."

Claire laughed. "She didn't want to come with you?"

"I didn't ask."

Claire said nothing and Tess now laughed. "You so want to know but don't want to ask."

The color rose in Claire's cheeks. "I do not."

"Well, I'll tell you anyway. Mel is a city gal through and through. The idea of her here on this ranch would not appeal to her. And honestly? I'm not sure I would want her here."

"Now I will ask. Why not?"

Tess gazed around the vast landscape; she could feel Claire

watching her. "Can I offer an explanation?"

Tess looked at her. "Please."

"I think this land is very special to you, and I think you'd want someone to appreciate it as you do."

"Yes, you're right."

"And it's annoying you."

"Oh, yeah." Tess finished her beer and stole a glance at Claire. "Anyway, I settled into a comfortable life that I don't think I could have had in Montana twenty or thirty years ago. It might be different now, but back then—"

"Twenty years ago?"

Tess laughed at the incredulous look. "Yeah."

"How old are you?"

Again Tess laughed. "Forty-nine. How old are you?"

"Forty-one. You certainly don't look your age."

"Thanks. Neither do you. Must be clean living."

Claire laughed then. "Must be. Didn't you want to run the ranch?"

"It was never asked of me. Stephen was the only boy. Dad wanted him to run it. I can't blame him. It was in Steve's blood. He took to it naturally, so I can see why my father wanted him to run it."

"You're the oldest," Claire pointed out the obvious.

"That doesn't mean much. I'm not a man. It hasn't been easy gaining the respect of ranchers. Women are frowned upon when we show our brains or our brawn... Or our differences," she added and drank her beer.

Claire sighed heavily and moved to the opposite porch railing and leaned back, stretching out her shorter legs next to the tall ones of Tess.

"Why is that? What is the big deal? So many women in the world are businesswomen and leaders. God, look at Eleanor Roosevelt or Amelia what's her name, the aviator. Hillary Clinton and..."

"Martha Stewart?"

"W-well..."

"Lady Gaga?"

Claire nearly fell off the porch in laughter. Tess joined her. "You know what the sad thing is?" Tess asked through her laughter. "I have no idea who the hell she is."

Claire roared and slapped at Tess's knee. Claire took a deep breath and stopped laughing. "Seriously, if that's possible, what would your father do right now if it weren't for you? My God, you handle this ranch single-handedly. You ride like a man, you work like a man. I bet you could stand up to any one of them and..." She stopped, knowing she was on her soapbox. Tess just watched her, smiling.

"Sorry, it just irks me to no end. Why can't people just accept each other as they are? Why can't it be all right for a woman to do a man's work?" She snorted rudely as she drank her beer, realizing it was empty. "It's okay to have the babies, keep the house, and I'll bet your mother and grandmother had a big hand in keeping the Double R going. Don't tell me they just sat in the house and cooked, cleaned, and bore children!"

Tess just kept smiling as she listened and drank the last of her beer. She got up with a groan, took the empty bottle from Claire, and went inside.

"I'll bet your father and your grandfather were plenty glad they could," she called to the back door. "And why can't you be proud of who you are? You're a strong, attractive woman who can do just about anything. Well, except cook," Claire said thoughtfully, then realized she was alone.

She looked up to see Tess coming out with two more bottles of beer. Tess grinned and handed Claire the icy bottle. Claire took it, knowing she was blushing horribly.

"You turn a nice shade of red. It nearly matches the bandanna in your hair."

Claire immediately put a hand to her hair and drank her beer.

Tess groaned again as she sat down. "Continue," she said. Claire felt the heat rising in her neck. "I think you left off at, I'm an attractive woman who can't cook," she said with a smug grin.

Claire hid her embarrassment in her beer. "I shouldn't drink."

"Oh, no, I think you should drink more. If you sing my praises with one beer, imagine how you'll turn my head with two," Tess declared with a tease.

"Are you flirting with me, Miss Rawlins?"

Tess's mouth dropped. "Uh, well, no. I mean, I don't think so. I—"

Mercifully, Jack came bounding up to the porch. "All done!" he announced.

Claire stood and opened the kitchen door. "Good, go wash up. Dinner will be ready soon."

She stood by the kitchen sink and slugged back the icy cold beer. Her heart was racing and her body tingled as she peeked out the kitchen window to see Tess laughing and talking with Jack.

"God, she is beautiful." She sighed and turned away to get supper ready.

Chapter 8

May shaped up to be a very busy month for Tess. After making sure all the calves were tagged and matched with their mothers, it was time to make sure they didn't over-graze each pasture. And that meant moving the herd every few weeks from the north pasture to the south and rotating the herd around their five thousand-acre spread. It was a long hard time in the saddle— thank God for Jack, Tess thought. And for Manny and Pedro. They were tireless in their efforts. And Jack, well, Tess never saw a more natural horseman.

"What are you thinking?" Chuck called out as he rode up to her.

Tess watched Jack and the rest of the men as the herd moved toward the south pasture. "Jack. He's a natural."

Chuck nodded as he took off his hat and ran his forearm across his brow. "Like Steve."

"I was just thinking that, too."

"After all these years, decades really, I can't believe how green and thick this pasture is. Your great-uncle sure knew his stuff."

Tess nodded. "I know. It's kept our cattle healthy and fat for seventy-five years. I think we'd have gone under long ago without it."

"But it ain't enough, is it?" he asked in a soft voice.

"I don't think so, Chuck. We have about a thousand head, and the taxes on the ranch alone will eat up much of our profit." She leaned on the pommel and looked at the old house in the distance at the foot of the Bitterroots. "I stopped by the old place when I first got back. It seems to be in great condition, considering no one has lived there in thirty years."

"It's your dad. He and Steve made sure it was kept up. Then after Steve died, your dad went there faithfully and had the men paint it and make sure the plumbing and all was in working order. I stopped asking why a long time ago."

"I know why," Tess said. "Because it was the house he was born in, like his family before. It's why Steve helped him. And I left."

Chuck turned in his saddle to face her. "Cut that shit out right now. You followed your heart just like your Uncle Jeremiah did and anyone else in this family."

"I know. I just feel so selfish sometimes. And now I don't know if I can make it right."

Chuck grabbed her arm and gave it a healthy yank. "There is nothing to make right."

"Maybe Steve would still be alive if I hadn't left."

"That's the biggest pile of cow dung I've ever heard and you know it. Whatever happened that night, it would not have mattered if you were here or not. And don't let your father hear you talkin' like that, either."

Tess felt the tears sting her eyes; she knew what Chuck was saying was true. Her head knew it, now if she could only feel it. "Anyway, as I was saying. I was at the house, thinking how gorgeous it was with the Bitterroots and the stream that runs through it."

"What about it?"

Tess shrugged. "Some other ranches are doing it."

"Doing what?"

"It could supplement the cattle and maybe bring in a little extra."

"What could?"

Tess looked around at the scenery with the cattle spread across the pasture. "It might work."

"If you don't tell me what in God's name..."

Tess laughed. "Turn the Double R into a working ranch."

"A dude ranch?"

She raised an eyebrow at the incredulous tone. "Now hold on."

"Aw, Tess. I'm too old to be playing nursemaid to a bunch of

New Yorkers who have never seen a cow and…"

Tess laughed and held up her hand. "Take it easy. It's just a thought."

Chuck scratched his chin as Tess stole a glance at his thoughtful pose. "You figuring on turning the old house into like a guesthouse?"

"Maybe. Maria will be coming back and Claire could stay on…"

Chuck grinned slightly. "You would need a reason for her and Jack to stay on. We certainly don't need two cooks. Plus she's nice to look at."

"What do you mean?"

He rolled his eyes and gently nudged her; Tess had to grip the reins to stay in the saddle. "Don't be an old fool. She's a widow, for chrissakes, and has a son."

"And a very nice woman."

"Yes, she is."

"And a real looker."

Tess smiled reluctantly. "Yes, she is. And that's enough, you dirty old man."

The next few days found Claire watching with a worried eye over Tess. She would wake at night to find Tess sitting at the big desk, frowning and mulling over the bills. Many times, she wanted to go to her, but she felt it wasn't her place. Sometimes Tess just looked lonely.

One night, she woke and found Tess sitting on the back porch. It was a chilly early May night; Claire pulled her robe around her as she watched Tess from the kitchen door. She shook her head, and as she was about to go back to her room, she decided enough was enough.

Tess gazed at the moon as she rocked back and forth. She just couldn't sleep. It was well after midnight as she listened to the crickets chirp and the lone coyote howl off in the distance. With that, she heard someone moving about in the kitchen. As she looked up, she saw Claire struggling with two glasses of milk and the apple pie.

She grinned and shook her head as she came to her aid. "Hi. I was starving and I couldn't sleep. I saw you sitting out here. How about some nice cold milk and apple pie?"

Tess took the glass and the plate. "I will never refuse your cooking or your baking, Claire."

They sat in silence for a few minutes. Claire glanced over at the worried look and broke the silence. "You've been scarce lately. Is everything all right?"

Tess hesitated for a moment, then the stoic look appeared. She smiled as she took a bite. "Everything is fine."

Claire took a deep breath. "I can help," she said in a small voice.

Tess looked over at the pretty face half hidden by the moonlight. "Help with what?"

Claire drank her milk and held the glass in both hands. "You're paying me too much, Tess. I-I don't need this. Jack and I are living here in a very comfortable room. We have no expenses, so…"

"No," Tess said angrily and drank her milk. "I can afford your wages."

Claire rolled her eyes. "I'm just saying I—"

"No, damn it!" Tess barked and stood. She leaned against the porch railing and looked out into the moonlit night.

Claire narrowed her eyes at the stubborn pose. "Then I'll quit."

Tess whirled around and glared at her. "You will not!"

Claire stood in defiance. "You can't run roughshod over me, Tess Rawlins. I'll fire myself!" She stopped abruptly when she realized what she said.

Tess blinked while breathing heavily, then chuckled and leaned against the post.

Claire was now embarrassed and angry. "Don't you laugh at me."

Tess walked up to her and stood much too close. "I would never laugh at you. If I'm laughing at anyone, it's me," she said tenderly. "I'm sorry. I appreciate your trying to help. Why? Why do you care?"

Claire took a deep shaky breath and answered as honestly

as she could. "I don't know. It's just since I came here, I've felt wanted and needed, alive almost. It's been so good for Jack. Helena was just too big. He was lost, but in the past month or so, he looks older and healthier. Don't you see it?"

Tess smiled warmly as she searched her face. "Yes, I see it. I see it in you, as well. You have some nice color. You look healthy. The Montana weather suits you."

"Yes, it does. I love it here," she said and looked up at the full moon. "It is a beautiful moon."

"Yes, beautiful is the right word."

Claire looked up to see Tess watching her; the sadness in her eyes pulled at Claire's heart. "Let me help, please. I can help..."

Tess smiled fondly. "You've helped in so many ways, Claire Redmond, you will never know," she said in a tender, honest voice. She put her hands on the smaller shoulders. "I can afford your wages."

She continued quickly when Claire started to argue. "If it comes to that, I will let you know, but for now, I appreciate the offer and I'm awfully beholden to you. Awfully beholden."

Claire noticed a tear in the crystal blue eyes. "I'll hold you to that," she whispered and found herself staring at her full lips.

"I'm sure you will. I'm beginning to know you. You get that determined tone in your voice."

"I know. Jack says the same thing."

Tess saw the faraway look and took a chance. "What happened to his dad?"

Once again, Claire stiffened. Tess went on quickly, "I don't mean to pry."

"I know you don't." Claire walked over to the porch railing and leaned on it.

Tess watched as she stared out into the darkness. Since she first asked Claire about her life, Tess felt she was holding back. "I know it's none of my business. I don't know why I need to know."

Claire looked at her. "What do you mean you *need* to know? I'm not a murderer or a thief. I have no criminal background."

Tess was shocked, and her face showed it. "I didn't mean that at all. Good God. I just see a loneliness in you, that's all. I'm sorry you think that of me."

As she turned to leave, Claire held her arm. "Tess, I'm the one who should be sorry. That was out of line for me to say."

Tess regarded her for a moment before speaking. "You don't open up to many people, do you?"

Claire looked down at the railing and shook her head. "I need to make sure Jack is okay."

"Jack is a fine young man. You've done a great job with him. I can't imagine how you've done it all alone." She was stunned to see tears spilling down Claire's cheeks. Instinctively, Tess reached for her and gently pulled her into an embrace.

Claire clung to her, sobbing into her shoulder. "It's okay. Let it out," Tess whispered into her hair. "You gotta let it out."

For a few quiet moments, Claire cried mournfully until she pulled back. "I'm so sorry. I have no idea where that came from."

"I do. You probably haven't cried like that in a while." Tess reached over and brushed the back of her fingers against Claire's cheek, wiping away the tears. "It's a good cry."

Claire chuckled nervously. "I never have a tissue when I need one."

"No one does," Tess said with a grin.

"I..." Claire stopped and shook her head.

"What? Please tell me." Tess was still standing so close to her, she got a hint of the subtle fragrance of Claire's perfume.

Through teary eyes, Claire looked up at Tess, who cocked her head and smiled. "My God, you're beautiful, Claire."

Claire lowered her head. "Thank you," she said in a small voice.

"I take it you haven't been told that lately. What's the matter with the men in Portland?" she asked playfully.

"I don't care about the men in Portland or anywhere else for that matter," Claire said; she looked anywhere but at Tess.

Tess grinned; she was pleasantly surprised, yet she was still unsure. "A bad marriage might do that for you, but not all men are bastards. You're young. You can meet the right man. Look at my

79

father, he's a good guy, so is Chuck. Even Kyle Mathis, though he's a kid and a flirt, he seems—"

Claire looked up then. "Are you being purposely obtuse?"

Tess blinked and closed her mouth. "No, ma'am. Just making sure."

"S-sure of what?"

"That when I summon the courage to kiss you, I won't get slapped."

Claire laughed then, a genuine amused laugh that had Tess joining her. "I'm not a violent person."

Tess put her hands on Claire's shoulders. She looked down into her blue eyes. "I know that. I think you're a compassionate woman and a good mother who needs to be told more often just how good and kind she is."

"And are you taking on that role, Miss Rawlins?"

Tess pondered the question for a moment. Was she? Did she want to? Wasn't there enough of her plate with the ranch, her father, and Steve's death?

Claire raised an eyebrow. "You're taking just a tad too long to answer."

Tess laughed nervously and scratched the back of her neck. Claire reached up and placed her warm hand on her cheek. "You're a sweet woman, Tess. With a great deal to contend with now. If you ever find that courage, rest assured I wouldn't slap you. Now good night."

"Good night, Claire. Oh, don't forget we have the barbecue in a week for sixty people. It's on Memorial Day, uh… "

Claire's smile faded quickly. "A week?"

Tess winced at the squeak in her voice; she backed away. "Um, yeah. Didn't I tell you?"

"In passing, yes." Claire closed her eyes in frustration.

Tess grinned and quickly leaned over, giving her a peck on the cheek. "G'night." She pulled open the screen door and made her way to her bedroom.

Jed sat at the kitchen table watching Claire dash back and forth.

"Sixty people," she mumbled as she made her list. Jed grinned as he drank his coffee and watched. "Tells me one week before and expects… Who does she think I am?" she complained and checked her supplies.

"Jack!" she called out the kitchen window. Jed jumped and spilled his coffee. "I'm sorry, Jed. Jack!"

Jack and Tess were practicing roping. Jack almost had it when he heard his mother bellow.

"Boy, she does not sound happy," Tess said as she chewed on a piece of hay. She pulled in the rope. "You'd better run along."

"Nice knowing ya," he said, and Tess chuckled as she continued to rope the fence post.

Jack took off and headed for the kitchen. In a moment or two, he came running out.

"Mom wants you," he said with a flushed face.

Tess's back stiffened. "Me, why?" she asked nervously.

Jack shrugged. "She just said, 'Tell the Duke I have sixty questions for her.' I think she was being sarcastic."

"Hmm, was she mad?"

"I have to go into the cellar and check on supplies. She's all upset about something," he said and scratched his head.

Tess had already mounted Stella. She pulled her black hat down over her brow and leaned down.

"You never saw me," she said nervously and gave the stunned boy a wink. She pulled on the reins, gave the mare a quick kick of her heels, and took off down the dusty road.

"Jack!"

He winced and slowly walked back to the kitchen.

Tess was nowhere to be found when suppertime came. Claire was doing a slow burn as she slammed the steaks onto the ranch hand's plates. Each man mumbled his thanks and ate in silence.

"Who wants dessert?" Claire asked angrily, and each man declined and made a quick exit.

Chuck lagged behind, drinking his coffee. Tess had told him what happened about the barbecue and offered him a day off to get her off the hook. The things I do for my job, he thought.

Actually, he had never seen Tess Rawlins so scared. She'd faced mountain lions, wolves, and a few drunken ranch hands in her younger days, and he'd never seen her flinch.

He watched and winced as the pans got some rough treatment. This woman was the object of Tess Rawlins's only sign of weakness. Upon seeing this, it answered his questions about Tess's interest in Claire Redmond. As another pot received a dent, he wondered about it.

When he was in the Army during Vietnam, he saw a few men who were homosexual. The Army did not treat them very well, and once it was in the open, they were given a dishonorable discharge or a Section 8. He didn't think Tess was crazy, but he sure didn't understand it, and he knew her father wasn't thrilled with it, either, wanting an heir and all, but there you have it. Chuck Edwards saw a good deal of life and death far away from home in Vietnam. He had enough death.

Tess was a good devoted woman, but he also knew she couldn't tell anyone back then. Hell, he thought, even now there is still unwillingness among folks. She'd have been run out of this part of the state thirty years ago. No wonder she wanted to stay in California. Well, if it meant anything, he may not understand, but he certainly wouldn't judge. The Rawlinses had been like family to him and his father for nearly seventy years.

He took a deep breath. "I'd like some pie, if you don't mind," he said as he drank his coffee. He walked over to the stove, poured another cup, and opened the top cabinet. He took out a brown bottle and walked back to the table.

Claire angrily cut the pie and slapped it on a small plate, setting it in front of him without a word.

"Sit down for a minute, Mrs. Redmond," he said. Claire was about to say something and he looked up. "Please."

She grumbled for a second, then sat. He pushed the cup of coffee in front of her and pulled the cork on the brown bottle, pouring some in her cup. Claire raised an eyebrow as she watched.

"It'll cure what ails ya," he said seriously and poured much more into his own coffee. Claire raised the other wary eyebrow.

"I have rheumatism."

Claire laughed as she took a sip and cleared her throat. Chuck ate a bite of pie and nodded. "You're a good cook, and Tess Rawlins is, well, Tess," he added with a shrug. Claire narrowed her eyes as she drank her coffee.

"She sent you, didn't she?"

Chuck laughed and nodded. "I'm gonna tell ya something. Quite a few years ago, we were out on the south pasture. It was just winter with a good amount of snow. A few cattle strayed, and when we got there, a couple had been killed, a wolf, we suspected. Tess Rawlins took a rifle, and she and I went looking for this wolf. You know what she did?" He leaned in.

Claire was enthralled. She drank more coffee and leaned in, as well. Chuck poured a little more into her coffee.

"What?" Claire asked with wide eyes. "You're a very good storyteller."

"Thank you. She faced that wolf head on, not flinching one bit. She stood there, just a few feet from this snarling animal, and in a flash, reached for the rifle and shot it right between the eyes as it lunged for us. I soiled myself," he admitted and took a drink, pouring more than a drop in his coffee.

"No!" she gasped and took a drink.

Chuck nodded seriously. "Yep, that woman knows no fear. She gets it from her mother and grandma. Those women were tough as nails. I remember Lucy Rawlins. She was an older woman when I came on this ranch. She could shoot with any man. She's the one who taught Tess how to handle a rifle."

"She was a regular Annie Oakley, huh?" Claire asked with more than a trace of sarcasm. Chuck lowered his head and chuckled. "What's your point?"

Chuck looked into her deep blue eyes. "She's scared."

Claire looked around the kitchen. "Of what?"

"You," he said simply and took a very long drink of his coffee. He watched the blank look on Claire's face as he retrieved the coffeepot and took it back to the table. He refilled the cups and sat down, glancing at the confused woman.

"See, Tess is well…" He laughed nervously and scratched the

back of his head.

"It's okay, Chuck. She told me."

"Told you what?"

"That she was gay."

"Did she?" He sat back, contemplating this development. "And how do you feel about that?"

"Chuck, it doesn't matter to me. I…"

"Yes?"

"Nothing. I don't hold it against her, nor do I think badly of her."

"What do you think of her?" He drank his coffee.

Claire sat back, looking somewhat stunned. "I think Tess is a fine woman who cares deeply about her love of teaching as much as her love of this land. She loves her father, misses her brother, and is trying to find a way to save the ranch."

Chuck nodded his approval. "Very concise and accurate. She's also worried that you're angry, and she doesn't know how to handle you."

Claire snorted into her coffee, which tasted very good right now. "I am angry. She tells me five days before this big annual event that we're hosting, by the way, and I'm supposed to jump through hoops…" She stopped short. She was getting angry all over again.

Chuck hid his grin. "Tess has been out of the loop for a long while. She's not very good at the domestic end of the ranch. Her mother, then Maria took care of that. Tess is more suited for the, well, more toward the physical and business part. Getting her back into the saddle and handling the roping and herding has been hard enough. Now she's also checking the stock, the bills that come in, ya know. Remember, she's had a lot on her mind lately, especially with her dad. So whattaya say? Go easy?"

Claire wanted to stay angry with her. "Scared of me, huh?" she asked, and Chuck nodded.

"Between you and me? She was petrified, said she'd rather face that wolf than your temper," he said and both laughed. "I believe her. You scared the hell out of the boys tonight!" he said through his laughter. Claire chuckled and agreed with a shameful grin as Chuck continued, "They didn't even want dessert."

They both howled with laughter.

Outside, Tess stood in the early evening twilight listening to the laughter coming from the kitchen.

"Boo," Jed hissed in her ear.

Tess jumped and fell over a bale of hay. Jed laughed and offered her a hand. "Damn it, Dad!" she grumbled as he helped her to her feet.

"What are you doing lurking around?"

She looked skittish and nervous as she brushed herself off.

"Answer me. Why weren't you at dinner?"

Avoiding his face, she shrugged. Jed gave her a wary look. "What's the matter?"

"Nothing, for chrissakes. I was just checking on Clover. The poor thing misses Jack."

Jed rolled his eyes. "Don't give me that."

She stopped, then explained her predicament. Her father listened and glanced every now and then at the house. Tess finished as she ran her fingers through her blond hair.

"So it's just Claire."

Tess kicked at the bale of hay. "Oh, I know. I just don't want her mad at me, I guess," she mumbled and jammed her hands deep into her pockets.

"Then be a grownup and go talk to her, for chrissakes. You're her boss, Tess. It's not like you're..." He stopped as Tess avoided his face completely. He blinked a few times in wonderment.

All Tess's young life, Jed wondered about her. So did Emily. She never wanted to date. Never wanted to get married. Went all the way to California to go to college when she could have gone right here. She would have stayed out there if not for Stephen's death. Jed didn't want to think about it. It was wrong and unnatural, for chrissakes. That sort of thing just didn't happen to your daughter.

He frowned deeply and looked at Tess. All her life...he thought. He then remembered what Em had told him, just before she died—

"Tess will be the one to count on, Jed. Stephen is a good

boy, and he loves this land, but in the end, Tess will be the one. She's different, Jedediah Rawlins, and we both know it, though we won't talk about it. My time is growing short… Promise me you'll love her always."

"Christ, Em. I love her, you know that," Jed said with tears in his eyes as he sat on the edge of the bed. His wife looked so small, so pale. All her strength seemed to vanish, but her eyes still sparkled. Jed leaned down and kissed her deeply.

"You know what I mean. There'll come a time, you mark me. She'll need your love. Be strong for her. Be strong for me," Emily pleaded, and Jed nodded in understanding. "I love you, Jedediah. Love your daughter unconditionally for both of us."

Jed now looked at his daughter, who was looking down at the ground in shame. A feeling of guilt swept through him that was so palpable it nearly made him sob. He stood tall and ran his finger under his nose as he sniffed.

"You get in there, young woman. You're a Rawlins. We fight and stay together," he ordered.

Tess's head shot up and searched the watery blue eyes.

"You're a grown woman. How dare you hide in a stable? Didn't your mother and I teach you?"

"Dad. You don't know…"

"I don't care. You're a Rawlins. You're my daughter and someday you'll own all this. You can run a ranch, handle ten men and me, and be a big professor. Are you telling me you can't handle a woman?"

Tess blinked and took a deep breath. "She's not just a woman to me, Dad. At least I don't think so."

Jed struggled with his reaction. He didn't like it. He didn't understand it. He didn't want anyone to know. Em's words bombarded his brain; this was his time. God, how he needed Em.

"Tess, you must understand what's happening. I love you and I will always love you. But you must…"

"If Warren Telford gets wind of this. Dad," she started sadly, "why do you think I went to college in California? Not just to follow Uncle Jeremiah's idea about agriculture. Don't you think it's been on my mind for as long as I can remember? It's not easy for you. Imagine how hard it was for me," she finished and slumped against the bale of hay.

"I don't give a damn about Warren Telford. I'm talking about you and your life. If this is what you want, you must be sure. Because I know you, Tess. It's all or nothing. That's what I mean, sweetie. Does Claire know this?" he found himself asking. "And look at me when you talk to me. Don't ever hide."

Tess looked into his eyes. "No, I don't know. Shit, what am I thinking?"

Jed took a deep breath. "I've long since given up on figuring you out."

Tess laughed along with her father. "I don't know what Claire is thinking."

"Then find out." He reached for her and Tess flew into his arms. He rocked her for a moment, then held her away.

"Nothing about me has really changed," Tess said in a pleading voice, willing him to understand. He smiled sadly, gave a disbelieving snort, then chuckled. Tess blushed and chuckled along. "Well, maybe a little thing, but I'm still Tess Rawlins. I'm still your daughter and I'm still gonna fight for this land."

"I love you and I believe you. Now quit feeling sorry for yourself and get in there. Get," he said, turned her around, and gave her a shove.

Jedediah Rawlins stood there and watched as his daughter stood tall and walked toward the kitchen. Well, Em, he thought. I did it. I don't know if I did the right thing, but she's a good woman like you. She'll make a fine...he didn't know the right word. Well, she'll make a good partner for someone. Like you, Emily Richardson. You were a good partner through thick and thin, good and bad. You were at my side. That's what I hope for our Tess. Isn't that okay? God, did I do right by you?

He smiled as Tess walked confidently to the porch, walked up two steps, and abruptly did an about-face, walked down them, and headed around the front of the house. Jed hid his face and laughed.

"Em, we raised an idiot child," he mumbled to the heavens.

"She gets it from the Richardson side of the family, not mine."

After walking around the house a few times, Tess decided to go in; she was starving. She cleared her throat as she opened the kitchen door, announcing her arrival.

Chuck looked up and stood. "There you are. Got the herd all settled?" he asked and winked. Tess grinned and avoided Claire, who was putting the cups in the sink.

"Um, yeah. Had a few strays that I had to round up all by myself." She glanced at Claire, who was washing the dishes. "It was dark and..." She stopped, knowing she sounded like a fool.

Chuck rolled his eyes. "Well, I'm off. I'll make the rounds and head for bed. Thanks for the coffee, Claire," he said, and Tess frowned noticing him calling her by her first name.

"You're welcome, Chuck," Claire said happily over her shoulder.

Chuck slapped Tess on the shoulder and walked out. Tess stood by the sink and absently picked at the corner of the countertop.

"Did you eat?" Claire spoke first.

Tess sighed with relief. "No," she said in a low voice.

"Sit down, I'll make you something."

"No, you don't have to do..." Tess started, then stopped as Claire gave her a firm look. "Okay, thanks," she amended and quickly sat.

"Wash up, please," Claire said over her shoulder and offered the bar of soap.

Tess dried her hands and sat back at the long table. Claire put a beer in front of her. "Join me?"

"No, thanks. I..." She stopped and laughed remembering her earlier conversation. "I'll just have coffee."

Tess sat in silence as Claire prepared the steak and eggs. She placed the large plate in front of her and sat beside her. Tess dove in with gusto. "I'm starved."

"Watching over the herd all this time must have done it," she said into her coffee. She hid her grin.

"Yeah," she mumbled with a mouthful.

She finished and Claire took her plate away. She came back

with a piece of rhubarb pie. Tess groaned. "I'm surprised I haven't put on twenty pounds. Claire, you are a wonderful cook."

"I'd better be if I'm feeding sixty people," she said evenly.

Tess stopped with the fork in her mouth. "I'm sorry about that. I don't know why I didn't tell you sooner," she admitted with a sigh. "I mentioned it in town, then completely forgot again."

Claire smiled and reached for her hand. Tess instinctively grabbed onto it. "I know why. You're doing too much by yourself. You think you don't need any help and you can run this ranch all alone. There's no shame in asking or needing help," she said and patted her hand. Tess pulled a childish face that nearly made Claire laugh openly.

"Now tell me about this barbecue," Claire said, mercifully changing the topic.

"The ranchers from the surrounding area all come over. The wives bring food, as well, so you won't be making too much. At least I don't remember Maria or Mom making too much," she said thoughtfully. "Anyway, we have a side of beef and a pig on the spit. Corn on the cob, baked beans, if I recall. Oh, and ..."

"Don't tell me, biscuits," Claire interrupted. Tess nodded helplessly and both women laughed. "Tomorrow, Miss Rawlins, you are taking me into town. I called Tom with a list, and it'll be ready in the afternoon. Now what do you do for entertainment?"

Tess nodded as she ate yet another piece of pie. "If I remember correctly, Tom plays the clarinet."

Claire gave her a curious look. "That's it? A clarinet?"

Tess laughed. "No, he's got a band. Ray plays the fiddle, my dad plays the guitar, and Stan plays the piano, sort of," she said happily. "There'll be dancing and ..."

She looked at Claire, who pulled a face. "What? Don't you like to dance?"

"I-I, no..."

Tess gaped at her. "You don't know how to dance?"

Claire glared at her. "So what? I'll be too busy cooking..."

Tess shook her head. "Oh, no, you don't." She got up and turned on the small radio on the counter. After searching, she found the right station and tuned in the Patsy Cline song. It was slow and rhythmic.

Tess stood in front of Claire and held out her hand. Claire cocked her head, then blushed horribly. "Tess..."

"Come with me," she said and pulled Claire by the hand.

"Oh, no, really..." She struggled as Tess pulled her outside.

They stood close to each other; Tess gently took Claire into her arms.

"We have plenty of room, and no one is watching. I know you've probably never danced with another woman before," Tess said tentatively and glanced at Claire.

"Yes, I have as a matter of fact."

Tess blinked in surprise and grinned wildly. "You have?"

"Many times, but it's been so very long."

"Then this won't seem awkward for either one of us, will it?" Tess asked with a soft smile.

Claire returned the smile and shook her head. "I have a feeling it'll be quite natural."

Claire relaxed as Tess masterfully waltzed around the yard.

"You got it," she whispered in her ear. Tess sighed openly as she waltzed near the corral. Claire smiled but said nothing. A shiver went up Tess's back when she felt Claire's hand caress the back of her neck.

The song ended much too soon but still Tess held Claire in her arms.

"It's over," Claire whispered.

A ghost of a smile touched Tess's lips. "Is it?"

Claire knew she was blushing; her entire body felt on fire. Tess gently slid her hand up and down her back, barely moving.

"I'd like to waltz with you all around Montana, Claire Redmond," Tess said.

Claire smiled tenderly at the admission. "Montana is a big state, Tess Rawlins. That could take a lifetime," she whispered. The look of pure devotion and desire spread across her tanned features, causing a shiver to run up Claire's spine.

Tess gazed at the red full lips and lowered her head. She stopped for a moment, their lips inches apart.

"Then let it take a lifetime," Tess assured her in a low confident voice. Claire sighed, slipped her fingers up the back of her neck, and pulled her close.

"Tess," Claire started. "I don't. I mean I do, but there's so much you don't know."

Tess stepped back. "I'm sorry. I got all caught up in the moment here." She laughed nervously and put her hands behind her back. "A little impetuous, sorry. You're just so pretty, and I'm starting to care for you."

Both women laughed, then Claire leaned against the corral post and looked up at the moon. "Life just can't be simple, can it?"

Tess cocked her head and stood next to her and rested her forearms on the fence. She stared out at the darkness. "No, it can't. Though I don't know much about your life, I can see it in your eyes that you've experienced some pain. If you ever want to tell me, you know I'll listen."

"I know you will. And I will tell you, just not tonight. It's been me and Jack for so long, and I haven't been with another woman in so long, I honestly don't know how to react to this," Claire whispered. She then looked over as Tess stared blankly into the night. "So you think I'm pretty, eh?"

Tess grinned but still did not look her way. "Yes, ma'am. I do."

"Thank you," Claire said in a quivering voice.

Tess turned to her then and stepped closer. "You're welcome. And I will listen when you're ready. But right now, Claire…" Tess's heart was beating like a drum as she gently pulled Claire close to her body. "Please tell me it's all right to kiss you. I mean no disrespect to you or your son. I want you to understand I care for you and…"

Claire smiled warmly and let go of Tess's hand to reach up and put her fingertips against the warm lips that she would soon know. "Yes, Tess. It's all right, please."

Tess sighed as their lips met in a warm brief kiss. She felt Claire shiver as she pulled back; her body was on fire with just one kiss. "It may be a long time for you, Claire, but my God, woman, that was a wonderful kiss."

91

Claire was trying to breathe as she laid her head against the post and closed her eyes. Tess smiled and lightly brushed the wayward strand of hair from her face. She couldn't help it; she leaned in and kissed her once more, moaning as Claire reacted by slightly parting her lips. With her heart pounding and her body on fire, Tess cupped her cheek, then lightly traced Claire's jaw with the back of her fingertips.

Claire whimpered, then placed her hand on Tess's shoulder, pushing her back. Resting their foreheads against each other, both chuckled.

"I feel like a schoolgirl," Tess said and pulled back.

"That was a lovely kiss, Tess." Claire looked up into her eyes.

"I hope there'll be more, but for now, we'd better get back inside before I forget myself."

As she took Claire's hand, Claire stopped her. "Thank you."

Tess was shocked to see tears in her blue eyes. She kissed the back of Claire's hand. "It was my pleasure."

They walked back into the kitchen where Claire put the plates and glasses in the sink. Tess turned off the kitchen light and led the way down the hall; she stopped by Claire's room.

Tess chuckled and scratched the back of her neck. "Well, g'night." She offered her hand.

Claire blushed horribly and took the offering. "Good night."

As she opened her door, Claire turned back and gave Tess a quick kiss, then quietly slipped into the room, closing the door.

Chapter 9

"Where's Jack?" Claire asked as she wiped her hands on the towel.

"In the stable. He's a little upset. They have to get Clover back in the herd. Tess is talking to him," Jed said as he read the paper. He looked over at Claire, who was looking out the kitchen window, and couldn't help but see the difference from the previous night to that morning.

"What is she doing?" Claire asked as she looked.

Jed walked to the back door and blinked. Tess had a rope around Clover's neck as she led the calf to the corral. She pushed the calf in and took off the rope. Jack was grinning as he jumped over the fence and hugged the calf around the neck. Tess was talking to him and wagging a finger in his direction. Jack nodded, then leapt at Tess, hugging her around the waist. For an instant, Tess did not know what to do. Then she wrapped her arms around the teenager and ran her fingers through his short dark hair.

She pushed him away then and wagged the warning finger once again. Jack nodded and grinned.

"Hey, Dad," Tess said as she came in and tossed her hat on the table.

"Take that dirty thing off my table," Claire insisted.

Tess laughed as she hung it on the back of the chair. "And good morning to you, too, Claire," Tess said, grinning.

Jed watched for a moment and cleared his throat. "I thought you were putting Clover back in the herd," he said with a stern voice.

Tess avoided Claire's curious look. "W-well, I tried a few times. No cow would let her near her milk. I'm thinking maybe one of them that was caught in the thicket might have been Clover's mama…"

Jed gave her a smug grin. "So?"

"So…" Tess countered. "I can't let the calf die, for chrissakes. She needs milk."

"Normally, we'd have veal for dinner," Jed said.

Claire dropped a fork with a clang and whirled around.

"Dad!" Tess argued and stole a glance at Claire's horrified face. "He's joking. Aren't you, Dad?" Tess glared at Jed, who chuckled.

"Yes, I'm joking."

Claire was not buying any of it. "You are not, Jed Rawlins. You…you can't be thinking of killing Clover?"

"We are not killing Clover. Are we, Dad?"

Jed couldn't help it. He started laughing. Claire just gaped at him, and Tess started to laugh, as well. It was true. When a calf could not be weaned back into the herd, it was sold to the butcher. However, Clover was different.

"She's family. We can't just eat her for dinner," Tess said seriously as her lips twitched.

"That is not funny, Tess Rawlins!" Claire scolded, and Tess stopped laughing. "Would you like to go out and tell that story to Jack?"

Father and daughter contemplated the idea. They looked out the back door to see Jack walking around the corral and Clover trotting behind him. He had the bottle of milk in his hand.

"Nope. I do not run the day-to-day business of the Double R," Jed said seriously and read the paper.

Later that morning, Claire was in their room stripping the sheets off the bed thinking of poor Clover.

"Mom?" Jack yelled from the hallway.

"Jack, stop yelling. I'm in here," she yelled back.

"Tess needs you. She's in the stable," he said and flounced on his bed.

"Why? I don't know anything about that stable."

As she neared the stable, Claire winced. "Smelly place," she

Sea Of Grass

said to herself as she tentatively walked in. "Tess?" she called out.

"Over here, Claire," Tess said; she was in a stall, brushing a black horse.

"Jack said you needed me," she said. "That's a pretty horse."

Tess grinned. "This is a stallion and he is handsome, not pretty."

"Okay," Claire said, watching Tess as she finished brushing the silky mane. "Now what do you want?"

Tess came out of the stall. "I want to ask your permission to do something."

Claire grinned. "You don't need my permission. After that kiss last night…"

"Oh, that's not what I'm talking about."

"It's not?"

Tess laughed as she put the brushes away. "You're kinda cute when you're all pissy."

"I am not …" Claire stopped and took a deep breath. "My permission for what?"

"Jack has been riding that mare, but I think this guy will suit him better. I'd like to give this horse to Jack."

"Give? Tess, I'm no judge of animals."

"Understatement."

"But this has to be an expensive animal. You just can't give it to Jack."

"Why not? He's gonna be seventeen in the fall, and he's taking to ranching and riding so quickly. He needs a reliable horse."

Claire ran her fingers through her hair. "This is very generous. I…" She stopped and chewed her bottom lip while Tess waited. "What happens when Maria gets back?"

"What about it?"

"The only reason I'm here is because Maria had to go home. When she gets back, I won't be needed. You don't need two cooks."

From the look on Tess's face, Claire knew she had not thought of the inevitable. When Tess smiled, Claire's heart skipped a beat. "We'll work something out when the time comes. Do you want to

95

go back to Helena?"

"What? Tess—"

"Do you like it here?" Tess now stood in front of Claire, who took a step back.

"Well, yes. Of course I do."

Tess took another step toward her and Claire stepped back again, this time bumping into the stall door. "Do you like me?"

Claire heard the vulnerable tone; her mouth was instantly dry. She merely nodded. When Tess cupped her cheeks with her hands, Claire's body temperature rose; her heart beat wildly in her chest.

"Then we'll work something out." Tess kissed her forehead, then her cheek. "I'm growing very fond of you, Mrs. Redmond. And I honestly don't want you to get away from me." She kissed Claire tenderly, her tongue lightly dancing across her lips.

Claire moaned and sagged against the door; she put her arms around Tess's neck and pulled her closer at the same time, deepening the kiss.

"God, Claire," she breathed as she pulled away for an instant. Claire grabbed her hair and pulled her back, kissing her deeply.

In a moment, Tess pulled back once again, barely breathing as Claire looked up into the crystal blue eyes filled with want.

"I'm sorry." Tess groaned and leaned against the opposite wall. "Since last night, I've tried, but I can't think of anything else but kissing you and holding you. I couldn't sleep at all," she mumbled and ran her fingers through her hair.

Claire smiled and walked up, gently cupping Tess's face.

Tess groaned and closed her eyes. "Don't touch me, Claire. I am not responsible for my actions right now. I'm on fire."

"So am I. You made me this way," she said in a low voice.

"I know I shouldn't have done that. I—"

Claire grinned and kissed her deeply. Tess swayed, then pulled Claire into her arms and kissed her again. Her tongue slightly begging for entrance, Claire shivered and parted her lips in submission.

"God, I need you so badly," she growled and kissed her neck.

Claire gasped as she threw her head back and buried her fingers in her blond hair. "Tess, so do I," she cried out softly. Realizing what she was doing, Claire then pushed Tess back. "We can't do this in a barn. This is a little much. We have to be careful. Jack."

Tess nodded quickly. "I know, I understand. We take this slow. I'm sorry, that was a selfish thing to do."

Claire laughed and tried to regain her composure. "It was not. It was extremely erotic, and my legs are shaking right now. Don't apologize, please."

Tess nodded and laughed nervously. "Does this mean Jack can have the stallion?"

Claire laughed along. "Yes, Miss Rawlins. Once again, you get your way."

Jack nearly swallowed his tongue when Tess handed the reins to him. "Are you kidding me?"

"Nope. A good ranch hand needs a good dependable horse. I think this stallion will suit you. He's even-tempered and has already been broken in. Just take care of him."

"I will. Thanks, Tess." Jack looked at Claire. "Thanks, Mom."

"You're welcome. Just be careful, please."

Jack swung up in the saddle, grinning like a kid as he petted the horse's neck. "Hey, I need a name for him. How about Zeus?"

"That's a great name, Jack." Tess slapped at the horse's flank. "Have a good ride, get acquainted with him. Why don't you go out to the south pasture and show him off to the boys?"

"Okay. Thanks again, Tess." Jack beamed with pride as he rode out of the corral.

Tess watched him as he rode out of sight. She glanced at Claire, who had tears in her eyes. She put her arm around Claire's shoulders. "He's a good young man. He'll be fine."

Claire sniffed and looked up into Tess's eyes. "You're a good woman. Thank you."

"I have an ulterior motive."

In a very natural move, Claire put her arm around Tess's waist as they walked back to the house. "And what is that?"

"Best way to the mother's heart is through the son."

Claire laughed as she mounted the back porch steps. "You think you're so smart." She turned back to Tess, who was standing on the first step. Claire pulled the old black hat off her head and ran her fingers through Tess's blond hair. "That's not the best way…"

"It's not?" Tess asked playfully as Claire tossed her hat back to her. She watched as Claire opened the screen door. "What is the best way to your heart?"

Claire laughed. "You're a college graduate, Professor Rawlins. You'll have to figure it out."

"That sounds like a challenge," Tess said as she followed Claire into the kitchen.

Tess was contemplating Claire's words as she shoveled the hay into the stall. "So what's the way to your heart, Claire?" She laughed. "I will find out. This could be fun."

It occurred to Tess she hadn't felt this alive in years. Though her passion was teaching, she loved being outdoors on the ranch. Wiping her brow, she stopped shoveling the stall and looked out the window at the landscape. It was amazing to her that she hadn't thought of Mel at all. It was the end of May; Tess knew Mel was in Hawaii. The thought was once extremely appealing to Tess— long warm days on the beach, romantic nights under a palm tree, sipping an exotic drink—just not with Mel. Tess suddenly had a vision of Claire Redmond clad only in a skimpy Hawaiian dress with a flower nicely tucked behind her ear. Tess closed her eyes and leaned on the pitchfork. Claire Redmond in a sexy dress, her long brown hair blowing in the summer wind, her blue eyes sparkling, her—

She fell forward, and her eyes flew open when she heard her father laughing as he kicked the pitchfork from underneath her. She stumbled into the stall door. "Damn it, Dad."

"What the hell were you thinking about? I called you twice," he asked, still laughing.

"None of your business," Tess said angrily and picked up the pitchfork. "You nearly gave me a heart attack and ruined a great daydream."

"Ahh, dreaming about Claire?" He sat on a bale of hay. "Well?"

Tess leaned against the stall. "I guess, yeah."

"Do you know now if she feels the same?"

Tess heard the compassionate tone mixed with concern. "I think so. It's just that it's been so long for her. Because she has Jack and I think she's been trying to protect him."

"It has to be hard with a child and to do it all alone. Your mother and I were very lucky to find a love that lasted. You never know what can happen. You two need some time alone to find out." He grinned and grabbed Tess by the hand.

"Dad, what are you doing? You're scaring me."

Tess followed him outside and around the back of the stable. "There," he said.

Tess looked at the dilapidated buckboard wagon. "There what?"

"It just needs a little fixing up." He walked over and shook the wagon, as if testing its sturdiness.

"Fixing up for what?" Tess watched him with a wary eye. "Dad?"

"This is what I took to pick up your mother when I proposed to her."

"So?"

Jed rolled his eyes. "You have no romance in your soul. You're a Rawlins, and we have romance."

"Okay, I still don't..." Tess scratched her head. "You want me to propose to Claire? Geez, Dad, we just kissed…"

"You kissed her?"

Tess blushed at hearing the incredulous tone. "Yes, and it doesn't mean marriage—"

"Not yet."

Tess took a deep breath and shook her head. "Okay, let's get back to your original idea, which scares me."

Jed laughed. "Fix up this wagon and take Claire for a ride. Have some time alone. Pack a picnic lunch."

Tess thought about it and smiled.

Chapter 10

The day before the big barbecue, Claire was busy in the kitchen when she heard a noise outside. She looked out to see Tess in a wagon, driving it up the dusty trail to the house. What is she doing? Claire asked herself as Tess led the team of two horses. She hopped down and walked up the back porch.

"Claire?" Tess called out and smiled when she saw her in the kitchen. "You look wonderful."

Claire looked down at herself. "Thanks, but blue jeans and a white shirt wonderful? What are you doing with that wagon?"

Tess paid no attention as she opened the refrigerator and smiled. "A-ha!" she said triumphantly.

Claire watched as Tess took out the fried chicken and potato salad.

"Hey! That's for the barbecue tomorrow," she protested.

Tess put up her hand. "A few pieces won't be missed. Good Lord, you've been at that stove for two days straight. You have everything ready and you've planned everything down to the last fork. Now enough work. No arguing," she said firmly and gathered the little feast, included a few bottles of beer, and placed them in the picnic basket. "Ah, I nearly forgot," she said and walked out of the kitchen.

Claire stood there, her hands on her hips as she waited.

"Jack? Dad? I'm taking the buckboard. Claire and I are going for a ride. We will not be back until suppertime. I suggest you go into town for dinner." She heard Tess's voice call out and her heart beat wildly in her chest.

Tess came back with two blankets and a smile. "Let's go." She grabbed the picnic basket and Claire, pulling her out the door.

"Where are we going, may I ask?"

Tess climbed up next to her; Claire heard the painful groan and hid her grin. Tess held on to the reins and roughly slapped them against the horses. She sported a wicked grin.

"Nope," Tess said simply and guided the horses around the corral and down the dusty trail.

"It's beautiful, Tess." Claire sighed as they drove the small trail through the grassland. The cattle dotted the landscape as they lazily grazed. "I can see why your family fought so hard to keep it."

Tess looked around as she held the reins in her hands. "Since the 1880s when my great-grandfather Ned Rawlins gambled with his small fortune in Missoula. He won big and bought this."

Up on the sloping ridge, a lone huge oak tree stood out. "We use it as a marker. It separates the north and south pastures. It gets dark as pitch at night." She stopped the team at the bottom of the slope. "We'll walk from here."

Tess spread out the large blanket on the grass and under the lone oak tree. It was a beautiful late May afternoon. A few scattered clouds drifted through the blue sky. The sun was warm and the sweet smell of honeysuckle filled the air.

Claire looked around in all directions. Off in the west stood the Bitterroot Mountain range, part of the Rockies. The snow-capped tops majestically reached for the heavens. The grassland below contrasted the rugged mountains wonderfully. "My Lord, Tess. This is heaven," Claire said in awe as she shielded her eyes from the noon sun.

Off in the distance, at the foot of the mountains stood a huge log house. Behind it, a small river snaked between the house and the grove of trees that seemed to line the foot of the mountains. "Whose house is that?" She knew Tess need not look to know.

"The original Rawlins house. Nobody lives there now. Five children were born in that house. Ned Rawlins built it almost by himself. That's where the first herd of Double R started. When we were kids, we'd have to avoid many a cow pie, believe me, when we played around that yard." Tess laughed and opened the picnic basket. "I'll take you down there later. Now get over here. I'm starving."

"What else is new?" Claire sat next to her on the blanket.

"I think I'm falling for you, for one," Tess replied, not looking at her as she ate her chicken. "This is good."

Claire was dumbfounded as she took a chicken leg. Tess looked up and grinned as she opened a bottle of beer and handed it to Claire, who took a long drink.

"Why doesn't anyone live in the house?" Claire asked, avoiding her declaration. Her heart was pounding in her ears as she tried to eat the chicken.

Tess shrugged and took a mouthful of potato salad. "Everybody's either gone or moved away. Dad built our home when my mother was pregnant, so we'd have a place of our own. Now I think my father would like to move back. He and Steve took care of it all these years." She laid back and put her hands behind her head. "God, what a glorious day."

Claire looked around and had to agree. The warm breeze blew gently and Claire closed her eyes and lifted her head toward the sun. "Mmm. I agree." She glanced at Tess, who was staring up at the sky. "This is quite romantic, Miss Rawlins."

Tess grinned but did not look at her. "Just trying to figure out a way to your heart, Claire."

Claire lay on her side next to Tess. "You're getting closer."

Tess closed her eyes and smiled. "I don't give up easily."

"Thank God for that."

Tess turned her head. "I thank God for many things lately."

"Like what?" Claire reached over and traced the outline of Tess's jaw with her fingertips.

"Like my good fortune to come back home. And while I miss Maria, her leaving brought you and Jack into my life."

"What about Melanie?"

"Since it's been over a month and she has not contacted me nor I her, I think we both realize what our relationship was, or more accurately was not."

"Is she pretty?" Claire gently ran her hand through Tess's blond hair and grinned when Tess actually purred.

"I don't want to talk about Mel or anyone else. And if you don't kiss me soon—"

Claire leaned over and placed a gentle kiss against her warm responsive lips. After a few minutes of heavenly kisses, Claire pulled back. Both women were breathless.

Tess let out a sigh. "C'mon, I'll show you the house. If I can walk."

They gathered the picnic basket and headed down the ridge to the old house. "The weather is turning," Tess said and looked up at the dark clouds.

No sooner did she say that than the clouds opened up. "Shit!" she exclaimed as the rain started. Claire laughed openly. Tess slapped the reins and the horses took off. "Hold on." Tess laughed, and Claire grabbed her arm and did just that.

Tess pulled tightly at the reins and stopped outside the empty house. "Get the blankets in before they get wet."

Claire jumped out, grabbed the blankets and basket, and dashed up on the porch. Tess was soaked as she quickly un-harnessed the horses, slapped them on the flanks, and they took off.

"Won't we need them?" Claire asked the obvious as she pushed the wet hair from her face. She was not as soaked as Tess was. At least the blankets were dry. Tess pulled her hat down over her eyes and dashed onto the porch, breathing heavily.

"Shit, it came down fast. And yes, they'll be back." Tess took off her wet hat. "Let's get in out of this." She opened the door.

They walked in and Claire looked around in wonder. The foyer was huge. Directly in front of them was a long wide staircase. At the top, she saw three bedroom doors spread across the expansive hallway. She looked to the left. A double door closed off the room, and to the right, the same huge doors hid the room behind it.

"This is magnificent," she exclaimed as she looked around. "It must have been wonderful living here."

Tess nodded and walked to the left, pulling the double doors open. Claire followed and saw the living room. It was as everything else, very large. The stone fireplace took up most of the outside wall. Arranged around the room were sheet-covered pieces of furniture. There was a large rolltop desk over in one corner with a desk chair.

Tess ran her fingers through her wet hair as she loaded the

fireplace with the wood that was still lying in the bin. "I'll get this going."

Claire walked into the spacious log-sided room. She looked around and took the sheets off the old furniture that smelled musty. "Your great-grandfather must have loved your great-grandmother very much to build something like this. It must have taken him months to build this."

"As far as I can remember, it took him the better part of the spring and summer. And yes, he loved her very much."

Claire heard Tess walk up behind her and gasped when she felt Tess's arms around her waist. "My father says the Rawlinses are all romantics."

Claire turned in her arms and wrapped her arms around Tess's neck. "I sincerely hope so. But for now, you need to get out of those wet clothes." Claire said seriously. "Take them off and we can dry them by the fire. Here, take the blanket. I'll check out the rest of this mansion." She avoided Tess's grinning face as she walked out and slid the doors closed.

Tess struggled out of her wet boots, denim shirt, and jeans, then her underwear. She slipped the wool blanket around her shoulders and placed her clothes on the fireplace screen to dry. She stood there for a moment and watched the flickering flames as they danced in the huge fireplace. She smiled as she remembered how much fun she had in this house when she was a girl. How her grandparents were always hugging or touching, kissing each other.

As a kid, she thought it was mushy adult stuff. Now as an adult and on the verge of being in love truly for the first time in her life, she felt she understood all the elder Rawlinses. She looked around the large living room and pictured all her uncles and aunts, all her cousins before they moved away. The house seemed lonely now. She understood as well her father's need to keep it up.

This was the idea she had when she talked to Chuck. This big house was ideal for a guesthouse for the Double R. "It could work," she whispered as she looked around. Everyone should be seeing this magnificent Montana landscape and this house, preserved so well.

With that, Claire opened the sliding door and poked her head in. "C'mon in. I'm decent." Tess laughed as she wrapped the blanket around her and sat on the couch facing the fire.

Claire sat on the opposite side and Tess gave her a smug grin but said nothing. "Check out the rest of the house?"

Claire nodded. "There are six bedrooms…"

"Seven actually. When Grandma got sick, Granddad made the back storage room a bedroom. They slept there from then until Grandma died. She couldn't make the stairs anymore. C'mon, I'll show you."

She walked out, pulling the blanket around her as Claire followed. "And, yes, Claire. I am naked under this blanket."

"Don't start, Tess."

Tess laughed and opened the door at the end of the hall. Inside was a huge bedroom.

"He knocked out a space for the windows and put a small fireplace in for her. Isn't it cozy?"

Claire looked around the large room. A four-poster bed was on the far wall. The fireplace was on the outside wall, a small overstuffed chair in front of that. One lone dresser stood on the opposite wall from the fireplace. It was cozy, warm, and very inviting.

"Yes, it's very cozy. You said no one lives here, but the entire house seems lived in."

"Dad's been coming here. I'm sure he hated to see everything covered in sheets. So he and Steve had been sort of looking after it."

"I guess the romantic soul runs deep in the Rawlins family. C'mon, let's get you back in front of the fire," Claire ordered and ushered her out.

Tess retrieved two beers from the basket. "A little warm, but what the hell," she said and offered one to Claire.

They sat on the couch as the lightning flashed and the thunder rolled. Claire jumped and scooted closer to Tess, who welcomed the closeness. She snaked her bare arm out of the wool blanket and reached for Claire's hand, which was shaking.

"You afraid of storms?" Tess asked quietly.

"Yes. It's stupid I know, but when I was a girl on Long Island, it seemed it was always raining. You'd think I'd get used to it." She chuckled nervously and drank her beer.

"I thought you were from Portland."

Claire pulled away from her and stared at the fire.

"Tell me about your life," Tess said. Claire shrugged but said nothing. "And don't give me the short one-word answers like last time. Tell me about you, about your life."

Claire pondered this for a moment. She knew Tess had a right to know about her life. She also knew that she'd tell her all of it someday... Maybe.

"It's boring stuff."

"But you were married. You must have been in love," she gently prodded.

Claire took a deep breath and a long pull on the beer bottle. "Tess..." she began and stopped when the thunder cracked overhead. She jumped straight up in the air and Tess followed her, holding on to her blanket.

Claire immediately clung to Tess, the blanket confining her movements. "It's all right," she whispered into her ear. She saw the faraway look in Claire's blue eyes as she gazed into the fire.

"My word, what's going on in that pretty head of yours?" Tess walked over to her clothes. The shirt and undergarments were dry, but the heavy denim jeans were still damp. She turned them over and set them once again on the fireplace screen.

She turned to see Claire watching her. "You'd best turn around," Tess offered as she held up her shirt and undergarments. Claire raised an eyebrow and stood still. Tess swallowed but was up to the challenge. "Suit yourself," she said with a shrug. It was actually a shiver.

Standing in front of the fire, she slipped the blanket down to her waist and secured it, then pulled her shirt on over her head.

"Beautiful," Claire murmured as Tess buttoned her shirt.

"I am not beautiful, Claire Redmond. I'm afraid that word can only describe yourself," Tess said in a low voice. She ran her fingers through her hair and turned to her.

Claire slowly walked up to her and finished buttoning her

shirt. "All right, then you're a handsome woman, Tess Rawlins. Is that better?"

Grinning with embarrassment, Tess said nothing. She reached out and held Claire's hands. With that, both heard the sound of horses outside. Tess whirled and grabbed her jeans, struggling into them. She dashed for the door just in time to see Chuck and Stan dismounting. She noticed they had Stella with them, saddled and ready.

"It's the herd, Tess. Somebody was shooting and they took off. The cattle are restless, and I'm ..."

On that, they heard it. Claire had no idea what was happening. It sounded like thunder.

"Stampede, shit!" Tess cried out and grabbed Claire. "Stay up here. Do not get off this porch."

"But..." Claire started, but Tess had already swung up on Stella.

"Stay put. I'll be back to get you," she yelled, and all three galloped through the grassland.

Off in the distance, on the high ridge, Claire saw it. She blinked several times in amazement. The rain had stopped, and the late afternoon sun tried to peek through. It seemed like thousands of them... The herd was on a stampede heading right for the old house.

What happened next was remarkable. Two other riders had joined Tess, Chuck, and Stan. They fanned out, riding right at the stampeding cattle. Waving their cowboy hats and screaming like banshees, they rode closer to the charging herd.

Claire held her breath as she watched Tess galloping, clicking her legs wildly against the horse's side, her white shirt billowing in the wind as she yelled, screamed, and waved her hat furiously against the oncoming herd.

It was amazing. The cattle nearly came to a halt as they dispersed and ran in every direction. The force of the stampede seemed to dissipate, but they still came in her direction. In a heartbeat, the herd was almost at the front door, running in all directions, kicking up dirt and grass.

Claire stepped back and plastered herself against the front

door, petrified. The thunderous sound was all around her. She was helpless but to watch through the dust as the cattle streamed by the house. With a crash, she looked over to see the buckboard rolling over, the cattle trampling it into kindling.

She then saw Tess riding like the wind in the wake of the stampede. She came to a screeching halt, pulling on the reins.

"Are you all right?" she called out.

Claire nodded. "I'm fine!" she yelled back and Tess nodded.

"Stay right there. I have to go with them. Don't worry."

Claire nodded. "Go!" she called, and Tess took off around the house.

Claire watched her ride out of sight. She finally breathed as the dust cleared. She sat on the porch steps before she collapsed. I don't know how that woman does it, she thought as her entire body shook with the adrenaline that surged through her body. "I think I may faint," she said seriously.

An hour later, Claire heard her. She ran to the front door to see Tess and Stan riding up slowly. Tess looked like hell. She was filthy and sweaty as was Stan. Claire dashed onto the porch to greet them. She stopped when Tess swayed slightly in the saddle. Stan reached over and caught her before she slipped off the horse.

"What happened?" Claire exclaimed as Tess shook her head.

"I'm fine," Tess said, and Claire saw the lines of pain etched in her face. Stan quickly dismounted as Claire ran down to help. "I fell off my fucking horse," Tess said through clenched teeth. "And if you repeat that, Stan, you're fired." She looked at the mangled wagon. "What happened to the buckboard, Claire? Did you try to drive it?"

Stan laughed and saw the look from Claire. "Sorry…" he mumbled as he helped Tess up the steps.

"Go into town and get the doctor, Stan," Claire said firmly, and he nodded. Tess stopped.

"I'm fine, just sore. I don't need a doctor," Tess argued as they guided her through the front door.

"Stan…" Claire said in a warning voice.

"Stan…" Tess said in a threatening tone.

Claire put her hands on her hips and glared at Stan, who swallowed and nodded. "I'm going," he said and took off.

"Quit telling my ranch hands what to do," Tess mumbled childishly.

"Keep still and get in," Claire ordered. She put her arm around Tess's waist as she let out a muffled cry of pain. Claire immediately pulled her dirty shirt up and saw the deep dark bruise. "Damn it, Tess..." she whispered. "Come on down the hall to the bedroom. Now," she insisted, and Tess walked slowly to the room.

"Stand still." She threw back the covers and gently got Tess to sit on the bed. "Hurts?"

"No, I'm fine," Tess insisted as she breathed heavily through her nose. Claire lifted the dirty shirt over her head, trying not to notice the naked upper torso. Tess chuckled at the blushing woman. "I had other plans for this moment, Claire Redmond," she said in a painful voice.

Claire chuckled nervously. "Lie on your stomach and quit talking," she whispered, and Tess, through a grimace of pain, obeyed. Claire gasped as she watched the bruise spread across her lower back. "Tess, I hope nothing's broken."

"So do I," she said in a muffled voice. She turned her face to see Claire. "I'll be all right."

Claire couldn't help it. Tears sprang into her eyes as she only nodded. Tess strained her neck to see her. She lifted herself up.

"Claire, please don't. I'm fine, really."

Claire wiped the tears away and gently pushed her back down onto the bed. "I know. I just hate to see you hurt, damn you. Riding in front of a stampede. What were you thinking?" she said angrily and walked across the hall to the bathroom.

Tess smiled slightly as she listened to her ramblings.

She came back into the room with a bowl of water, soap, and a cloth. Tess was grinning wildly as Claire set the bowl on the nightstand next to the bed. "Honestly," she scolded as she wrung out the cloth.

"Honestly, you hate to see me hurt? Why?" Tess asked as she looked back.

"Shut up and lie still." Claire gently wiped the dirt off the

109

exposed tanned cheek.

"There is nothing broken, though I don't know how, just a deep bruise." Doc Harris sat on the edge of the bed. "How the hell did you fall off your horse?"

"I have no idea," Tess mumbled into her pillow.

"Too much time sitting in the classroom. I'm glad you're back, by the way. I know this might not be a good time, but your father has skipped two appointments over the winter. He blamed it on the snow."

Tess looked over her shoulder, then with his assistance, she turned over on her back and winced. "What's wrong with him, Doc?"

"Besides the mild heart attack, I won't lie to you, Tess. He may have the onset of Alzheimer's." He stood and rolled down his sleeves.

"What do we do?" Tess glanced at Claire, who smiled.

"Not much to do right now. He just needs to come to me regularly, just for a checkup. We'll take it from there. Now you stay put, ice your back. I've left a few pain meds for you. Take them as needed, you know."

He looked up at Claire. "I suppose you'll have your hands full with this one." He motioned to Tess, who was scowling.

"I'll do my best, Doctor, thank you." Claire followed him out of the bedroom. She poked her head back in and smiled sweetly. "Don't go anywhere. I'll be right back."

"She'll be fine. It'll take more than a stampede to hold that idiot down. Maybe you can talk some sense into her. I think you may be the only one," he said, giving Claire a curious smile. Claire felt the color rise to her cheeks. The doctor looked around the landscape.

"God certainly was in a generous mood when he created this." He sighed as they gazed at the late afternoon sun lazily hanging over the mountains. Claire took a deep happy breath.

"Yes, he was, Doctor. Can you see why they fight so fiercely for it?"

Dr. Harris nodded. "Yes, I do, but it's a way of life that's dying, Mrs. Redmond. With Tess back from college to help, I'm sure she can turn this ranch around. It'll help the town, as well. I hope she has a few tricks up her sleeve to keep it going. People are talking about moving away to the big cities. Helena, Butte, Missoula. I'd hate to see that happen. Ah, well." He sighed and winked. "Take care of that pain in the ass."

"Will you be at the barbecue?"

"Yep. Wouldn't miss it."

Claire watched the car drive down the dusty trail and waved as Stan and Chuck rode up to the house.

"How is she?" Chuck asked as he dismounted.

"She'll be fine, boys. Just a deep bruise, but she has to stay in bed. She probably shouldn't be at the barbecue, but I don't think she'll listen to any of that."

"I just need to tell her what's happening with the herd. Stan brought a few things for the night. We figured she was going to stay put and you'd stay with her. We already told Mr. Rawlins and Jack. They'll come by in the morning," he said, and Claire nodded.

"Check this out, Mrs. Redmond. If ya need anything, I'll bring it by." Stan took off his hat. Both men disappeared into the house, neither wanting to face the rage they were sure to find.

"Tess?" Chuck called out as they entered the bedroom.

"I'm awake, Chuck. C'mon in," Tess said tiredly. "How's the herd?"

"All settled. Don't worry," he said and glanced at Stan.

Tess felt the tension in the air and struggled to move.

"Hey, you stay put."

"What's going on, fellas?" she asked painfully. "I said, what's going on?"

Chuck took a deep breath. "Someone spooked the cattle. We heard a gunshot, but I didn't see anyone. Luke told me he saw somebody in the grove of oak trees on the top of the north ridge. He couldn't be sure, but Marty thought the rider was on an Appaloosa."

"We all know the only asshole in this county that owns a

111

fucking Appaloosa!" Tess barked through clenched teeth.

Claire ran into the bedroom. "What's going on?" she asked as Chuck and Stan stepped back when she entered the room. Tess struggled to wrap the quilt around her as she tried to sit up. "Stay right where you are." She sat on the side of the bed.

"Does my father know?" she asked after taking a deep breath.

"Yeah, Luke was a blabbermouth," Stan said.

"Chuck, get back to the ranch, please. Make sure my father doesn't flip and head into town. Tell him we'll be back in the morning." She shifted angrily under the covers. "Have Luke, Stan, and Pedro stay with the herd tonight. Just in case."

"Already done, Tess. You relax. We'll see ya in the morning. G'nite, Claire," he said and both men walked out.

"How do you feel?" Claire adjusted the quilt around Tess's shoulders.

"Like I fell off my fricking horse," Tess said honestly.

"Stan was nice enough to bring over a few things. I'll fix something to eat, then you get some rest. I'd tell you to stay in bed tomorrow, but you won't."

"I'm the hostess. I have to make an appearance. Besides, I want to see if Warren Telford has the nerve to show his ugly face."

"Do you think he'd be stupid enough to have someone cause a stampede in the middle of the day with your men all over?"

Chapter 11

"Are you a complete idiot?" Warren Telford bellowed. Ed winced as he sat down. "Who told you to do something that asinine?"

"Um, you did, sir," Ed said in a shaky voice. Telford glared at him through the billow of cigar smoke.

"I believe I told you to put a scare into them, not cause a stampede! You fucking idiot!" He rubbed his sweating brow. "You see, Ed," he said very calmly, "the purpose of a stampede is to take them by surprise and have the cattle scattered all over the county. It's best done at night," he explained slowly as if poor Ed was a moron.

Ed nodded and looked as though he had an excellent idea. Telford held up his hand. "No. Do you think Tess Rawlins is stupid enough to leave the herd unattended at night now? The element of surprise is gone..."

With that, the phone rang. "Mr. Telford, Mr. Collins on line two."

"Get out of here, Ed. You've done enough for one day." Ed rose and made a hasty retreat.

"Collins? What have you got?"

"Nothing so far. I can't find anything on a Redmond in Portland killed in the time frame you asked. Claire Redmond lived in Portland for ten years, then in Helena until she came here. Nothing out of the ordinary. What exactly are you looking for?"

"She's hiding something. I can tell by the scared look in her eyes. Keep digging," he said and hung up the phone.

"I'll get that land one way or another," Telford vowed as he rocked in the big chair puffing his cigar.

113

Chapter 12

Tess woke with a heavy groan. "Falling off my horse. How embarrassing," she mumbled as she sat on the edge of the bed. She painfully slipped into her shirt, then struggled into her jeans and socks. Tess glared at the boots. "Those are going to be a problem."

"What are you doing out of bed?" Claire demanded from the doorway.

Tess looked up and grinned. "Good morning to you, too, Claire," she said with a grin. "Where'd ya sleep?"

"On the couch. Get back into bed," she ordered and walked into the room.

"You first," Tess challenged lightly.

Claire put her hands on her hips and just glared at her. Tess chuckled at the maternal posture. "Okay, at least help me with my boots."

"You can't even put on your own boots?" Claire picked up the dusty cowboy boots. "You need a new pair. I'd like to see you dressed up. I bet you clean up nice. Lie back and relax."

Tess did as she was told as Claire lifted a leg and slid on the old boots with a minimum amount of difficulty. Although when Claire looked up, Tess was grimacing. "What's the matter? Are you sore?"

"Nope," Tess grunted and smiled sarcastically. "Now please leave the room. I don't want to pass out in front of you."

Claire laughed openly and offered her hand.

Jed and Jack helped the others set up for the barbecue while Claire busied herself in the kitchen with the last-minute preparations. Tess was ordered to bed until the guests arrived.

"My Lord, is that a whole cow?" Claire asked as Jed instructed Jack how to baste the huge side of beef with the marinade.

"Isn't this amazing, Mom?" Jack took the marinade-soaked mop and basted the beef. "Mr. Rawlins said it'll be ready by five. It's my job to baste it every twenty minutes."

Claire watched Jack as he concentrated on his task. He looked older, much older than his sixteen years.

"Is he taller?" she asked Jed as he set up the horseshoe pit.

"He does look older in just the short time you've been here, Claire. He's really taken to ranching. Did you know Tess has him riding all over and even the boys have taken him under their wing?"

"Amazing," she said, shaking her head. "This is so good for him."

"Bet he misses his father. Or was he too young?" Jed asked.

Claire watched Jack and smiled sadly. "He was too young."

"Claire, I have to ask you something. Jack asked Tess if it was all right with you, if he could bunk with the boys occasionally. He needs a male figure and I'm not trying to tell you how to raise him. He's a fine young man. But he's at an age…" He stopped and took a deep breath. "Tess thought it would be good for him and I agree. The decision, of course, is yours."

Claire looked at Jed and smiled warmly. She reached up and kissed his cheek. "Thanks, Jed. I think it'll be fine. You're right. He needs a father or at least a man around. He is a teenager now. In a few years, he'll be all grown. God, if he gets any taller,' she said and both laughed as they watched the boy coming into his own.

"Well, we'd better go get cleaned up. Folks should start arriving in an hour or so." Jed put his arm around Claire, giving her a small hug. "I'm so glad you two are here."

Claire looked up into the watery blue eyes, so much like Tess's sparkling eyes. Jed smiled. "I know Tess is glad. I haven't seen her this happy since she got her first filly," he whispered, then walked away, leaving Claire just staring as he walked into the house.

"Holy cow, Mom, you look great!" Jack exclaimed as he walked around her.

"I do? Are you sure?" Claire asked nervously as she ran her fingers through her hair.

She wore a pale blue shirt with the tradition western-style black trim. Her jeans fit snugly, and Tess offered one of her belts. "I don't look too..."

"You look perfect. Like a real cowgirl."

Claire laughed. "Well, if you're sure."

"I'm sure," Jed called out from the kitchen doorway. Claire looked up and her eyes widened.

"My, you are a handsome man, Mr. Rawlins."

Jed stood tall and grinned. He wore brown slacks and matching cowboy boots. His brown shirt tucked in and the slacks belted with a large silver buckle. He held his brown Stetson in his hand. "Thank you, Mrs. Redmond," he said and bowed slightly. "Jack, you look handsome, as well, young man."

Jack grinned. He wore a pair a dark blue denim jeans and boots and a black cowboy shirt open at the collar.

"Where's Tess?" Jed asked quickly. "That woman is always late. Her mother said she was late for her own birth..."

"Stop your yammering, Dad," Tess called out from the hall.

Claire blinked several times and Jack whistled. Tess stood in the doorway dusting off her slacks. "I haven't worn these in years. I had no idea they'd fit. Maybe I have lost a few..." She straightened her collar and looked up to see three pair of eyes staring. "You look like a bunch of hoot owls. Oh, shit, did I forget to zip?" She quickly looked down.

"You are beautiful, Tess," her father said honestly.

Tess blushed and frowned. "I am not beautiful."

"Handsome then," Claire said and they exchanged grins.

Tess wore a pair of black slacks and matching cowboy boots. Her crisp white long-sleeved shirt, trimmed in black tucked in the turquoise belt with a small buckle, gave notice to her slimmer waistline and hips. She wore a matching turquoise stone necklace that accentuated her ocean blue eyes. Her blond hair was unruly and Claire Redmond never saw anything quite so captivating in her life.

Tess held a new black Stetson in her hand and dusted it off. She and Claire met in the middle of the kitchen. Tess smiled fondly. "Got a new hat. You are beautiful," she whispered emphatically, just enough for Claire to hear.

Jed slapped Jack on the back. "C'mon, son, time to tend to the barbecue."

Claire closed the distance between them. She reached up and straightened the collar and smoothed the shoulders of the white shirt. "And you are quite a handsome woman, Tess Rawlins."

Tess winked and put on the new black Stetson, pulling it low over her brow. Claire laughed at the cocky grin. "You do clean up real nice," she drawled, and Tess grinned deeper.

"I'd like to kiss you right now." Tess looked over Claire's shoulder and out the back door. "No one can see…"

Claire then pushed the hat on the back of the blond head and pulled her down for a searing kiss.

Tess's knees buckled at the unexpected kiss and moaned slightly. Claire pulled back and Tess swayed forward. "Whoa, now that was a kiss."

"Yes, it was," Claire said nervously and licked her lips. The Stetson was replaced to its original position. "Now let's get out of here before I forget myself altogether."

Claire Redmond had never seen so many people eat and drink so much. The music was lively and very good. Jed strummed his guitar, and Tom played a mellow clarinet. Even Stan played a mean piano.

Tess was a perfect hostess, dancing with all the older ranchers. By their looks, Claire could tell all the ranchers and their wives respected Tess. Not just for being a woman who came home to run one of the wealthiest ranches in the county, but for being warm, kind, and generous. Many came up to Claire, expounding on how the Rawlins family spread their wealth over the decades to keep many small farms and ranches going while helplessly watching others fall to Warren Telford.

As Claire handed out the fried chicken and corn on the cob, she listened to the ranchers' wives. Mrs. Hank Patterson was most entertaining. She was juggling a mug of beer and a plate of chicken.

"My dear, Mrs. Redmond, this chicken is heavenly," the older woman said. "And these biscuits are as light as a feather." She was on the short side but in tremendous shape. Her gray hair was pulled back in a scarf as she licked her fingers. "Where's Hank?"

They both looked and found him standing by the corral with Tess, Jed, and a few other ranchers. "Ugh, talking cows again." She sighed and Claire had to laugh as the woman sipped her beer.

"Tess Rawlins, my God, she's good-looking, isn't she?" She didn't wait for Claire to answer. "Never dated, never married," she said and shrugged. "Smart woman!" she exclaimed, and Claire laughed out loud. Miriam Patterson joined her.

"However, she is just like her mother, kind and gentle in a gruff sort of way. This life makes you a little rough around the edges. However, Emily Rawlins, now there was a woman. Three miscarriages before she had Tess. Four years later, along came Stephen. What a pair they were. Emily had a way with both of them. Not that Jed didn't, but he was too busy with the ranch."

Claire listened, getting insight into the family she worked for and the woman she was beginning to love. The idea came into her head, lingered for a moment, then faded. She watched Tess as she listened and talked intently with the other ranchers, every now and then taking a long drink from her beer mug. As Tess leaned against the fence, Claire had to laugh. She was eating a biscuit as she listened.

"Don't tell me a pretty woman like you has to stand here and not have any fun," a voice whispered behind her.

Claire whirled around to see a tall dark-haired man standing there smiling. He was tan with dark eyes and wore a black shirt and jeans. He took off his hat and offered his hand.

"Ethan Drummond."

Claire smiled and took the offered hand. "Claire Redmond."

"Well, dance with me, Claire Redmond," he said with a charming grin.

"I-I really can't. I'm working," Claire said, and Ethan shook his head and grabbed her hand.

He took her over to where Tess and the ranchers had gathered.

"Tess," he called.

Tess looked up grinning. When she saw his hand on Claire's, the grin faded.

"This charming woman says she's working. As her employer, I'm asking you to give her permission to dance with me," Ethan said.

Tess avoided Claire's red face. The other ranchers chuckled and drank their beer.

"Mrs. Redmond can do as she pleases. If she wants to dance with you, Ethan, it's up to her," Tess said with a tight grin.

Hank Patterson laughed. "You'd better just dance with him, Mrs. Redmond. He won't give up."

"This is true," Ethan admitted, and Claire laughed nervously and gave up.

Tess frowned even deeper and drank the contents of her beer. She tried to ignore the way Ethan Drummond held on to Claire's waist or how he whispered in her ear. She really tried to ignore Claire's laughter.

"Who needs a refill?" Tess marched up to the barrel of beer and angrily turned the spigot. She turned to see Claire dancing—again—with Drummond.

"Hey, Tess," Chuck said, waiting to get a beer.

"What?" she barked, and Chuck's eyes bugged out. Tess took a deep angry breath. "Sorry, what?"

"Nothing, I just want a beer," he said helplessly.

Then he saw the object of his boss's anger as he looked out on the dance floor. Oh, boy, he thought as he watched her jaw muscle twitch. The last time that happened, Tess nearly killed Warren Telford. The things I do for my job, he thought, and put his beer down. He walked up to Ethan and tapped him on the shoulder.

"Excuse me, Drummond. No fair monopolizing all the pretty ladies."

Without waiting, Chuck gently pulled Claire into his arms

and danced her away. Claire looked over his shoulder to see Tess sporting a happy grin as she sipped her beer.

Claire gave Chuck a dubious look. "Did she send you over here?"

Chuck laughed and shook his head. "No, but I saw the jaw twitch, which means certain death, Claire. No kidding," he said, and Claire laughed as he whirled her around.

For the next hour, each time Ethan Drummond walked toward Claire, Kyle, Pedro, Stan, and Luke made a beeline in front of him to dance with her. Each time, Claire shook her head at Tess, who raised her beer. She glanced at Jack, who was watching her. Jack stood by the horseshoe pit with Manny, waiting his turn. He watched Tess, then watched his mother as she danced.

"Hey, Jack." Manny punched his shoulder. "It's your turn."

"Oh, sure," Jack said, glancing at Tess one more time.

Tess drank her beer.

Just before sunset, Tess cornered Claire in the kitchen. Claire was getting the numerous pies and cakes ready. She turned to see Tess looming over her.

Without a word, she pulled the struggling woman out of the kitchen and into the hallway. Immediately, Claire was pulled into a crushing embrace with two warm lips smothering her. Claire reached up to put her hands around Tess, but Tess took her hands and pinned them over her head. Claire went weak in the knees and whimpered helplessly as she felt Tess's body moving against her while her lips moved down to her neck.

"God, Tess." Claire moaned.

"I couldn't bear it any longer," Tess growled in her ear. "I can't stand the way Drummond had his paws all over you. It drove me crazy."

"I was thinking of you the entire time. When we danced in the moonlight," Claire whispered.

Tess pulled back and looked into the deep blue eyes. "You were?"

Claire nodded, and as Tess stepped back, she reached up and

cupped her tanned face. "Yes, I was."

"Well, you were laughing with him and everything," she mumbled.

"I don't care about Ethan Drummond."

"You don't?" Tess looked at the floor.

Claire smiled inwardly at the vulnerable pose. "No, and if we could, I'd dance with you all night long and nobody else."

Tess grinned wildly. "You would?"

Claire returned her grin and nodded happily. "With all your ranch hands included. I'm surprised you didn't have Jack come over."

"Speaking of Jack. I think we might need to talk to him. He was watching me tonight. I'm not sure what's going through his mind, maybe nothing."

Claire leaned against the wall. "It will have to come. I know. He deserves to hear it from me. But for now, get back out there, Miss Rawlins, before you're missed." She pulled her down for one more passionate kiss, then let her go.

She was pleased to see the stunned look as she walked away.

Chapter 13

At the end of the evening, only Hank Patterson and two other ranchers—Mark Farrell and Claude Holcomb—were left sitting around the kitchen table talking to Tess and Jed. Tess was desperately trying to listen, but her gaze kept wandering to the yard where Ethan Drummond was talking to Claire for at least twenty excruciating minutes.

"Whattaya think, Tess?" Mark asked.

Tess felt a kick under the table and winced. She looked at the three men. "Sorry. What were you saying?"

"I was saying that Warren Telford has almost got Claude's ranch."

"I have to come up with seven thousand dollars now. Telford wants the land." Claude let out a sad heavy sigh.

"What about the cattle?" Tess asked. "Claude, you have at least a thousand head."

"Telford told me he's taking the whole thing if I don't come up with the money by week's end."

With that, Claire came into the kitchen. Tess gave her an odd look, which she ignored. "I'm sorry for interrupting. Seems like you're deep in conversation. Would anyone like some coffee?"

All agreed and Claire stood by the stove and listened.

"So what now? If Telford takes over Claude's place, he'll have water rights, Tess, Jed," Mark said helplessly.

Jed scratched his head and looked to Tess, who stood and walked over to the kitchen door and gazed into the darkness. In a moment or two, she spoke. "How much is your cattle worth?"

"Hell, Tess, you know the prices. I've got at least twenty to seventy-five thousand dollars in that beef. If not more."

"No, I think you only have seven thousand dollars, Claude. The Double R can afford seven thousand dollars." Tess walked over to the table and placed a booted foot on a kitchen chair and leaned in with a grin.

All three men sported confused looks. "I don't get you, Tess. That's nowhere near what it's worth."

"True, but it's all that Telford and the bank need. Now with my father's permission, I'll go to the bank tomorrow and buy your cattle for seven thousand dollars cash. I take your cattle and drive it to Colorado with ours. You get our price. The country gets quality beef. Telford gets his measly seven thousand dollars and you walk away with whatever your beef sells for and your ranch. All just for giving me the privilege of seeing Warren Telford's face turn red," Tess said with an evil grin.

"It's brilliant!" Hank slapped Claude on the back.

"I-I can't let you do that, Tess. We're all struggling. I know the Double R is one of the wealthiest, but I also know it's been hard on all of us. What if something happens? What if the price of beef goes down? What if…"

"What if you stop and listen to reason?" Jed interjected. He knew how much cash they hand on hand. It wasn't much. Tess was taking a gamble. "We're in this together, ever since our grandfathers started ranching. Now my daughter is a gambler, gets that from her great-granddad. He gambled on this land and won, so will we. We all need this cattle drive. It may be the last big one we have. With big companies buying up ranches and making corporations out of 'em. The Double R will hold out as long as we can, and as long as we can, we'll help our friends. If situations were reversed, you'd be helping the Double R," Jed said in a firm voice and stood behind Tess, who smiled and looked back at her friends.

"We gamble on each other. We stick together and fight. Right?" She looked at all three men.

"Right," they said collectively.

Claire stood there and watched Tess as she once again held their part of Montana together. Tess looked over at her and winked. Claire smiled and nodded as she served the coffee.

After all was settled and the ranchers gone, Jed yawned wildly. "I'm bushed. G'night, girls. Tess, lock up?" he asked and kissed her.

"Of course. Good night, Dad." Tess hugged him. "This will work."

"I know it will. Hank was right. It's a great idea. That California big city college was good for something," he said with a wink. "G'night, Claire, and thank you. You were marvelous."

"Thanks, Jed. I enjoyed every minute." Claire kissed his cheek.

"Well, I'd better check the stables. I'll be right back," Tess said and headed out the kitchen door.

As she fed Stella an apple, she heard the music.

Allegheny moon, I need your light to help me find romance tonight. So shine... shine... shine...

She grinned and walked out of the stable to see Claire standing there in the moonlight. She quickly stepped into Claire's outstretched arms and slowly waltzed by the stable.

Tess waltzed Claire into the stable as the song ended. They stood for a moment in the darkness barely seeing each other's eyes but looking deep into each other's heart.

"What's happening, Tess?"

Tess heard the wonderment in her voice and felt the same. "Could it be love?"

For an instant, neither said a word, but their heavy breathing seemed to fill the air around them. Claire reached up and touched her cheek. Tess sucked in her breath, feeling her blood rushing through her veins at the lightest touch.

"Tess..."

"Tess!"

Her head shot up at the sound of Chuck's urgent voice. "Shit!" she cursed and pulled back. Claire let out a disappointing groan as she quickly pulled herself together. Tess ran her fingers through her hair and ran from the stable.

"Chuck, what the hell?" Claire heard Tess hiss.

"Tess, we've got a problem. Stan was watching the herd. Somebody slaughtered a few head of cattle. Two steers and a cow."

"What? Where?" Tess yelled as she grabbed at his shirt.

"The north pasture."

"Let's go," Tess growled and ran back into the stable, quickly saddling Stella. She looked over at Claire with deep regret. "Claire…"

"Go, for heaven's sake. Please be careful," Claire begged as Tess swung up on the chestnut mare.

She smiled sadly and leaned down to Claire. "I'm sorry. Damn it. Tell Dad. I'll be back," she said firmly, kissed her, then let her go.

Claire stood there as both galloped out of sight into the darkness.

Chapter 14

As Tess and Chuck approached the north pasture, the glittering light of the flashlights led the way in the pitch dark. Luke, Stan, and Kyle stood holding the lights over the slaughtered cattle.

Tess pulled the reins on Stella and dismounted. "Anybody see anything?" She cursed under her breath. The cow's throat had been cut cleanly through.

"No. Stan and I heard the cattle making a bit of a ruckus. We thought for sure it was another stampede. We scouted around the pasture and came up to this mess," Luke said sadly.

"Ya think it was a wolf, Tess?" Stan asked.

Tess shook her head and ran her fingers through her hair in an angry gesture. "Look at that cut, boys. This was no animal. If it were a wolf, he'd have ripped her to shreds. Fuck!" she hissed. "Okay, Stan, go back to the ranch and tell my father what's going on. Then ride into town and bring that worthless sheriff out here, not that it'll make a difference. I'm going to the south pasture. The rest stay here. Go on," she said, and Stan swung up on his horse and rode into the darkness.

Tess held the flashlight and knelt beside the slaughtered animal. It was a gruesome sight. "I take it there's more?" she asked tiredly.

Chuck nodded sadly. "Two more, about fifty yards up on the ridge. It's the same thing as here. Clean cut right across the throat as if..." He stopped and Tess looked up at him and finished his sentence.

"Somebody knew exactly how to do it. Someone with experience in slaughtering livestock. Someone like Ed Chambers and Warren Telford."

Both men glanced at each other. "Tess, let's not fly…"

"I'm not going into town and kill Warren Telford, Chuck, if that's what you're thinking," she said and stood. "As much as I'd like to. Get to the south pasture and guard the herd for the rest of the night. You two stay here." She swung up on her horse. "I'll check out the south pasture and be back in a while."

Chuck and Luke watched as Tess galloped through the meandering herd and out of sight.

All was quiet on the south pasture. It was almost too quiet. The half moon that hung low in the sky illuminated the grassland as Tess slowly cantered through the herd. She saw nothing out of the ordinary as she pulled Stella to a halt and looked around, realizing that this is where they found Stephen's body. Damn Warren Telford and his money-grubbing ways.

Jed Rawlins paced back and forth in the big living room. Claire sat on the couch and watched him patiently. "Jed, you'll wear a path in the carpet."

Jed sighed and sat by the fire, glancing at the clock on the mantel; it was nearly two in the morning. With that, Stan came bounding in through the kitchen door.

"Stan! In here," Jed called out and met him in the living room. Stan, tired and dusty, explained the situation. Jed was breathing heavily through his nose as he listened. Claire noticed how much Tess was like her father. Tall and proud with a quick-fire temper.

"Damn that man," Jed said in a low angry voice that scared Stan and Claire. They let him rant and rave for a minute or two until Claire walked up to him, remembering what Tess had said about his heart. She put a calm hand on his arm. "Damn that man!"

"Jed, please take it easy," she said. Jed nodded and Claire looked at Stan. "Where is Tess?"

"She's out at the south pasture, rode out alone while…"

"Alone!" Claire barked, and Stan stopped, his mouth hanging open.

"Uh, yeah…"

"And you let her?" she continued angrily.

127

Both men exchanged hidden grins.

"Let her? Tess? My boss?"

"Damn that woman!" Claire exclaimed, and now Jed walked up to her and put a calming hand on her shoulder.

"Claire, please take it easy," he said with a small grin. He turned to Stan. "Now what?"

"Tess wants me to ride into town and get the sheriff."

Jed nodded his agreement and grabbed his hat. "I'll go with you. We'll take the Jeep. Claire, we'll be back. Don't worry. Tess will be fine, she can take care of herself." He gave her a reassuring hug.

Pat Hayward squatted down to examine the slaughtered cow. "Maybe it was a wolf. Ya know Marty Banks had one a while back…"

"This was no wolf and you know it, Sheriff," Tess said evenly.

He stood and took off his hat, running his hand through his sandy brown hair. "Did anyone see anything?"

Everybody looked at one another except Tess. She was staring a hole through Pat. "Would it make a difference if we did?"

Pat shot her an angry look. "Are you questioning my ability, Miss Rawlins?"

"As a matter of fact…" Tess said and took a step.

All three men took a step between them.

Pat didn't move. "Be careful. Threatening an officer of the law is a serious offense."

Jed turned to Pat. "Nobody's threatening anybody. No one saw anything tonight, but yesterday, one of my men saw someone on an Appaloosa riding away, just after a shot was fired that spooked the cattle into a stampede."

"Yeah, I heard that. I don't know what…"

"We all know the only one who owns that type of horse," Tess said angrily.

Chuck and Stan stood as cautious sentries.

"Well, now, that's not quite true. Don Milltown's wife just bought the prettiest little Appaloosa not two weeks ago. Ya think she caused the stampede?" he asked in amazement.

Tess let out a growl and started forward. Chuck and Stan physically had to restrain her. "You lying—"

"Watch it, Tess. I'm not in the mood. How would you like to spend the rest of the night in jail?"

When he grinned, Tess saw red. She struggled against Chuck, then winced as the pain shot through her bruised back.

Jed had enough. He stood between his angry daughter and the smirking sheriff. "Warren Telford may own many people in this county, Sheriff, but he doesn't own the Double R or me. You do your job and find out who slaughtered my cattle and who caused the stampede yesterday. That's all I want. Do your job. Good night, Pat," he said in a dismissive tone that Pat snarled at.

Jed gave Tess a stern look. She relaxed as Chuck and Stan let her go. "Let's go home," he said and put his arm around Tess.

She nodded and slipped an arm around his waist. Chuck and Stan smirked at the flustered sheriff and mounted their horses.

Pat stood there feeling stupid and useless as he knew he was. "Fuck you, Rawlins!" he growled, then kicked the carcass of the slaughtered animal.

Chapter 15

"Is Tess awake?" Jack asked as Claire cleaned up the breakfast dishes.

"No. Jed said to let her sleep and I agree. They didn't get back until almost daybreak and she looked exhausted."

She felt Jack watching her, and when she looked at him, he looked away. Claire then remembered Tess's comments the night before. Her stomach immediately knotted; she placed the damp towel on the counter to dry and took a deep breath. Although Claire was not looking forward to this, she knew it was time. "Jack, how about taking your mother for a stroll around the corral?"

Jack cocked his head. "Sure."

"Okay, Mom, we've walked around the corral, and I've given you the tour. What's up?"

"Nothing is up."

"Then why are you frowning so much. What did I do?"

Claire stopped and regarded him. "Sweetie, you've done nothing. I'm the one who did something and I'm ashamed of myself."

Jack put his hands in his pockets and leaned against the fence. When he said nothing, Claire wasn't sure if that was a good sign or not. "You were such a happy baby."

Jack turned bright red and kicked at the ground.

"Always laughing and playing. I remember holding you when you couldn't sleep and I sang to you. When you would fall asleep, I loved to hold your hand, look at your tiny fingers and toes. I'd say a prayer on each one, thanking God for giving me you."

Jack snorted. "I remember you kissing my feet."

Claire laughed along. "I couldn't help it, you had sweet feet."

"Mom…"

"And I look at you now, and I can't believe how grown you are and what a fine young man you've become."

"You helped," he said in a small voice that broke Claire's heart.

"I lied to you, Jack."

"I know."

Claire was stunned. "What do you know?"

Jack looked down at the ground once again. "That my father is alive and doesn't care about us."

Claire felt as though she might faint. Apparently, Jack noticed. He took her by the arm and led her to the bench outside the corral. "Sit down, Mom."

On shaky legs, Claire sat. "How? When?"

"When you sent him a letter to tell him how we were doing and he said he didn't want to know and that he was married and wouldn't give you any money."

Claire thought for a moment, trying to gather her thoughts. "That was over three years ago. You've known all this time? Why didn't you say something?" Claire hid her face in her hands. "I'm so sorry."

Jack quickly sat beside her. "It's not your fault. You were trying to protect me. It was better thinking my father was dead and loved me than to know he was alive and didn't want us."

"I should have been honest with you," Claire said, not able to look at him.

"If I knew that when I was a kid, I might not have handled it so good. Now being older and knowing he's a fucking loser…"

Claire's eyes bugged out of her head; Jack blushed. "Sorry."

"I understand, sweetie."

They sat in silence for a moment with Claire trying to wrap her mind around this. She almost missed her son's next words.

"It had to be so hard for you," he whispered. "Going through it all alone."

Claire reached over and ran her fingers through his dark

hair. "But I had you growing inside me. And that kept me going. When your father and my parents wanted nothing to do with me, I decided to take what money I had and move to Portland. I guess it seemed as far away from Long Island as I could get without falling into the ocean."

Jack laughed but said nothing.

"It wasn't such a bad life," Claire said, knowing it came out as a question.

"It was a great life," Jack said.

Claire saw his bottom lip quiver and turned toward him. Jack immediately flung his arms around her. Claire blubbered like a baby; she could tell Jack was trying to be strong and not cry.

"I don't need him, Mom," Jack said and sniffed. He pulled back and wiped his eyes.

"I've felt bad that you never had a man around." Claire shook her head sadly and wiped her eyes, as well.

"We had Brenda. She was more of a man than most, I think."

Her head snapped up so quickly Claire nearly threw her back out. "What...?"

Jack grinned sheepishly. "I've known about you and Brenda for a long time now."

"W-what...?" Claire hung her head. "I'm gonna be sick."

"Mom..." Jack insisted. "It's okay. I kinda figured it out on my own."

"How?" Claire looked at him then. "And just so we're on the same page here. We're talking about Brenda and I—"

"Being lesbians, yeah."

"Oh, God, that sounds so odd coming from my son," Claire said, shaking her head.

"Why? I'm practically seventeen. In a year, I'll be going to college. Now let me finish. I overheard you talking to her one night when you thought I was asleep. You said you loved her, but you and I were a package deal." He stopped and laughed at Claire's gaping look. "I remembered a lot then. How you never went out with men, only your girlfriends. Then when you met Brenda, she was always around. She would play football with me and watch all the sports on TV. Remember when she fixed the sink and the garbage disposal?"

Claire nodded emphatically. "She saved us a boatload of money on a plumber. Who knew that apple core would get stuck?" She playfully bumped shoulders with Jack, who blushed. "Remember the hideous noise it made?"

"Oh, my God, I had nightmares for a week."

Claire broke into a fit of laughter, as did Jack. "I nearly wet myself, it scared me so bad."

"I thought you were gonna kill me," Jack said through his laughter.

Claire put her arm around his shoulders, momentarily amazed at the broad muscles. "I'd never kill you, sweetie. I love you too much. I did want to spank you, though."

"I love you, too, Mom."

"So it doesn't bother you?" Claire looked anywhere but at Jack.

"No. But can I ask you a question?"

"At this point, I have nothing to hide."

"Why did you, ya know, with him?"

It pained Claire that Jack didn't say "my father." Not for his sake, but for Jack's. "Sit back. I'm going to tell you the whole thing. I was in college. I didn't start right after high school. I worked for a few years so I could pay my own way and not rely on my family. I met your father in my junior year. I guess I was trying to deny the fact I was gay. I know that sounds lame, but there you have it." She turned toward Jack again and took his hand in hers. "I honestly loved your father. His name is Lawrence Michael Redmond III. He was from a very wealthy family in Long Island. I thought he loved me. When I found out I was pregnant with you, I told him. I never wanted him to marry me because I was pregnant. I told him the decision was his. Well, you know his decision."

"What a loser."

"He wasn't ready to be a father."

"Were you ready to be a mother? Probably not, but you didn't abort me or give me up."

"No, I couldn't do that. When I realized I had a life in me, I just couldn't. I'm sorry we struggled so long. I tried to get good jobs."

"Mom, stop it. You took care of me and you love me. I always felt safe. I still do." He stopped and lowered his head. "I just feel so bad you had to give up your life with Brenda 'cause of me."

"Now just a minute, Jack. Look at me, please."

Jack lifted his head and swallowed. Claire shook her head. "What happened between me and Brenda had nothing to do with you. We just wanted different things from life. That's all."

"But I know you cared for her."

"I did. And I'll care for someone else again." She leaned over and touched his cheek.

"Someone like Tess?"

"I don't know. I love you, sweetie. And I think it's enough right now—"

Jack interrupted her. "Don't do that. If…" He stopped, seemingly formulating his next words. "If Tess makes you happy, it's okay with me. I like her. I like Jed and this place. But don't do anything for me. Do it for yourself, please. I'm nearly seventeen and I can take care of myself."

Claire brushed the tears out of her eyes. "Whatever happens between me and Tess, always remember. We're still a package deal because you're my son, and even if you go off to college and find a nice girl to marry, you'll still be my son. Okay?"

Jack grinned and kissed her on the cheek. "Okay, Mom."

As he started to rise, Claire held his hand. He looked down and cocked his head. "Thank you, Jack. I love you very much."

"I love you, too."

Claire sat back, once again wiping the tears from her eyes as she watched the boy she once knew become a compassionate young man. "I did okay," she said with a loud sniff.

Tess opened the bathroom door to see Claire slowly opening Tess's bedroom door.

"Boo!"

Claire let out a screech and whirled around. "Don't do that!" Claire exclaimed as she put a hand to her heart.

Tess chuckled by way of an apology and toweled her hair. "Just what are you doing lurking around my bedroom?"

"Making sure you're still breathing. After how angry you were last night, I thought you'd give yourself a heart attack."

Tess scowled, remembering a few short hours earlier. She wanted to strangle Pat. She walked by Claire and into her room, tossing the towel on a nearby chair.

"This is one hell of a situation, Claire. I know Telford's behind the stampede and last night. Geezus, he could have killed so many innocent people. In two months, we have to drive the herd to Colorado. We'll get a good price for the beef, then Telford can go straight to hell. Just two more months," she said wearily.

"You're tired, Tess. Why don't you take it easy today? Jack's taking care of the stable. Later your father is going to take him out riding. He's..." She stopped and bit at her bottom lip. Tess gave her a curious look.

"What? Tell me."

"Jack has hinted at the possibility of going on the drive to Colorado. I'm not sure about it, but he wants to and Jed's been teaching him how to handle a horse, and every time I see him, he looks older, and I'm wondering if I shouldn't let him go..."

Tess grinned at the adorable rambling and put her hands on Claire's shoulders. "If my father thinks he's ready and it's fine with you, then he can go. He's a young man and you have to let him grow up. My father and I have discussed it. We can't believe how quick he's taken to life on the ranch."

Claire walked away from Tess and stood by the window. "I had a talk with Jack a little while ago." She turned and chuckled at Tess's stunned look.

"And how did that go?"

Claire rolled her eyes. "It was unbelievable. He's turned out to be a very compassionate and intelligent young man."

"Who loves his mother."

Claire nodded. "Yes. We'll talk about it later. Right now, I'm emotionally drained."

"Was it a good talk?"

"Yes." Claire reached up and kissed Tess on the lips. "It was

135

very good. And we will talk. It's just a lot to absorb right now."

"I'm glad. For both of you." Tess pushed Claire toward the door. "I'm starving."

"Yes, ma'am."

Chapter 16

It was nearly five o'clock when Chuck and the men rode back, tired and dusty. Claire stood at the sink and noticed Tess was not with them. She knew Tess was out before dawn.

Pedro, Manny, and Kyle sat at the long table, talking about the day. Claire watched Chuck as he finished and walked to the kitchen door.

"Where is she, Chuck?" she asked.

"Out at the north pasture," he said tiredly as he looked out. "Luke and Stan are watching the herd at the south. When they're done, I'll send Pedro and Manny to relieve them. Me and Kyle will relieve Tess when she gets back."

They watched as Jack practiced his roping on poor Clover. The calf patiently helped her companion.

"He's getting good at that. I swear Tess is the only other young person who took to ranching as quickly as Jack has. He's a good young man. Reminds me a little of Stephen, gentle like, but mostly of Tess. He's got her spunk. Jed adores him."

"I know. We're so lucky to be here."

He smiled. "Oh, I dunno. I kinda think we're the lucky ones." He looked out the back door. "Speak of the devil."

With that, they saw Tess, Luke, and Stan riding up. All three were sweaty, tired, and full of dust. Tess slowly dismounted and Jack dashed up to take Stella. Tess smiled wearily and ruffled his head and petted Clover, then slapped her rump to get out of the way. The calf bleated her annoyance as she scooted.

All three riders immediately went to the horse trough. Claire grimaced. "What is it about that trough?" she asked completely confounded while she watched Tess grab a towel and dry her head. Chuck laughed quietly.

As Tess walked in, Claire had a plate ready for her. "Sit down and eat," she ordered. "Not on the table," Claire said over her shoulder. Tess set her Stetson on the back of the chair. The fact that Tess didn't argue was not lost on Claire; she watched her with a cautious eye.

"Okay, finish up," Chuck said, and every hand quickly went to the plate of biscuits.

Tess laughed tiredly. "I don't blame you. Just save me one."

"Go ahead, take them. I made more. I swear I've never made so many biscuits in my life." Claire poured Tess a cup of coffee.

"Chuck, make sure Stan and Luke get something to eat. They were up with me this morning." Tess rubbed her face. "Where's Dad?"

"He's in town with Claude. He wanted to be there when they paid the bank," Chuck said with a grin.

Tess grinned, as well. "Damn, I wanted to see Telford's face when he made the payment. When is he bringing over his cattle?"

"He said he'd drive them over tomorrow. It'll take the better part of the day."

"I'll go over there tomorrow. I think we can squeeze them in on the south pasture."

"I think so. Why don't you let me do it, Tess? Take a load off tomorrow?"

"That's a good idea," Claire said. "You've been running yourself ragged for the past three weeks."

"I know. I just want to make sure nothing happens. I have a bad feeling here with two months to go before we drive them to Colorado. I don't trust Warren Telford as far as I could throw him, the fat…"

"More coffee?" Claire gently interjected.

"Well, I'll get a few of the boys and head out."

"I'll swing by later tonight," Tess said between mouthfuls.

"You will not. You're taking a hot bath and going to bed," Claire said, dismissing the topic.

Tess glared at her and avoided Chuck's grin. "Claire," Tess started.

Claire ignored her. "Have a good night, Chuck. I'll keep the coffee on for anyone who wants it. If you guys are out too late and get hungry, just let the men know. Good night, Chuck," she said again.

Chuck shrugged and gave Tess a helpless look as he walked out.

"Now you go and get out of those filthy clothes. I'll run your bath." Claire walked out of the kitchen.

Tess sat there, frowning. "I thought I was in charge here."

She glared at the kitchen door as she heard Chuck's laughter.

Claude and Jed sat at the large desk waiting for their banker. The tall skinny man sat down with Claude's file.

"What can I do for you, Claude?" he asked sadly.

The owner of Holcomb's Farm grinned and took his billfold out of his jacket pocket. "Well, Mike, I'm here to pay my mortgage," Claude said too loudly. He saw Warren Telford standing by the teller's window. Both men knew he could hear them.

Mike tried to suppress his elation. "That'll be seven thousand dollars, Claude. How did you want to pay?"

"In good old American hard-earned dollars by good *honest* people," he emphasized, and Jed tapped his knee. Claude cleared his throat and started peeling off the one hundred-dollar bills.

Jed tried not to grin as Claude emphatically counted. Mike tried not to show any emotion at all. "Six thousand nine hundred and seven dollars," Claude finished and pushed the stack of money toward the banker.

Over in the corner, Warren Telford puffed on his cigar and watched.

"Uh, Claude, you could have just wired the money instead of all this cash."

"Oh, I know. Just making a point," Claude said with a satisfied grin.

"Okay, here's your receipt. Next payment is due on…"

"October 5, 2010. That's after the cattle drive. You'll have the next payment before that."

Both men stood. "A pleasure doing business with you. Have a

139

good day," Claude said happily. Jed shook Mike's hand.

Mike grinned and shook his head. "You and Tess are good people, Jed Rawlins," Mike whispered and gave his hand a healthy pump, then quickly dropped it, lest his boss see him.

As they walked out, Jed noticed Ethan Drummond follow Telford into his office.

"What's the Drummond boy doing with Telford?" Claude asked as Telford grinned and closed his door.

"I don't know. He's been away for nearly two years. Now he's back, and it looks like he's in tight with Telford. Kinda curious, though," Jed conceded as they walked out of the bank.

Tess lay in the steamy bubbles. "I haven't had a bubble bath in ages." She sighed and put her head back on the deep old claw-footed tub. She grinned evilly as she heard the knock at the door. Closing her eyes, she heard the door creak open.

"Tess?" Claire whispered.

Tess feigned sleeping as she lay still. She heard Claire giggle and desperately tried not to follow suit.

She heard nothing but very heavy breathing and the sound of a bottle being opened. Then she heard nothing but the deep breaths.

"You going to give me that beer or just stare?" Tess asked with her eyes closed.

"Oh! Damn you, Tess Rawlins," Claire said, trying not to laugh. Tess opened her eyes and laughed as she reached for the icy cold beer. Claire handed it to her as she sat on the edge of the tub.

Tess took a long pull from the cold bottle. "Ah! That's good. Thank you." She sighed and closed her eyes once again. She ran the cold bottle across her forehead. "Now tell me what you and Jack talked about."

Claire took a minute to start. Tess figured she was choosing her words. "You can say anything you want."

"I know. I suppose I thought Jack was innocent and knew nothing. That I was being careful, trying…"

"To protect him."

Tess saw the sadness in her eyes and reached over to take Claire's hand.

"Yes, I suppose I was trying to protect him. But he figured it out on his own."

"Figured what out?" Tess leaned back in the bubbles and closed her eyes.

"That I'm a lesbian and he's okay with that."

Tess opened her eyes. For a moment, she said nothing. "He's a good young man. You've done a fine job with him."

"I'm not sure about that, but I agree with you. He is turning out to be a fine man."

Tess waited, hoping that Claire would expound on what she and Jack talked about. When Claire remained silent, Tess grinned. "Wash my back?"

Claire laughed and picked up the soapy cloth. "Do not challenge me, Miss Rawlins."

"Who's challenging? I'm asking…practically begging."

Both women laughed, then stopped when they heard Jack and Jed's voices in the living room.

"Fun's over," Claire said sadly and stood.

Tess leaned back and slid under the steamy water as Claire left.

After the hot bath, Tess felt much better—tired but no longer exhausted. The night was warm and the sun was still hanging in the western sky. Claire was sitting on the back porch with Jed. Tess walked out and stretched.

"What a glorious night. It'll be a wonderful sunset. That bath did the trick."

Jed stood and stretched, as well. "You worked hard today, Tess. Claire's right. Take a day off tomorrow. The boys can handle things. Listen to Claire."

Tess frowned and avoided Claire's look of superiority. "I'm fine."

"And you're stubborn," he said. He winked at Claire. "Gets it from her mama."

Claire laughed and rocked in the chair. Tess stumbled forward as Jack opened the screen door. "Oh, sorry, Tess."

Jed laughed. "It's getting crowded. Jack, how about a game of gin?"

Jack glanced from Tess to Claire. "Um, maybe later, okay, Jed? I need to talk to Tess."

Claire stopped laughing. The look of terror on her face had Tess chuckling.

"That's fine, son."

When Jed was out of sight, Jack looked at Tess. "Would you take a ride with me?"

Claire looked as if she was about to be sick. Tess now felt about the same. "Sure," she said, trying not to sound petrified. She absently looked around for the shotgun.

"Great. I'll go saddle the horses." He kissed Claire on the cheek before walking to the stables.

Tess glanced at Claire, who still looked ill. "Well, this should prove very interesting."

As she stood, Claire reached over and grabbed her arm. "What do you think he wants?"

Tess heard the terror in her voice and had to laugh. "Claire, he's your son. Don't worry." She bent down and kissed her gently on the lips. "But if I'm not back by sunset, send Chuck."

By the time Tess got to the stable, Jack had saddled Stella and was finishing up with Zeus. He looked up and smiled. "All set." He led both horses out by the reins; Tess followed behind.

"Where would you like to go?" Tess asked as they mounted their respective horses.

"I thought the south pasture. I love it there."

The late afternoon sun was warmer than expected as they neared the pasture. Jack stopped Zeus and Tess followed. For a moment or two, neither said a word; Tess got worried and stole a glance at Jack, who was gazing out at the green pasture. She smiled slightly as he pushed his cowboy hat off his forehead.

"Sure is beautiful here. I can see why you love it," he said.

"I do," Tess said; she now looked around. "I remember as a girl, I'd ride out here and lie in the tall grass and look up at the clouds passing by. I felt like I was swimming in a sea of grass."

"That's very poetic," Jack said with a laugh.

Tess laughed along. "My great-uncle Jeremiah said that first. It always stuck with me."

"And you'd fight to take care of this and make sure nothing happens to it."

Tess cocked her head and looked at him. "Yes, I would."

Jack nodded, still not looking at her, which made Tess more nervous. "I remember when I was a kid, Mom would always make sure I was safe. It was only the two of us. I'm not sure what she's told you."

"Not much," Tess said. When Jack frowned in concentration, she smiled, thinking how much he looked like Claire. "I'll tell you what I told your mom. I'll listen to whatever you have to say."

"No matter what?" Jack looked down at his hands as they rested on the pommel.

"No matter what."

He looked up once again, studying his surroundings; Tess sensed he was picking his words cautiously. It seemed a lifetime before he spoke once again.

"Mom is always protecting me, not wanting me to get hurt. Like with the knife and the apple." He laughed. Tess laughed, as well, but said nothing. "I overheard her one night. It was maybe three years ago. She thought I was sleeping and was talking to her friend, Brenda. I remember Mom saying, 'Jack and I are a package deal.' I wasn't sure what she meant, but then I remembered seeing Mom kissing Brenda, then I knew." He looked at Tess and smiled. "I always kinda figured. Mom never dated guys, ever. And on the rare occasion when she went out for fun, it was with women. But she never let on and never had anyone stay over. But I remember, when she broke up with Brenda, I remember hearing her cry and I wanted to go to her, but I didn't know if she'd be embarrassed or not."

He stopped for a moment and took a deep breath. "When I was little, she told me about my dad. Said he loved us but had an accident and died before I was born."

"I'm sorry, Jack," Tess said.

Jack shook his head. "No need. A few years ago, I found a

letter. He's alive." He looked at Tess. Tess was stunned; she could feel her mouth hanging open.

"So I did a little digging without Mom knowing. I found out he's some rich asshole on Long Island. He knows all about me, and in the letter, he said 'I've told you for the last time, I don't want anything to do with you or him. I'm married and have a family. And you won't get any money.'" He shook his head again, this time in disgust. "He's a bigwig in some law firm, and he married into a political family."

"Shit, Jack, I'm sorry." Tess felt stupid repeating the same thing, but she had no idea what else to say.

"In the letter, Mom said she just wanted to let him know how I was and what a good young man and all that and she didn't want any money." Jack shrugged. "He doesn't care."

"What did your mom say when you told her?"

"I didn't."

Tess leaned in. "You never told her about the letter?"

"Nope. Or hearing her talk with Brenda."

"Why not?" Tess asked. When she saw the tears well in his brown eyes, her heart ached. She reached over and placed her hand on his forearm.

"She was protecting me, telling me he loved us and died in an accident so I would grow up thinking he loved me. And if I told her, she might be ashamed and that would hurt her." He looked at Tess. "And I won't let anyone hurt her ever again. She gave up her whole life to make me happy and safe. Gave up Brenda and who knows who else, for me. Anyway, we finally talked about it earlier, and I did tell Mom. She felt bad and ashamed. I know she hasn't told you."

"I can understand her apprehension in telling me."

He smiled then, as if remembering some happy time; this too broke Tess's heart.

"She always had daisies on the kitchen table. No matter where we lived or how broke we were, Mom always had daisies." He took his hat off and angrily slapped it on his thigh. "And it really pisses me off now thinking that she had to buy them for herself."

He jumped off his horse and turned away from Tess, who

immediately dismounted Stella and rushed to him. She pulled him into her arms and held him as he cried.

Jack pulled back and sniffed as he wiped the heel of his hand across his eyes. "I'm okay."

"I know," Tess said. "I know you love your mother very much."

Jack nodded and took a deep breath. He glanced at Tess, then looked away. "I know you do, too, but I won't see Mom hurt anymore. You protect and fight for this land. That's how I feel about her."

And there it was.

Tess stepped back; actually, she nearly staggered and put her hands deep in the pockets of her jeans. She gazed out at the pasture and the mountains in the distance. Myriad situations flashed through her mind, all of them too fantastic to comprehend. She thought of her own childhood and how safe and happy her parents made her and Steve feel, how Uncle Jeremiah, even as an old man, lifted her onto his lap and told her about the land, and how important it was, but family, he said, family was everything. And their land was part of that family. That's why she went to the same university he did and learned what he had learned so many years before. She was more useful there than on the ranch. And now, with Steve gone, she was needed back here with her father and—she looked at Jack who was staring at the ground. And who? she asked herself.

"Walk with me, Jack," she said, motioning with her head.

Jack dutifully walked beside her in the tall grass. They walked with their horses trailing behind them, neither of them speaking for some time. They stopped by the huge oak tree. Jack leaned against it and absently kicked at the ground with the toe of his boot.

"I do love your mother," Tess said, nearly shocking Jack and herself.

His head shot up at the declaration and he nodded.

"And I admire you for protecting her and loving her. It couldn't have been easy for her or you. I admire you both."

"I know I'm just a kid and you probably don't think I know

much about such things, like lesbians, ya know…and maybe I don't. All I know is she's my mom and been alone all her life. I love her, and if you love her, too, then it's okay with me. Someday I won't be around, and I'd like to think she's happy with someone. She deserves to be happy." He looked at her and shrugged, then smiled.

Tess grinned, as well. "You know, I told your mother the best way to her heart was through you. But she told me it wasn't the only way. I guess I'll just have to figure that out."

Jack walked over and mounted Zeus. He pulled on the reins, smiling as he looked down at Tess. "Make sure she has daisies on the kitchen table, Tess."

Tess stood there, dumbfounded as she watched Jack ride through the pasture and away from the house. She leaned back against the tree and shook her head. "That young man is no kid." She mounted Stella. "Now where am I gonna get daisies?"

Chapter 17

"Where have you been?" Chuck asked.

Tess swung the saddle over the post and picked up the brushes. "I was out riding with Jack. It was very enlightening." She shook her head in amazement and started brushing Stella.

"Enlightening how?" Chuck asked.

"What's enlightening?" Jed asked as he walked into the stable.

Tess groaned and put her head on Stella. "Nothing."

"Tess went for a ride with Jack that was very enlightening," Chuck said to Jed.

"Really? Enlightening how?"

"That's what I asked, but she ain't sayin'," Chuck said.

Tess heard them snicker and raised her head. "Will you two go away?"

"I don't think so," Jed said. "Now tell us."

Tess looked from Jed's eager face to Chuck's innocent grin. "Jack told me about his father, which I can't go into until I talk to Claire. So don't even ask." She took the brush to Stella once again.

"That can't be all," Chuck said.

Tess felt Jed's gaze and looked up to see him smiling. "It's not, is it?"

"Nope. It appears that young Mr. Redmond is quite the worldly fellow and is in tune with his mother, whom he adores." She smiled fondly, remembering their conversation.

"And whom you adore, as well," Jed said.

Tess avoided both men but nodded obediently while she continued to brush Stella.

Chuck's mouth dropped. "You adore Claire?"

Jed slapped his back. "Of course she does. You don't think Tess is just after sex."

Tess felt the color flood to her face. She looked around for a hole to jump into.

"Of course I don't," Chuck said. "I'd never think that of Tess." He looked back at Tess. "So now what? Does Claire adore you, too?"

"Guys," Tess said.

"Of course she does!" Jed exclaimed. "What's not to adore about my daughter?"

"Dad…" Tess tried again.

"I didn't say there wasn't. I'm just askin' if Claire adores Tess, too," Chuck said angrily.

Both men looked at Tess. "Well?"

"I don't know," Tess said slightly amazed and very petrified that Claire might not.

"Then you'd best find out," Jed said.

Chuck agreed. "How?"

Tess shrugged and nervously played with the brushes and mumbled, "Jack says she likes daisies."

"Daisies, huh?" Chuck scratched his chin. He then slapped Jed on the arm. "The north pasture by the fence up on the ridge."

Tess frowned, trying to think of the spot. She didn't remember seeing any wildflowers up there. However, she really never looked.

Jed raised an eyebrow. "How do you know about daisies?"

Chuck turned bright red. "Remember that little brunette a few years back? We were up…"

Tess put her hands over her ears. "Oh, my God. I don't want to hear this…" She hummed loudly and walked in a circle.

Jed laughed and fished the keys out of his pocket. "C'mon, we have daisies to pick."

Tess gave him a disturbed look. Chuck grinned and grabbed the keys.

"Guys…" Tess tried to argue while they pulled her out of the stable.

Claire was still sick to her stomach. Tess had not come back from her talk with Jack, and Jack was not telling Claire what they talked about. When he came back, he grinned, kissed her cheek, and grabbed an apple.

Claire decided on a shower and a good book. It was only eight o'clock, but no one was in the house. She had no idea where Jed and Chuck had gotten to, and Jack was in the bunkhouse with Manny and the other men.

An hour later and freshly showered, Claire grabbed her book and had a taste for the cookies she had made earlier. "I'd better get one before Tess smells them."

Claire walked into the kitchen and stopped dead in her tracks when she glanced at the kitchen table. In the center of the table was a beautiful vase, and in the vase were white daisies.

Claire smiled. "Jack, you son of a gun," she whispered.

As if on cue, Jack walked into the kitchen. Claire put her arms around him and kissed his cheek. "Thanks."

"For what?" he asked. "And please don't go kissing me. What if the guys walk in?"

"Oh, shush. Thank you for the daisies."

Jack looked at the table and shrugged. "I didn't do it."

Claire now was confused. "Then who did?"

"Beats me. Yum, cookies." Jack walked over to the counter. "What kind?"

Still staring at the daisies, Claire slowly responded, "What? Oh, oatmeal raisin and wash your hands."

Jack grumbled but obeyed. He grabbed a few cookies from the plate on the counter and walked out of the kitchen.

Blinking back the tears that flooded her eyes, Claire reached over and plucked one daisy from the vase. She didn't even dare think who left them, but she sincerely hoped it was not Jed or Chuck. She walked outside and stood on the porch, twirling the flower. When she heard the screen door creak, she turned to see Tess standing there, a sheepish grin covering her face.

In an instant, Claire's body temperature rose perceptively. She knew she was blushing and tried to hide it in the daisy she held.

"Hi." Tess walked onto the porch and leaned against the

railing, her hands deep in the pockets of her jeans.

"Hi," Claire said. Her heart was pounding, and she only hoped Tess was on the verge of a mild heart attack, as well. "Did you do this?" She offered the daisy.

Tess grinned. "That depends on if they please you or not."

Once again, tears leapt to her eyes. Claire only nodded; she didn't trust her voice just then, and blubbering like a fool was not an option. When Tess didn't answer, she knew she had to say something. "Yes, they please me very much."

Tess let out an audible sigh of relief. "Then yes. It was me."

Claire laughed nervously, reverently holding the flower. Tess closed the distance between them but looked out at the setting sun, her hands resting on the railing. Claire did the same but reached over and placed her hand on Tess's; their fingers immediately intertwined.

Tess looked down at their hands. "Please tell me this is the way to your heart, Claire."

When Claire heard the quiet plea in Tess's voice, she couldn't control the sob that seemed to come from her soul. "Yes," she said, trying not to cry.

In the next instant, she was in Tess's arms, crying into her shoulder as Tess stroked her hair. "How did you know?"

"I have my ways. I'm a college professor, remember?" Tess tightened her embrace.

Claire looked up and studied her face. "I never realized how blue your eyes are."

Tess raised an eyebrow and leaned back. "I hope when you realize more, it won't send you screaming into the night."

Claire chuckled and pulled Tess back in her arms. "I doubt that, Miss Rawlins, but I'll let you know."

"I love the feel of you against me." Tess placed a soft kiss on her forehead.

"I do too." Claire sighed. She immediately thought of Jack and pulled back. "Tess, what about Jack? I need to—" When she felt Tess's warm lips against hers, she melted. Her mind reeled and her body betrayed her as she fiercely clung to Tess and returned her kiss.

It was Tess who now pulled back. "Jack loves you very much and he's very intelligent."

"You're finding that out, too, huh?" Claire took a step away from Tess. Suddenly, she felt the distance between them was needed right now.

As if sensing the same thing, Tess stepped back and leaned against the railing.

"There's so much I need to tell you. I'm not sure what Jack said." She stopped for a moment. "It's been so long. I haven't been very forthcoming with you. I wasn't with Jack."

"You were protecting him. It couldn't have been easy for either of you."

Claire looked into the darkness. "I was running from what I was. Coming from a wealthy Long Island family, being a lesbian was just not acceptable. So I tried not to think about it and deny it. As I'm sure many women have. I met a man who was from the same background as I was. I thought I loved him and everything would be fine, everyone would be happy.

"I got pregnant, and Lawrence did an about-face. He questioned whether he was the father." She laughed and shook her head. "I suppose that was predictable. I realized then he would never be the man I thought he was or the father my baby needed. I decided I'd lived a lie long enough. It was time to realize who I was and what I was doing. I even went to my parents for help and foolishly told them the truth."

"About the baby and you?" Tess asked.

"Yes. I knew if I was going to have this baby, I needed to be honest. That proved a disaster. They practically disowned me, told me to give the baby up for adoption." She laughed again, this time with more than a trace of sarcasm. "They're old money and very Catholic, and my father suggested an abortion. I was shocked, and that's when I knew the only thing to do was to do this on my own. I had some money. I left college in my senior year and contacted a friend who lived in Portland and the rest, as they say, is history."

"So you did this all on your own with no help from anyone but your friend."

"Yes. It's what thousands of women do every day, Tess, so

don't go thinking I'm someone special—"

"Too late."

Claire looked at Tess and smiled. "Thank you for that."

"You're welcome, now continue."

"Well, I had Jack," Claire said; she couldn't help the grin that spread across her face. "He was such a gift, and he changed my life. I knew there was more than my feeling sorry for myself. I had a son."

"You made the effort with his father, and I use that term very loosely, and he took the low road and denied both of you. So you told him his father died before he was born, and he loved him very much."

Claire looked down. "I see he told you everything."

"Yes, because he loves you and he understand what you did and why. If I were in your place, I think I would have done the same thing."

"I know you have a great deal going on with the ranch and your job at the university—"

"And the idea of turning said ranch into a working ranch and my great-grandparent's house into a guesthouse."

Claire's head shot up then. "Really? That's a wonderful idea."

"I haven't completely thought it out yet." Tess scratched her head.

"It's a wonderful idea. It'll take time, but the ranch is already well known in Montana. It'll generate more income."

"It'll take money to get things going, but I have a good savings, which I've already…"

Claire cocked her head and smiled. "You used your money for Claude, didn't you?" She could see Tess's embarrassment. "You did."

"I transferred some to Dad's account. I knew he wouldn't find out. Anyway, I think this might work. There's one thing. I-I need someone to help me and you know how hard it is to ask for help."

Claire wasn't sure what Tess was asking. It was so long for her; Claire didn't trust her heart, but she knew she was falling in love with Tess. She needed to know. "What kind of help?"

"I need a partner, someone I can trust."

"A financial partner?" Claire counted the number of planks in the porch.

"No, Claire. I need someone I can love. Someone who might love me, too. I thought maybe you and I could be partners."

Claire grinned and put the daisy to her nose. "Are you saying you love me?"

Tess chuckled and folded her arms across her chest. "I drove out to the north pasture with Dad and Chuck, for chrissakes, and picked daisies for you. So, yeah, damn it, I'm saying I love you." She looked at Claire from across the porch and whispered, "Do you love me?"

Claire slowly walked up to her. "You did find the way to my heart."

"That must count for something."

Claire hesitated, her mind racing, as well as her heart. She turned and walked to the opposite side of the porch.

"Claire, I know you have so much to think about. You have Jack, and as you said, it's been so long for you. If you tell me to back off, I-I will—"

Claire heard the resignation in Tess's voice, and all at once something inside broke. She whirled around and ran to Tess, who seemed stunned and took a step back.

"No," Claire said frantically, trying not to cry. "I-I don't want that. I don't want to be like Billy Bigelow—"

"Who?"

"I don't want to be like that," she cried and held on to Tess's shirt. "I don't want to say, if I loved you and th-then it be too late and say soon you'd leave me, off you would go in the mist of day."

"Claire—"

"And you'd never, never know how I loved you," Claire said, tears streaming down her face. She sobbed mournfully into Tess's shoulder.

Tess held her and whispered, "Claire, sweetheart. Please don't cry."

Claire couldn't stop the tears. All the lonely years suddenly caught up with her; she desperately clung to Tess.

"You don't have to worry, honey." She sniffed loudly and held Claire at arm's length. She wiped the tears from her eyes with the heel of her hand. "I'm not leaving in the mist of day, or night for that matter. And we won't let..." She stopped, her gaze darting back and forth in a panic. "...our golden chances, um, shit, I can't remember the next line."

Claire laughed and cried at the same time at the helpless tone in her voice. She stopped crying and took a quivering breath. "I guess I must love you."

Tess took her hand and brought it to her lips. She gently smelled the daisy, then kissed Claire's hand. "Yes, you must."

Claire touched Tess's cheek. "Jack and I are a package deal."

Tess nodded. "So is my father and Chuck and Pedro and..."

Claire let out a genuine laugh along with Tess. "Then we have the beginning of a wonderful partnership, Tess."

"Thank God." Tess pulled her into her arms.

"Kiss me, please," Claire whispered against her lips. She threw her arms around Tess's neck, leaving Tess no choice.

After a moment, Tess pulled back and whispered, "Am I going to have to memorize all of the Rodgers and Hammerstein musicals?"

Chapter 18

"You think Mom knows?" Jack and Tess rode to the north pasture.

"Not a chance. She'll be very surprised. Now let's get to work. Take that calf right over there." She pointed in the direction.

Jack nodded and took the rope off the pommel. Swallowing hard, he pulled his hat down low on his brow. Tess smiled at the serious posture. "Now remember, quick release and snap it back. Watch their hooves. Ready?"

Jack nodded and sat tall in his saddle. "Go!"

He clicked the mare's sides and took off. The calf, sensing his presence, made a beeline for the herd. Jack swung the lariat over his head a few times, then he slung it at the hooves of the calf. Immediately, he pulled it back and tightened the noose around the hooves.

"Tie it off quick!" Tess said as she watched. Jack did just that and flew off the horse. He ran and got the calf on its back and hogtied it. He raised his hands when he finished and Tess stopped the time clock she held in her hand.

"Yeehaw!" she exclaimed, and Jack untied the calf. He slapped its rump as it took off. Running back, he was laughing and jumping.

"I did it!"

"You certainly did and a great time. You'll be all set for the Fourth of July Rodeo. I'm proud of you," she said as he mounted his horse.

"Boy, I never thought I'd be roping in a rodeo. I wish my Mom was here."

"Then it wouldn't be a surprise. Now let's try it again while we still have some light." She gave his cowboy hat a playful tug.

"So you gonna do the barrel racing at the rodeo?" Chuck asked Tess as they sat on the back porch. Tess was sitting on the top step, leaning against the railing, her long legs stretched out in front of her, her Stetson drawn over her eyes. Essentially, she could have been asleep.

"I am not," she grunted. Claire was sitting in the chair peeling potatoes. Chuck was helping.

"What's barrel racing?" she asked absently. Chuck glanced up and grinned.

"Tess here was the champion, three years running—"

"When I was twenty."

"She raced 'round a few barrels and competed against other ladies. No one came close."

"Doesn't seem that hard." Claire winked at Chuck.

"Nah, it's not. But it's the only competition for women," Chuck teased and got a grunt from the dozing Tess.

"Must not be much competition," Claire added.

Tess slightly lifted her Stetson and peered at Claire. She smirked slightly and settled down again.

"Why don't you enter in the baking and cooking?" Tess drawled lazily.

Claire cocked her head in thought. "What would I enter?"

"Biscuits," both said at the same time.

Claire raised an eyebrow. "No! My biscuits would never win," she said halfheartedly.

"Maria enters every year and wins. Seems only right you should defend the Double R." Tess yawned and shifted comfortably against the post. With her arms folded in front of her, she lazily waved off an annoying fly.

"Tess, I can't do that," she argued. "Can I?"

Chuck grinned and nodded. Tess lazily nodded.

"Hmm. Well, maybe I could enter the biscuits. I-if you think they're good enough. I don't want to embarrass the Double R."

"You could never embarrass the Double R, and your biscuits are heavenly. Enter them," Tess said.

It was all set. For the next two weeks, Jack was nowhere to be found. He'd finish his chores, then hop on the black horse and ride off. Claire wondered what in the world he was doing. She was so grateful to Tess, Jed, and Chuck for taking him under their wings. It made her so happy to see how much he'd matured in a few short months.

She was finishing up with the dishes when a voice called from the back porch. "Mrs. Redmond?"

Claire recognized the voice. It was Ethan Drummond. She walked to the screen door to see him standing there, his hat in hand. She had to admit he was a handsome man. "Mr. Drummond, good afternoon. Come in." She opened the screen door.

Ethan walked in smiling. "I was in the area, thought I'd stop by. Boy, it's hot out there." He wiped his damp brow. Claire offered him a seat.

"How about some lemonade?" she asked, and Ethan agreed.

She sat across from him, and they absently sipped the lemonade. "So, Mr. Drummond…"

"Ethan, please. And I'd be honored if you allowed me to call you Claire," he said, smiling. Claire smiled back and nodded.

"Ethan, what brings you here?"

"I had such a lovely time at the barbecue, I just thought perhaps, well, maybe you'd like to go out for dinner sometime. You spend too much time in the kitchen. Tess is a slave driver," he said with a smirk. Claire laughed.

"Not really, it is my job," she pointed out the obvious.

"Then you need a break. I insist," he said just as Tess walked through the kitchen door.

She was dusty and sweaty. Her white shirt wet with perspiration. She took off her hat and ran her forearm across her damp face. "Ethan, this is a surprise."

Tess smiled thinly and glanced at Claire, who was oddly aroused by Tess's jealousy. Tess walked to the sink and picked up a glass.

"Have some lemonade," Ethan offered happily. "Claire was so kind to make some."

Tess turned and saw the pitcher and glasses. Her jaw twitched. "No, thanks, this'll do me. I've got to get back."

Ethan smiled. "Tess, take a rest and…"

"I'm fine, thank you," she said evenly and drank the water.

Claire glared at her but said nothing.

"So, Claire, how about it? Dinner in town and a movie? Tess, you shouldn't work this adorable woman so hard. She needs a night off," Ethan said.

"Mrs. Redmond can come and go as she pleases. She doesn't need my permission."

Claire closed her eyes and counted to ten.

"Be my guest. We can fend for ourselves for one night. I'm sure we won't die. Have fun," Tess said and refilled her glass.

"Wonderful," Ethan exclaimed. "How about tonight?"

"Fine," Claire said, watching Tess.

Tess finished and set the glass in the sink. She grabbed her hat and gloves. "Nice to see you, Drummond. Have a nice time, Claire," she said without looking at her as she walked out of the kitchen.

Claire watched as Tess mounted the chestnut mare and took off in a flash, leaving behind a trail of dust. Claire let out an exasperated sigh.

"Geez, she rides like a man," he said.

"Better," Claire said. "Why don't you pick me up at six?"

Tess stayed at the north pasture when the men were leaving. "Not coming to dinner?" Chuck asked curiously.

"No, I'll stay. Send one of the boys out when they're finished with supper."

"What's wrong?"

"Nothing! Shit, I'm just not hungry," she said angrily.

Chuck raised both eyebrows. "Since when? I hear Claire made chili and biscuits. The guys have been talking about it all afternoon. What in the hell is wrong with you? You've had a burr under your saddle since you came back this afternoon."

Tess gave a hard yank on Stella's reins. "Nothing is wrong. I'll see ya later. I'm taking a ride." She kicked Stella's side sharply and took off, scattering the cattle as she rode southward.

Chuck scratched his chin. "Now what?"

When he got back just in time to see Claire get into a convertible with Ethan Drummond, he knew. Jack was at the stove stirring the chili. "Where's your mom going?"

"Out with that Drummond guy. I don't know why. She didn't look like she wanted to go. Where's Tess?"

"She's out riding. Says she won't be back for dinner."

"Hmm."

"She'll come back when she's hungry, which I am."

Jack laughed and handed him a bowl. "Me too. I hope Mom has fun."

Claire sat at the restaurant and absently sipped the iced tea through her straw. Ethan watched her carefully as he sipped his whiskey.

"Well, I'm having a marvelous time," he said.

Claire chuckled. "Sorry, Ethan. I'm not very good company."

"Nonsense. Now tell me all about yourself. Don't leave anything out," he said as the waitress set the menus on the table. "May we have a bottle of wine, please?"

After two glasses of wine, Claire felt a little more at ease and not so angry over Tess's reaction.

"So you left Portland with Jack and headed to Helena," he said and cut into his steak.

"Yep. That's pretty much it," she said as she ate.

"Well, there was something else. You were married," he said, stealing a glance at the pretty woman across from him.

"And I am no longer. Now that's it," she said, trying to change the topic. "So what about you? You don't look like a rancher to me."

"God, no. I'm a businessman. There's so much happening in this area, so much money to be made and I, Mrs. Redmond, intend on cashing in," he said and raised his glass. Claire gave him a wary look as she toasted with her glass. "I went to college, got a degree in business and marketing, and I plan on making a fortune by the time I'm forty-five."

159

"Very ambitious, Ethan. Just how do you plan on making your millions?"

"Oh, I have a few ideas. But enough. Tell me how you came to be at the Double R with Tess, the taskmaster."

Claire told him enough to keep him satisfied. She was very leery of saying too much to anyone. "I got a job as a waitress and advanced to cook in Helena. There's no big story, a boring life. Maria is a friend of one of the workers at the hotel and told me of this job. I thought it would be a good change for Jack. I was right. He's filled out so much since being here."

"Ranch living. It'll make a man out of you. Look at Tess," he said dryly as he drank his wine.

"That was an unkind thing to say," Claire said evenly.

Ethan looked up and realized what he had said. "Truthfully, I like Tess. Stephen and she were my two favorite people growing up in Silverhill. However, you're absolutely right, but everybody knows about Tess Rawlins," he said as he drank his wine.

Claire watched this man curiously. There was no judgmental tone in his voice. She couldn't understand the sudden faraway look in his eyes, however.

"It's not a big mystery. She never dated. She'll never marry." He chuckled quietly. "You know I don't think I've ever seen her in a dress."

"That's a good criterion for marriage," Claire countered sarcastically.

Ethan smiled and agreed. "Don't scold me. As I said, Tess and I go back a long way. Steve was a good friend of mine," he said, and Claire saw the look once again.

"I understand it was an awful accident," Claire said as she watched him. His face darkened as he merely nodded. "I was told he was an excellent horseman, much like Tess."

He smiled then. "No one was as good as Tess. And if you ever tell her that, I'll deny it."

Claire laughed and agreed. "I've never met anyone like her."

Ethan raised a curious eyebrow as he watched the smile spread across her face. "Well, you two couldn't be any different. You're attractive and very feminine. No man would want a woman who rides better, shoots better, and probably swears better than he does. Tess's passion is that ranch. Well, that was long ago. She left for college and virtually never came back."

"She still loves the ranch and her family."

"So did Steve. He used to tell me how he loved taking care of what his father and those before him did for this country. He would have made a good ranch owner for this community, like his father and grandfather before. I wish he had that chance." He frowned deeply as he toyed with his wineglass.

"What are you thinking?"

Ethan looked up and smiled slightly but said nothing.

"Steve Rawlins?" she asked, and Ethan leaned back against his chair. "Are you of the opinion that he was too experienced to be thrown from a horse?"

"Yes, but Pat Hayward said otherwise. Too many people were talking about Stephen Rawlins and his untimely death. It's been more than hinted at that he was not merely thrown from his horse. But there was no real proof, only hearsay, and that means nothing. Perhaps...." He stopped abruptly as he looked at Claire, who gave him a questioning look.

"Do you know something?" She leaned forward.

Ethan regarded her for a moment. "I know many things," he said lightly. "Now finish your meal and we'll talk of more pleasant things."

"If you know something, why aren't you telling Jed or Tess?"

Ethan stopped with his fork in his mouth. He blinked several times before he set his fork down. "I don't know what you're talking about."

Claire leaned forward. "I've been on my own since I was seventeen. That's a good deal of time to get to know people. I know when someone is lying to me and you, Ethan Drummond, are lying. I care very much about the Rawlins family. I will not see them hurt. So start talking."

Ethan tossed his napkin down and drained his wineglass, then refilled Claire's and his own. "Steve had some information on Telford. He never told me what it was, but he was sure. When he died, I told Tess and Jed. We all went to Pat, who denied ever talking to Steve and who said there were fifteen witnesses that heard Steve tell Telford he'd never cheat anybody again. To Pat, that sounded like a threat. He told the Rawlinses and me that Telford came to him and he was worried about Steve and his threats. Afterward, it was determined that Steve's horse must have been spooked and threw him. The U.S. marshal in Helena had no reason to doubt the sheriff. It was dropped. I honestly thought Tess was going to kill Pat Hayward. Jed had a small heart attack recently, and now I suppose Tess has decided to stay on and take care of things. I'm not one of Tess's favorite people."

"Why? You tried to help," Claire said, not understanding why Tess would feel this way.

Ethan shrugged and drank his wine. "I'm working for Warren Telford."

Claire watched him curiously as he seemed bored with the conversation. One minute he was trying to solve the mystery of Stephen Rawlins' death, and the next, he was working with the very man who may have murdered him.

"I suppose I can see her point," he added dryly.

The drive back to the Double R was quiet. Ethan pulled behind the house and jumped out to open Claire's door.

"Thanks for nice evening, Ethan," Claire said as they walked up the porch steps.

"I'd like to see you again," he said. Claire looked up into the brown eyes, and as she opened her mouth to say something, Ethan reached down and took her hand in his. Claire winced inwardly. Oh, boy, Tess will have a stroke if she sees this.

"Ethan, I don't think so. I have so much to do here and…" she started, not knowing how to say no gracefully.

"Is there a reason you don't want to see me again?"

With that, the screen door opened and banged into him. Tess stood there sporting a smirk.

"Oh, I'm sorry, kids, I didn't see you," she said lightly, avoiding the glare.

Ethan rubbed his shoulder. "No problem. Shouldn't you be

getting your rest?"

Tess walked right between them, ignoring Ethan, and headed for the stable.

"Where are you going so late at night?" Claire asked through clenched teeth.

Tess whirled around and marched back up to the porch. Ethan shook his head at the angry bull in Tess. He leaned against the railing, folded his arms across his chest, and watched the reason Claire would not be seeing him again. He might as well have been invisible.

"If I remember correctly, Mrs. Redmond, I own this ranch. I don't have to explain to anyone where I go or what I do."

"It's just that it's so late," Claire hissed.

"Then you'd better say good night to Drummond. You've got a job to do, you know," Tess retorted.

"I know very well what my job is…" Claire started, and Tess walked back up the steps and yanked the screen door open as she marched into the kitchen. The screen door slammed and Ethan winced.

Claire was furious as she stood there swiping the long hair from her face. "Oh, that woman!"

"Yes, that woman," Ethan agreed and stood in front of her. He took her hand and gave it a healthy pump. "Good night, Claire, thank you for a wonderfully enlightening evening," he said as he chuckled. "We'll see each other again."

"Good night, Ethan. I-I'm…" Claire stammered, and Ethan put his hand up.

"I understand," he said. As he walked down the steps, he called over his shoulder, "I'm leaving, Tess, so there's no reason for you to have a stroke."

Claire hid her eyes in embarrassment, then gave Ethan a weak smile. He waved as he pulled away from the house.

"Tess Rawlins," she hissed as she closed the back door. She turned into the darkness of the kitchen. "What is the big idea…?"

Tess stood in front of her, pinning her against the counter. "Did you enjoy your evening?" she asked in a dark voice.

163

Claire swallowed. "Actually…" she started, then gasped openly as Tess loomed over.

"Do you love me?" Tess asked in a low voice. Claire nodded. She tried to speak, but all the moisture left her mouth. Her body once again was on fire. "Then you will not see Ethan Drummond again. Do you understand me? I love you, Claire. I…" Tess stopped and took a deep quivering breath. Her body started to shake and Claire wasn't sure if it was from anger or fear. She remembered Chuck's words. *She's petrified.*

Claire reached up to the trembling cheek and cradled it tenderly in her hand. "I'm sorry, Tess. I let my anger get the better of me when I said I would go to dinner with him, you seemed not to care, and I…"

"What could I say? God knows I wanted to pick him up by his nose and throw him through the screen door," Tess said angrily. Claire caressed her cheek, instantly calming her. "God, when you touch me, Claire," she whispered helplessly.

They stood in the dark kitchen. The only sound was their breathing and hearts pounding. Claire rested her forehead on Tess's chin and sighed deeply. "I need you, Tess. God, I'm constantly thinking about you touching me," she whispered as Tess lowered her head and kissed her neck, her warm lips searing the soft skin. Her tongue lightly bathed the silky skin, causing gooseflesh to pop out all over Claire.

"I can't take much more of this," she whimpered as Tess unbuttoned the first few buttons of her blouse. She pulled it back and lowered her head, lightly kissing the top of her breast. Tess groaned as she tasted the soft flesh, sending a shiver through both women. Claire ran her fingers through the blond hair as Tess reached in and slipped Claire's breast out of her bra. Claire bit at her lip to avoid crying out as Tess sucked hungrily, her teeth gently pulling the tender flesh into her mouth. Claire flinched, knowing Tess would leave a mark; she couldn't care less. She held the damp head in place, silently begging her to continue.

Claire pulled her head back as the playful nip got too playful. Tess was panting as Claire held her face between her hands. "Leaving your mark, Miss Rawlins?"

A look of pure want and desire filled the crystal blue eyes. "You're mine, Claire Redmond," Tess growled sensually. She reached in and palmed the heaving breasts; Claire shivered. "Say it. Tell me, Claire," Tess nearly begged. "Please…"

"I'm yours, Tess. God knows I am," she whispered breathlessly.

Tess lay naked in bed, her hands behind her head, staring at the ceiling. The humid night breeze that blew through the curtains did nothing to cool her overheated body. Something definitely had to be done. She needed Claire, wanted her in her bed every night. The thought of Claire down the hall from her drove her crazy. She growled lowly, pulled the pillow over her head, and let out a muffled frustrated scream.

Chapter 19

It was time for the Fourth of July Rodeo in Silverhill. The Rawlinses packed up the station wagon and hauled the trailer, which housed Jack's black stallion.

"I don't know why you had to bring Jack's horse," Claire said as they pulled into Silverhill.

"He's proud of Zeus. Let Jack show him off a little," Tess said.

Silverhill was buzzing. The crowd of people milled through the one-street town. "Holy cow! I didn't know Silverhill had this many people," Jack exclaimed as Jed steered the wagon by the rodeo stands.

"There are people from all over the county. Even tourists who have never seen a rodeo," Jed said and parked the car.

Tess agreed. There were tons of people taking their vacations, wanting to get a glimpse of what was left of the Old West. Then it started again, that nagging thing running around in her mind. Time after time, she'd get an idea and couldn't quite put it together. She had much too much on her mind right now with the impending cattle drive.

"You still thinking about what I think you're thinking about?" Chuck asked.

Tess laughed. "Yes. If I'm thinking what you're thinking."

"You are."

Jed and Jack exchanged glances.

"Tess?" Jed said loudly.

"Sorry, my mind was wandering," she said as she got out.

Claire slipped her arm in hers. "Quit thinking and have fun. Now show me where to go to enter my biscuits. They'd better stay warm." She held the covered basket. Tess licked her lips as she tried to sneak a peek and got her hand slapped for her trouble.

Chuck and Jed stood by Tess and Jack as the judges tasted the contestants' bread, pastries, and biscuits. Claire stood behind hers and bit at her bottom lip as the judges walked up and down. She glanced at Tess, who winked and smiled. Jack gave her the thumbs-up.

"Well, I think we have a winner..." Old Henry Colton said as he slipped his fingers in his suspenders.

"You looked like the cat that swallowed the canary, Mrs. Redmond," Tess whispered as she stole a kiss on the cheek from the beaming winner.

"I am! I can't believe I won my first time out! Maria will be so happy. I can't believe it. I mean my first time," Claire rambled as she proudly displayed the blue ribbon on the winner's cup.

Tess laughed and Jack grinned. "Mom, of course you won," he said and hugged her. Claire wrapped her arms around him and hugged him back.

"Okay, now what?" Jack asked.

"I'm starved, and since I didn't get any of your mother's biscuits, I guess we'll just have to settle for some barbecue," Tess said and led the way.

As they sat at the table eating ribs and hot dogs, a voice came over the loudspeaker.

"All right, folks, the ladies barrel racing is next. Contestants, please step up and get your entry numbers. And I understand we have a past winner here. Tess Rawlins from the Double R Ranch. Tess won this event three years running back in... Well, it was a long time ago."

The crowd clapped and laughed. A few people sought Tess out and shook her hand. Tess, completely embarrassed, graciously chatted for a few minutes.

They watched the event with Tess ignoring the grunts from Chuck. When it had finished, Chuck took off his hat and sighed. "You could have won that easily, Tess."

"Oh, Good Lord, Chuck," Tess said. "I haven't done that in over twenty-five years. I'd have made a fool out of myself."

Chuck and Jed would have none of it as they continued until Tess put up her hand. "Guys, I love you both, but please remember." She leaned in for emphasis and said slowly, "I fell off my horse recently. And I wasn't racing around barrels."

Claire laughed and handed Tess a bag of popcorn.

Once again, the announcer's voice called out over the loudspeaker. *"Next event, calf roping for boys ages 14 to 17. Contestants, please sign up and get your entry numbers. Good luck to you young folks, the future of Montana Rodeo!"*

Claire looked up from her ice cream. "Where's Jack?"

Tess gave her a shrug. "Don't know. I think he's looking around. C'mon, let's go see the calf roping."

Claire pulled a face and Tess laughed. "C'mon. I'll buy the beer."

"Deal," Claire said and followed.

As they sat in the stands, Tess started to walk away. "I'll be right back. I'll get us a beer."

Claire sat next to Jed, who nodded with a small grin as Tess winked.

Jack was sitting behind the stall waiting his turn. Tess could sense his nervousness as he tried to spit.

She smiled slightly. "You all set?" she asked, and Jack nodded quickly. "I know you're nervous, only natural. Now just do exactly as we did out on the range and how you did with Pedro and Kyle. Quick release, watch their hooves, and a quick pull. You'll be fine. I'm proud of you," she assured his questioning face. "It's just like out on the pasture."

"Yeah, but no one was watching. Look at all those people."

"They're all just friends," a girl's voice called out quietly.

Both turned to see a redheaded girl standing behind Jack. She looked to be about the same age as Jack, who for some reason blushed furiously.

"My brother is in this, too. He's so nervous he threw up this morning," she said, and Jack chuckled.

Tess said nothing as she watched them.

"My name is Rebecca Riley," she said.

"J-Jack Redmond. Hi." He offered his hand. Just before she took it, he took off his hat. Tess smiled inwardly and stepped out of the way.

"We just moved from Three Forks, my father bought the hardware store in town."

"I work at the Double R," he said in manly fashion. "Oh, I'm sorry, this is Miss Rawlins. She owns the Double R."

Tess shook hands with the girl. "I'd better get back to your mother. She'll come looking for me. Now remember…"

"I know. Quick release, watch their hooves, and a quick pullback. Thanks, Tess," he said, and Tess nodded.

"It was a pleasure meeting you, Miss Riley. After Jack wins," she said and winked, "you're welcome to join us at the barbecue."

"Thank you," Rebecca said. "Well, I'd better get back to the stands, my parents will be wondering. I-I hope you do well, Jack."

Jack shrugged. "Thanks, but I don't know…"

"You'll do well. I-I know you will," she said, smiling as she backed up. "See ya."

"See ya," Jack said nervously and watched the redhead dash through the crowd.

He turned to Tess, his face flushed. "Okay, I better get going."

"Good luck, son."

Tess made her way back to Claire and the others—without the beer.

"Hey," Claire complained.

Tess laughed. "Sorry. We'll get it afterward."

Claire glanced at Jed and Chuck, who were fidgeting in their seats. "Okay, what gives with you guys? Why are you so nervous?"

With that, the announcer's voice called out, *"This is the first time for our next contestant. Jack Redmond from the Double R Ranch is up. Let's give the young man a hand."*

Chapter 20

Claire nearly dropped her ice cream; Tess saved the cup and smiled sheepishly. "Jack? My Jack?"

Tess, Chuck, and Jed all nodded. Claire was stunned as she watched the starting gate. In a flash, she saw the calf run out, and there was Jack, his tan cowboy hat pulled down low and racing Zeus while his lariat swung over his head.

"Oh, my God!" Claire exclaimed and stood.

Jack let the noose fly and snapped back as he caught the leg of the calf. He quickly jumped off Zeus, got the calf on its back, and pulled out the rope, hogtying its other legs. He stopped and threw his hands up, signaling his finish.

Tess whistled and cheered. Claire screamed and laughed. She had no idea why she was screaming. "Did he do all right?" she yelled to Tess, who was still whistling.

"He did great!" she exclaimed, and Claire once again looked out at Jack, who was grinning from ear to ear as he took off his hat and waved to Claire.

"That's my boy!" she yelled out to him.

"One second," Jack muttered as he took off his cowboy hat and hit it against his leg. Claire put an arm around his shoulders.

"I'm so proud of you. I can't believe you did that. You were magnificent."

"I was?"

Claire nodded and kissed his cheek. "Mom…" he complained halfheartedly.

Jed walked up to him and stuck out his hand. Jack took it and looked up at the older man. "If I ever had another son, I would want him to be just like you. I'm proud of you. Today, you became a man. You earned the right to go on the cattle drive to Colorado."

Tess fought the tears that welled in her eyes as she watched Jed fight with his emotions. Claire didn't fight, she started to cry.

Jack put his arm around her. "Don't cry." He looked back at Jed. "Thank you, Mr. Rawlins, that means a lot to me. I won't let you down."

"I know that, son."

Chuck was sniffing behind them and Jed gave him a look. "I can't help it," he said and walked away.

"Who is that redhead?" Claire asked suspiciously. Rebecca and Jack stood by the soda stand. Jack handed Rebecca a bottle of Coke and took one for himself.

"Rebecca Riley, just moved here from Three Forks. Her father bought the old hardware store," Tess said as she dipped into the bag of popcorn.

"Mom? This is Rebecca Riley," Jack offered the introductions. Claire smiled at the redhead and took her hand.

"It's nice to meet you, Mrs. Redmond," the girl said with a smile.

"It's nice to meet you, too, Rebecca."

"Jack almost won," she said and blushed. Jack drank his soda.

"Yes, he sure surprised me," Claire said.

"Mom, would it be okay if I walked Rebecca around? You know she just moved here," he said in a hopeful voice.

"Sure, Jack. The fireworks start in an hour. We'll sit by the car and watch."

"Okay, thanks."

"It was nice to meet you, Rebecca."

"Same here, Mrs. Redmond. Bye," the girl said and followed Jack.

"He's growing up so fast," Claire whispered as she watched Jack walk beside Rebecca. Tess saw the forlorn look on Claire's face.

"Today was a rite of passage for him. He wanted so much to surprise you," she said in a soft voice.

Claire gave her a playful scowl. "And you… How long did you know about this?"

"About a month."

"That's where you two have been?"

Tess nodded and ate the popcorn. Claire reached over and gently touched the denim-clad knee. "Thank you."

"My pleasure," she replied in a quiet voice.

"Well, good evening," Ethan Drummond's voice called out.

Both women looked up. Tess's face was void of emotion. "Drummond. How are you?"

"I'm fine. Saw your event. I know how you pride yourself on your horsemanship, Tess. I'm sorry you didn't ride."

Tess looked at him and heard the honesty in his voice. She actually smiled slightly. "Thanks, Ethan."

Ethan nodded and looked at Claire. "Claire, and how are you? I saw your son compete. He's very good. He must have had a good teacher."

"Thanks. I'm very proud of him, and yes, he had an excellent teacher."

He studied both women for a moment or two. "I must be going. It was nice seeing you again, Claire. Tess, a pleasure as usual."

"As usual, Ethan," Tess agreed dryly.

They exchanged looks, then Ethan nodded and walked away. Tess narrowed her eyes at his retreating figure. "I've decided I don't like him."

"Tess, Ethan told me what happened after your brother died. He tried to help…" Claire started, and Tess shot her an angry look.

"Then he quickly started working for Telford when it was all clear. Just when did you two talk about all this?"

"Will you please stop with this jealously? I don't care about Ethan Drummond," Claire said seriously.

Tess turned to face her. "You don't?"

"What do I have to do to assure you?"

Tess leaned closer and whispered in her ear, "A night with only you and me and waking up in my arms."

"Oh, God, Tess. I want that so badly," Claire said, looking into her eyes. "You must believe that."

"I do. I—"

"Hey, Mom, Tess. Fireworks!" Jack called out, causing both women to jump. "C'mon, they're starting."

He pulled at both women, who locked gazes for the briefest of moments. They smiled and headed back to the car.

As the fireworks ended, Tess and Jed heard the whistle from the old steam engine blaring. "What's going on?" Jed asked.

"I heard they're starting a tour of the Bitterroots by rail. It starts in Helena and stops in Silverhill, then off to Three Forks and around again. It's something the city council thought was a good idea for tourism. Get folks to come out and see the Old West," Chuck said.

"People will pay for that?" Jed asked, scratching his head.

"Sure, folks who've never been out this way get a chance to see what life was like in the West," Tess agreed thoughtfully.

Jed shook his head as he started the station wagon and waited for everyone. "Seems like a waste of money to me."

Tess slipped into the front seat and shook her head. "No, Dad, it makes perfect sense." She nodded and smiled. "Perfect."

Chapter 21

Warren Telford sat in this office watching the fireworks. How appropriate, he thought as he grinned evilly.

"I'll get you Rawlinses yet," he vowed.

He turned back to his desk and leafed through the pages of Collins's report. Claire Redmond, Long Island, New York. Son, Jack Redmond, 16. Father unknown. Lived in Portland, now Helena. Occupation: Food Service Industry. Currently working at the Double R Ranch in Silverhill, Montana.

"Father unknown," he said as he continued reading. With that, there was a knock at his office door. "C'mon in."

Ethan Drummond walked in and lazily sat in the chair by his desk. "Mr. Telford."

"Ethan, what have you got?"

"Nothing really."

The old man's head shot up. "I thought you were dating Mrs. Redmond."

Ethan shrugged and twirled his hat. "I tried. I don't think I'm her type."

"Then I was right. Tess Rawlins is her type." Telford grinned wickedly and sat back in his chair. "Tess Rawlins and the cook. Ha!" He let out a laugh. "Who, by the way, has a son."

Ethan frowned deeply, trying to avoid punching Telford dead in the face. "Mr. Telford, that is an ugly rumor," he warned.

Telford grunted. "Who knows? It might be true. If it's not, then let them deny it. Oh, this will be good. I wonder what Jed Rawlins would do to keep this bit of information a secret."

"That stretch of land? The north pasture?" Ethan offered.

Those hundred acres were prime in this state. Developers had been screaming to get their hands on it. Warren Telford wanted it.

"Maybe, Ethan my boy, maybe." Telford sighed and puffed on his cigar.

August turned out to be a dry, hot month. They had spent the time getting Claude's cattle branded for him and getting an accurate head count. The Double R herd was all set. In two weeks, they'd be on their way. The cattle along the north pasture bathed in the Bitterroot River that flowed adjacent to the old mansion.

Tess rode Stella along the river, stopping for the horse to drink. The idea of turning the old house into a guesthouse was a sound idea. Over the past month, she had talked to other ranch owners in other states who had done the same thing, and all of them had the same thing to say—it saved their ranch.

She knew raising cattle alone would not be enough, and turning the Double R into a working ranch and guesthouse would work. As Stella lazily loped the high ridge, Tess heard a car and shielded her eyes with her hat against the hot afternoon sun. She smiled as she saw Claire driving the Jeep as far as she could.

Claire honked the horn once or twice, and Tess waved her hat, quickly riding up to the Jeep.

"What are you doing out here?" Tess looked down from atop Stella, leaning on the pommel of the saddle.

Claire swallowed hard as she gazed into her blue eyes. Tess wore a white sleeveless undershirt, her sweat-soaked denim shirt draped across the saddle in front of her. Looking farther, she noticed the leather chaps that covered a pair of old Levi's. Tess Rawlins was a beautiful woman. Though she argued she was not, Claire Redmond knew differently.

"It's about a hundred degrees, and I knew you wouldn't have enough sense to get into the shade. Follow me on that beast. The men can watch the herd for a few hours."

She started without waiting for a reply and drove the hilly pasture to the old house. It was a bumpy ride.

"God, you need to get a road or a path or something up here," she groaned as she got out of the car.

175

Tess swung off Stella, tying her to the porch rail. She noticed Claire had a large picnic basket.

"What are we doing?" Tess followed Claire up the steps.

"You are taking a cool bath and having something to eat. I brought you a change of clothes. Everyone else has had lunch. You haven't come back for lunch in four straight days. You'll collapse before you get that herd to Colorado."

She walked into the old mansion and straight to the bathroom. Running the tepid water, she called out to Tess.

"Okay, in you go."

Tess walked into the bathroom and smiled. "You are sweet, Claire Redmond."

"I know," she said and kissed her chin. "Now strip."

Tess's eyes nearly bugged out of her head, but she obeyed. She unbuckled the leather chaps and Clair took them from her. "Shirt and jeans, they're filthy." She held out her hand.

"I-I'll be naked," Tess said.

Claire raised an eyebrow. "A bath works better that way. I'm waiting."

Tess shrugged and stripped off her shirt and undershirt. She sat on the edge of the tub and yanked off her boots. "Stop drooling, Claire."

"Continue."

Tess complied and slowly unzipped the dusty jeans and pulled them down her hips. "You're going to watch this whole thing, aren't you?"

"Oh, yes." Claire tossed the dirty shirts aside and walked up to Tess. "Let me help." She gently pulled the jeans down the rest of the way. "You're beautiful, Tess. Now get into the tub."

Tess tried to swallow but found it impossible as she slipped into the tepid water. Claire sat on the edge of the tub and soaped up a cloth. "Lean forward. I'll get your back."

Tess obeyed without a word and sighed when Claire gently rubbed the cloth down her back. She pulled her knees up and wrapped her arms around them. "Oh, God, Claire, that feels so good. Man, I'm sore."

"You're not getting any younger."

"This I know," Tess said dreamily.

Claire washed her back and shoulders. "Put your head back, sweetie."

Tess whimpered and did as she was told. Claire took the old pot sitting there and poured the water over her head, then lathered her hair. "Oh, God, that feels good."

"You said that already," Claire said and rinsed her head. She then stood. "I think you can wash yourself the rest of the way."

Tess ran her fingers through her wet hair and laughed. "Yes, but it won't be as much fun."

"Next time." Claire kissed her shoulder. "I'll go make lunch."

After the cool bath, Tess dressed in fresh clothes. "Thanks, I feel much better. And I'm starved."

Cold beef, potato salad, and lemonade rounded off the picnic lunch.

"My, that was good. Now I'm pooped. Thanks. I have to get back..."

Claire walked across and sat on Tess's lap. "Not so fast. You're going to rest for a while." She got up and took Tess by the hand. She compliantly followed her down the hall.

Claire threw open the windows, allowing the warm gentle breeze to circulate through the room. Tess sat on the bed and Claire gently pushed her back against the pillows. "Join me."

"I was hoping you'd say that," Claire whispered and lay next to her on the big bed.

Tess let out a contented sigh as Claire cuddled up to her, nestling her head into the strong, soft shoulder. "This will be our place. What do you think? We can come here. No one will bother us. Just for the afternoon or..."

Claire shifted and loomed over her. "That was the general idea. I thought of the same thing this morning. All this time, we had this right in front of us."

Tess smiled and reached up to stroke the soft cheek. Claire lowered her head and kissed the warm lips briefly. As she pulled back, Tess put a strong arm around her back and pulled her on top of her.

In a few short moments, tender kisses turned decidedly more

177

passionate as Tess rolled over, taking Claire with her. Now she was on top, kissing Claire's neck, her jaw, up to her ear where she nibbled the sensitive lobe.

"Make love to me, Tess. Please," Claire begged.

Tess groaned and shivered at the plea in her voice and eagerly tried to unbutton her blouse. Claire chuckled at her fumbling and gently pushed her hands away and sat up. Tess blinked as she watched the woman she loved slowly unbutton the cotton blouse and slip it off her shoulders. She reached around and the white bra was next. Tess now was trying to control her breathing as she watched Claire stand and slip out of her jeans and panties.

"Oh, God, Claire, you are beautiful." Tess moaned as she stripped her shirt off, then her bra. Claire nearly laughed at how quickly Tess got herself naked.

In a flash, Tess's body covered Claire's, both gasping at the virginal feel of their bodies touching intimately. Claire shifted her leg, and Tess groaned as she felt Claire's thigh rubbing against her. If she weren't careful, this would all end much too soon.

She shifted and lay next to Claire, partially covering her. Her kisses seared the soft flesh as she licked and nibbled every inch offered to her. Her fingers wandered over the lovely body, memorizing each curve, each line.

Claire moaned into the sensual kiss as their breasts pressed against each other, nipples aching with desire. She naturally parted her legs as Tess's fingers moved south, reveling as the muscles in her belly quivered from her touch. "Now, Claire. I need to touch you now," she whispered, and Claire nodded helplessly, then gasped and arched her back into the heavenly touch.

Tess loomed over Claire's body. "Open your eyes," she demanded. Claire's eyes flew open. "I love you always."

Claire's violet eyes filled with desire, pleading for release. Claire bit at her bottom lip as she felt the strong fingers sliding through her. Her hips bucked, seeking more contact, and Tess smiled as she easily slipped two fingers in. Claire cried out as she felt Tess moving within her, loving her, controlling her body and soul.

Tess could feel the inner walls contracting around her saturated fingers as they slowly moved deeper. Claire cried out, her fingers digging into Tess's shoulders. "Tess!" she said helplessly.

"Claire, Claire," Tess whispered tenderly as she watched her. Claire looked up into the blue eyes with an astonished look.

"Tess! I-I..." she nearly screamed as they never lost eye contact.

"Now, Claire," Tess whispered in a low voice. Working her fingers faster, Claire bucked her hips in rhythm with the passionate thrusts.

"Oh, God," Claire cried out in amazement. "Don't stop!"

"Never," Tess whispered in a ragged voice. "I'll never stop loving you." She kissed her deeply, her tongue plunging deep. Claire was shaking with the onset of her orgasm. Tess pulled back and gazed.

"Claire," she whispered her erotic command. "Come for me, please." She placed her thumb over the engorged clitoris and stroked in rhythm with her thrusts. Claire arched her back and became completely still. Then she cried out, clawing at Tess's back, knowing she must be bruising her.

Tess winced but continued loving her; how could she stop? Claire's body surrendered completely. She came, helpless to stop, for Tess—only for Tess. As she cried out her name, Tess kissed her deeply, swallowing her cries of ecstasy.

Tess slowly brought Claire down, her body still trembling with the aftershock of the most powerful orgasm she'd ever known. Tess clung to her as she lay on her back, taking Claire in a warm embrace. Both women were perspiring and breathless.

"Oh, my God, Tess," Claire's voice was a mere whisper. She cuddled into the hot body and threw a shaky leg over Tess's thigh. "I love you," she said tenderly and kissed the salty neck.

Tess moaned and pulled her close. "I love you, too."

Claire reached up and placed her palm over the larger breast. Tess arched her back into the touch. Immediately, her breathing became ragged and her body shook.

"Relax. It's my turn." Claire quickly straddled the muscular thighs. Tess looked up and grinned. She reached up to cup her large breast; Claire held her hands over her head, kissing her deeply. She kissed down her neck, to the top of her breast. All the while Tess's body jerked with anticipation.

"Claire." She sighed and closed her eyes. Claire wasted no time. She eagerly took the aching nipple into her mouth and suckled. "Yes!" Tess hissed through clenched teeth as she writhed beneath her.

"I believe you left your mark a few weeks ago, Tess Rawlins. I think it was right about here," she added in a seductive whisper and sucked the warm flesh into her mouth. Tess wriggled and groaned as Claire hungrily feasted.

"Ah!" Tess cried out. "Geezus, woman."

Claire released the bruised flesh and gently licked the area, causing a deep groan from Tess. She then proceeded to feast on the other breast, leaving Tess gasping and aching for more.

Lowering herself, Claire kissed her way down the long muscular torso, flicking her tongue against the quivering stomach muscles. She hesitated at the top of the dark blond curls. Tess had her legs spread so far apart she thought she'd break something, still Claire hesitated. Tess could feel her soft, warm breath on her and moaned helplessly.

She opened her eyes to see Claire gazing at her with a questioning look. She gently prodded with her smile and Tess groaned and flopped back. Claire teased her mercilessly with her warm breath and light kisses around the curls and upper thighs. With every touch, Tess twitched uncontrollably.

"Damn it, Claire," Tess hissed as she bucked her hips into the elusive tongue.

"Hmm?" Claire mumbled her question. Tess looked down once again to see the evil grin on Claire's face. Her tongue appeared and made a licking motion in the air.

Tess groaned and nearly whimpered as the throbbing between her legs became unbearable. She knew what Claire wanted.

"Your tongue, please," Tess begged, and she got her wish. Claire licked her like a starving cat. Her tongue snaked in and out, invading every inch of Tess's overheated flesh.

Tess was a mass of quivering flesh as Claire feasted, bringing her to an unbelievable height. Soon the exquisite feeling became too much to bear. With her last ounce of strength, Tess grabbed

Claire and tossed her on her back, pinning her arms over her head and breathing as if she was having a mild stroke.

"Enough! My God," Tess exclaimed in a ragged voice. She slumped over Claire's smaller body and let out a deep groan.

Claire grinned as she wrapped her arms around the strong sweaty shoulders. "You made me beg," Tess's muffled voice called out quietly.

Claire chuckled and ran her fingers through the damp hair. "Yes, sweetheart. Yes, I did," she agreed, earning a chuckle from Tess.

For the rest of the glorious afternoon, Tess and Claire thoroughly explored each other's bodies and the rest of the mansion.

Tess walked onto the porch, her chaps slung over her shoulder. She set her Stetson on the back of her head and took a deep happy breath.

Claire followed her out and spun her around. "We still have three bedrooms to go," she reminded the chuckling Tess.

"I don't know, the way you were screaming, we might have scared the poor cattle," Tess teased.

"Cattle nothing. Every ranch hand..." She stopped abruptly and gave Tess a wild-eyed look of horror. Tess laughed and pulled her into her arms.

"I don't care. At this very moment, I don't have a care in the world but you," she said, and Claire sighed helplessly.

"You and that Rawlins charm. Get out of here and go do whatever it is you do with your cows." She gently kissed her, then pushed her off the porch. "I'll see you at dinner."

Tess grinned and swung up on Stella without using the stirrups. In one swift movement, she leaned down and pulled the stunned Claire up into her arms and kissed her, then deposited her on the porch steps. "And I didn't fall off my horse." She gave her a wink and galloped toward the herd.

"See ya!" Tess happily called out over her shoulder and waved her hat.

Claire shook her head and waved. "Oh, God," she said with a laugh. "I'm so in love with that goof."

Chapter 22

"Will ya stop that infernal whistlin'?" Chuck pleaded.

Tess laughed and slapped him on the back as they rode along the ridge. "I'm happy. In two weeks, you'll have the herd on its way to Colorado, and I've found a way to keep the ranch going. Why shouldn't I be whistling?"

"You're going with us on the drive?"

"No. You don't need me. Jack is doing fine, you'll have enough with Claude's men, as well. I need to get everything set to turn this place into a working ranch. I need to get our lawyer in on it. And there're renovations to be done."

"And just how are we going to afford that?"

"I've been saving over the years."

"Your dad will not let you use your pension."

"I'm not. Just my personal savings. We'll be fine. So there's no reason not to whistle."

Chuck laughed. "I don't suppose Claire Redmond has anything to do with it."

Tess smiled. "She has everything to do with it. I never thought I'd be this happy or content."

"I'm happy for ya. And Jack seems to be okay with it, as well."

"I know. Claire and I are very lucky in that regard." She saw the glance from Chuck. "What? Has Jack talked to you?"

"No, no. He admires you, Tess, and Jed. He loves his mother. It's just that…"

"What? Will you spit it out?"

"Tess. He may be only sixteen, but he still considers himself the man of the family. Now he's said nothin' to me, but I see he wants to make sure his mother is cared for and happy."

Tess chewed on that for a minute or two. "You're right. He's been the only man in her life. I'll have a talk with him. As an adult. He deserves that." The idea of actually talking to Jack about this made her insides flip.

Mercifully, Chuck changed the topic. "This cattle drive might be the last one the Double R has." He looked around the landscape. "I remember when I was a kid. Your granddad used to let me ride the herd with him. He told me this would be here forever. People gotta eat and they love beef. His beef was the best in these parts," Chuck said, and Tess listened as they trotted along. "Jeremiah did good things with this grass. Took a few years, but look at it. Green and healthy and the cattle love it. Look how healthy they are compared to Claude's."

Tess glanced at the small herd and had to agree. "But he'll get Double R prices. Claude will keep his ranch. I don't know how much time we have left in this business. It's changing and we have to change with it."

"Mmm," Chuck grunted. "Wet nursin' a bunch of New Yorkers."

For the next few days, Tess and Claire grinned like two schoolgirls every time their gazes met. Claire would grin and look down at her plate, and Tess smiled as she drank her coffee. One afternoon, however, the serious side came out in Tess while she and Claire were sitting on the back porch. She explained her conversation with Chuck.

"Tess, we're adults. Jack understands perfectly."

"I know," Tess said as Jack rode back from the herd. "Here he is." She waited until he got to the corral. "Jack, I need to talk to you," Tess called out from the porch. Claire groaned. "It's fine, sweetie. I have to talk to him."

"Tess, this is unnecessary, honey."

"No, it's not. Now trust me." She ignored Claire's sarcastic grunt. "Let me do this. It's important."

Jack took off his work gloves and nodded. He slapped Zeus on the flank, sending the black stallion into the corral. Taking off his hat, he wiped his brow with his forearm. In that one gesture, Tess was amazed how much he looked like his mother and how much older he seemed. He was on the verge of going to college, an intelligent young man, and he deserved to be treated as such. He was Claire's only child.

Claire shook her head. "Tess, really. It's—"

"What's up, Tess?" Jack walked up to the back porch; he looked from his mother to Tess.

"I, we'd like to talk to you," Tess said, finding no moisture in her mouth at all. Her hands were shaking, as well. Maybe this wasn't such a good idea…

"Sure," Jack said and climbed the steps.

"What's going on?" Jed asked as he walked onto the porch.

Chuck was right behind him, eating a bowl of ice cream.

Realizing too late just how bad an idea this was, Tess hung her head. "Nothing is going on. Claire and I—"

"This was your idea," Claire reminded her.

Tess rubbed her temples. "All right. I'd like to talk to Jack."

"About what?" Chuck asked. "Claire, where did you get this ice cream? Is it peach?"

"Yes. Isn't it great?"

"Okay. Hold on now," Jed said. "Tess wants to talk to Jack alone."

"Thanks, Dad," Tess said with a sigh of relief.

"But that's not going to happen, so continue," Jed said and sat in the rocker.

Tess looked at Claire, who was trying not to grin. Tess blushed furiously when she saw the confused look on all three men. "I'd like to talk to you about your mother and me."

With that, Jed and Chuck stood and rushed for the back door. Bumping into each other, they finally got the screen door open and made a quick exit.

"So okay," Jack said to Tess.

"As you know." She cleared her throat. "I, uh." She looked at Jack, who looked as though he was trying to comprehend what she was saying, if his deep frown meant anything, that is. Tess tried another tack. "You know I'm fond of your mother, Jack."

"Sure."

"And, well, I just want you to know I'm fond of her."

"O-okay," Jack said slowly; he glanced at Claire, who smiled happily, watching Tess struggle. "Are you saying you want to date Mom?"

Tess chuckled. "I want to do more than that."

Jack's eyes bugged out of his head, as did Claire's. All of them heard the clang as the spoon hit the kitchen floor.

"What's wrong?" Tess asked both of them. Then it dawned on her. "Oh, my God! No. No. I mean, yes that, but no..." She stopped and painfully rubbed her forehead. This was not going how she imagined. "I love your mother. Love like, ya know love, in love, not love, like just love."

"Good Lord," Claire mumbled, avoiding her son.

"Okay, I get it," Jack said. "You're in love with Mom, right?"

"Yeah, um, right."

"And, Mom, are you in love with Tess?"

"Yes, sweetie. I'm stuck."

Jack laughed along with his mother, then grew serious. "As long as you take care of Mom and make her happy, it's cool with me. If that's what you were gonna ask."

Tess nodded, holding her hands out in a helpless gesture. "Pretty much, yeah."

"Great." Jack kissed his mother's cheek. "I'm gonna take Zeus for a ride."

"Okay, sweetie. Dinner at six."

Jack turned to Tess and kissed her cheek, as well. "Welcome to the family."

Tess laughed. "Same to you." She watched Jack bound off the porch. "What a kid."

Claire walked up to her and put her hands on her shoulders. "Nice speech."

"It kinda got away from me."

"So you want more of me, huh?" Claire whispered against her cheek.

"Hell, yeah. Now that it's okay with your son."

Chapter 23

Jed paced back and forth on the small platform and heard the whistle blow. His head shot up in the direction and smiled. He would always think of Emily when he heard that. Though he could not remember where he put his hat that morning or his wallet, he hoped he would never forget the first time he met Em.

Suddenly, he realized how he missed Maria Hightower, even though the summer flew by, and they had received a few letters from her.

In a few moments, the train chugged into the Silverhill station. Jed couldn't help himself. He smiled happily as the train stopped at the platform. It was only three cars long, but Jed found it amazing the amount people that streamed out of the doors.

Rick Cumberland seemed like he was holding court as he spoke to the tourists. "Now, folks, this is Silverhill, Montana, a throwback to the Old West. It's cattle country and many a cattle drive passed through here, thousands of head of cattle sent on their way to the cattle towns of the Southwest. Silverhill was founded in 1835 by a man who was prospecting for silver…."

From engineer to tour guide, Jed thought he looked like he enjoyed his new job. He scratched his head as the stream of visitors snapped pictures and followed Rick through the station.

"I'll be damned." Jed scratched his head. "I guess Tess was right."

"It's not a good sign for a man of such wealth to be talking to himself," Maria's soft voice called out behind him.

Jed whirled around and gazed at the smiling familiar face. He realized just how much he missed her. "Maria" was all Jed could say. He took off his hat.

"You look well, Jed." Her soulful brown eyes smiled warmly.

"You look different. What is it?" he asked curiously as he searched her face.

She wore the same wide-brimmed sage green cowboy hat that she always wore, the eagle feather lying on the crown. Her long silky brown hair with gray streaks gracefully running through it lay comfortably in a long braid down her back. Her white shirt tucked in to her mid-calf denim skirt rounded off her look of a typical western lady. However, her air of regal Cherokee heritage was predominant.

"You're a fine-looking woman, Maria."

"Am I, Jed Rawlins? I must go away more often," she said with a small grin.

Jed returned the grin. "Oh, no, never again. I hope everything is all right with your family?"

"Yes, now. Thank you for asking. So how are things at the ranch? How is Claire doing?" Maria asked as they walked through the station. "Do I still have a job?"

"Things are going very well. Claire is doing a wonderful job. And you will always have a home on the ranch. You know that. Tess has a wild idea for the old house." He then thought of Tess and Claire. "Um, things around here have changed."

He gently guided Maria out of the station and placed her suitcase in the Jeep. "Walk with me?"

They walked to the outskirts of Silverhill and Jed glanced at the woman he had known since Emily's passing. He remembered when Maria Hightower came to the Double R. She fit right in with his family. Taking Tess and Stephen under her wing, teaching them about the Cherokee way of life, showing all of them how to live in peace with the land and one another.

"You're scaring me," Maria said.

"I don't mean to scare you, though when I'm done telling you this, you very well may be." He took a deep breath and explained Tess's idea of turning the old house into a guesthouse for tourists and turning the Double R into a working ranch. He also told her about Tess and Claire and their love for each other.

Maria listened intently, raising an eyebrow once. She then nodded and smiled slightly. "I assumed as much. I sensed it from Claire when I first met her."

Jed gaped at her. "What? How? My Lord, that's exactly what Emily had said about Tess. What is it with women?"

Marie chuckled openly. "Men are too busy being logical. You don't listen with your heart," she said. "Do I still have a job at the Double R?"

"Yes, thank God. I've come to love Claire, but I really missed you."

"Thank you." Maria smiled. "I've missed you and the ranch."

"Well, good, because like I said, you're not going anywhere. If I'm not mistaken, I think Tess and Claire will move into the old house and take care of the guests. I'm sure Claire will take care of the house and the cooking. Tess will look after the activities. You should see her. Remember how she and Steve used to fish in the stream? Well, who knew that would be an attraction. Fly fishing. Tess got one of her college friends to work on the computer, I guess, for a Web site and all that."

"What will she do about her job at the college?"

"That's the best part. Her contract will be up soon. She's been in contact with them, and the agriculture department is going to let her to do some sort of independent study for students and use the ranch as their playground."

He laughed along with Maria. "She's got a mind, that girl. Gets it from her father," he said, stealing a glance at Maria.

"My goodness, it's been busy. But Tess found a way to keep the ranch. This is good."

"Yes, it is. And it's good to have you home again. And you won't ever leave?"

"I'll never leave."

Maria slipped her arm in Jed's as they walked through town.

"Maria!" Tess called out as she dashed off the porch and hugged her old friend, lifting her off the ground and twirling her around. Jed laughed as he took the luggage out.

"Put me down, you idiot!" Maria exclaimed as Tess set her down.

"Boy, I've missed you." She kissed her cheek.

"I've missed you, as well. I understand you've been a busy woman," she said and glanced at Claire.

Tess blushed deeply. "More than you know." She stopped short, not knowing what in the world to say.

Maria laughed and took her hand, leading her to the porch. "Your father has told me all about your new venture with the ranch. It's good." She noticed Claire and smiled. "This is good, as well."

Claire hugged Maria. "I'm so glad you're back."

"Thank you, Claire."

Maria took her hand and reached for Tess's hand, as well. "It will not be easy, but to find love is wonderful. To keep it is hard work. Be partners."

"Hey, Maria!" Jack's voice called out as he rode up.

"Good heavens, is that Jack?" Maria asked in amazement.

Claire nodded. "Unbelievable, isn't it?"

"He looks like a young man, not a boy."

Jack swung off his horse and hugged Maria. "Let me look at you. Jack, you are so handsome. I see your mother in you now. More than ever," she whispered, and Jack's grin covered his face.

"Let's get you settled in your room. Jack is staying in the bunkhouse, Claire and I, well, we're staying in the old house. And…"

Claire mercifully stepped in. "I think she gets the general idea, honey."

Jed drove into town to meet with Tom about the last-minute preparations for the cattle drive. After settling everything, Tom shifted uncomfortably in his chair. His old friend gave him a curious look.

"What's the matter with you?" he asked lightly. He was in too good a mood. Tom was about to change that.

"Jed, we've known each other all our lives. I consider you

one of my closest friends. And what I'm gonna tell you is for your benefit."

Jed sat tall in the chair and studied Tom. "Okay." He knew what was coming.

"A few people saw Claire and Tess earlier…"

"So?" His voice was even and clear. His anger rose.

Tom took a deep breath. "Jed, there's talk. Tess was kissing her…"

Jed leaned forward in the chair. "This is no one's business but Claire's and Tess's, who I might add will inherit the Double R Ranch someday, the ranch that gives a good many people their livelihoods. Now what is your point?"

Tom rubbed his face tiredly. "I like Claire. I respect Tess, and I don't care who she fools around with."

"Fool around! I'll have you know those two women are deeply in love. If it were possible for them to marry, they would. So be very careful how you choose your next words," Jed said in a controlled voice.

"Marry her? Jed, are you trying to give Warren Telford ammunition? It's bad enough they're talking about them behind your back, do you want…?"

Jed stood and banged his fist on the desk. "Enough! What my family does is my family's business. We don't expect anyone to live by our rules and expect the same in return. My family has practically kept this town alive for over a hundred years with our sweat and blood and sharing our good fortune…"

"Please listen to me. Telford's already talked to some of the ranch owners in town today. The rumor is spreading like wildfire. I overheard him talking to the Drummond kid. He's threatening to expose the whole thing unless…"

"Unless?" Jed asked slowly, keeping his fists clenched at his side.

"Unless you give him the north pasture. That's what he told Ethan Drummond. There are a couple of ranchers who are backing him," Tom said. He walked around the desk and held out his hand. "I for one am not. I love Tess. I'm telling you this to warn you. Telford will stop at nothing. We both know he was involved with

Stephen's death. Please be careful."

Jed hesitated for a moment, then took Tom's hand. "Sorry if I got a little riled."

Tom chuckled and placed his other hand on Jed's strong shoulder. "Just one thing?"

"What?"

"Can they get married?"

"Tom, I never thought Emily would die so young. I never thought I'd see the day when cattle ranching would become a thing of the past. I never thought I'd be struggling to keep my family's ranch. So I have no idea what's possible anymore."

As Jed walked out of Tom's store, he noticed Ethan Drummond getting into his convertible.

"Good evening, Drummond," Jed called out.

Ethan's head shot up and he smiled slightly. "Good evening, Mr. Rawlins. How are you?"

Jed watched him for a moment, remembering how he used to come by the house as a kid. He and Stephen were good friends.

"I'm doing just fine. I haven't seen you in town the last few days. How's business at the bank?"

Jed noticed his hesitation and placed his hands on the car door. "I hope whatever you're doing, you know what you're getting into, son."

Ethan swallowed and nodded. "I do too, Mr. Rawlins. Just remember..." He stopped and grinned. "You take care. It was good to see you. Say hi to Tess and Claire for me," he finished and put the car in gear.

Jed nodded and stepped back, allowing Ethan to pull out of the space and head out of town.

Chapter 24

"So what are we going to do?" Ethan asked lazily as he lounged in the chair. Telford regarded him with interest.

"What do you want out of this, Drummond?"

Ethan looked up and sported a thoughtful pose. After a second, he answered. "Money, pure and simple. I don't want land. I don't want cattle. I just want money." He yawned.

"And it doesn't matter that you're ruining Mrs. Redmond's life and that of her son? What about Tess? I thought you…"

Ethan snorted. "We both know what she likes, Mr. Telford."

Telford watched him, then laughed. "You have a wonderfully twisted sense of having no conscience. I like that. We'll get along just fine." He walked over to the window and looked out at the sleepy town. It was well after midnight and not a soul in sight.

"I hate that Rawlins family. They've been a thorn in my side for over fifty years. I thought for sure when Stephen Rawlins died and Jed had a heart attack, they'd be through. But no, Tess comes back from her decadent life in California with her ideas from all her queer friends. God, I hate her!"

Ethan watched him carefully. "Did you really have something to do with Stephen's death?" he asked, completely intrigued.

Telford smiled evilly and liked the look on Drummond's face. He was eager. "Now that is an ugly rumor, young man."

"There's been talk that you had something to do with it, Mr. Telford. I don't care," Ethan said with a noncommittal shrug. He watched Telford move about his office as he always did. If there were any documents, he'd have to keep them close by and locked up. It wouldn't be easy. It took Ethan over a year just to get into Telford's good graces and into his office.

"Every ranch owner and farmer who didn't have the guts to make it work needed someone to blame for their failure. Look at this recession, my boy. Those fools kept holding on to the land when money made the difference. When the banks started folding and they all lost their farms and their ranches, who had the money? Not the bank. I did. I was smart and shrewd. They were small and stupid, so naturally, I looked like the bad guy."

"What did you do?" Ethan watched the egomaniac sit behind his desk. He took out a long key and opened the bottom drawer. Ethan stood and walked over to the window and absently looked out. He glanced down and watched as Telford took a long pouch out of the drawer and unzipped it. He took out a small worn ledger, placed the stack of money into the pouch, replaced the ledger, and zipped it up. He then locked the drawer, placing the key in his vest pocket. Why would he keep money in a drawer and not in the bank vault? Ethan thought.

"I did what any other bank did that owned a mortgage, wasn't getting paid, and had no hopes of getting paid. I foreclosed and took the property fully within the law," he said and gave Drummond a challenging look.

"I agree with you. Don't worry, I admire your business ethic. I'm learning more from you than any college course I took," Ethan said, which was true. There weren't many courses on Embezzlement 101, which is what Ethan now was sure Warren Telford was doing. "I would like to know how you got away with Stephen Rawlins, though."

Telford let out a self-satisfying laugh. "So would everyone else, I'm sure. Let me tell you one major rule, Drummond."

Ethan leaned in for the words of wisdom that he hoped would hang this old murderer. "I'm all ears, sir." Ethan leaned against the desk as if settling in for a good story.

"Always have someone in your back pocket," Telford said as he lit up another cigar. He watched Ethan's questioning look and puffed at his cigar. He then sat back like a preening cat.

"Sheriff Hayward," Ethan whispered in astonishment.

"You're a very clever young man. We'll get along just fine. And we'll make millions," Telford assured him. "I have Pat right where I want him. Back about eight years ago, he got some girl pregnant, a minor. She was fifteen, I think. He needed money for an abortion. I gave it to him, and I've had him ever since. The girl died…" he finished with a shrug.

Ethan listened, tasting the bile in the back of his throat. Taking a deep breath, he shrugged, as well, and stood. "That's unbelievable," Ethan said evenly.

"That's enough for one night. Why don't you go get some sleep? Now Bob Nelson and Gary Whiting are the only ranchers I can get on my side. They'll be in town later today around four. Be here…" he said, dismissing Ethan, who nodded and walked out.

Chapter 25

Tess, Claire, and Maria were sitting on the back porch. Tess was gazing at the moon as she leaned against the porch railing. "What a handsome moon."

Claire sat across from her on the top step and nodded. She slowly slid her way across and finally wound up sitting next to Tess.

Maria smiled as she rocked on the porch swing.

"I fell in love—"

With that, they heard the Jeep drive up into the back. The door slammed and all three women jumped.

"That money-grubbing son of a bitch!" Jed roared.

"Oh, boy," Tess groaned and quickly stood. "Dad, calm down. What happened?"

Maria ran down the three steps to stand beside him. "Jed, please."

He took a deep breath and retold his conversation with Tom.

Tess's eyes grew dark as she breathed angrily through her nose. "That money-grubbing son of a bitch!"

Claire placed her hand on Tess's arm. She looked at Jed. "So what do we do?"

"We do nothing. Telford can say whatever he likes. It's the fricking twenty-first century, and if he doesn't like it, fuck him," Tess said.

Claire said softly, "Tess, he can cause trouble—"

Tess whirled around to her. "He can do nothing. We have Claude and his men take the herd. After the sale, he gets his share from his cattle. He pays his mortgage and keeps his ranch. We continue as we planned with our lives."

Claire bit at her bottom lip and nodded. She glanced at Jed, who frowned, seemingly deep in thought. In the back of her mind, Claire wondered what she would do.

The next morning, Tess woke to find Claire's side of the bed empty. She stretched and slipped out of bed.

"Claire? I don't smell coffee," she called out as she slipped into her jeans and shirt. She padded down the hall, rubbing her head.

Claire was not in the kitchen or anywhere else.

"Tess?"

She heard Jack's voice from the front door. He poked his head in.

"C'mon in, Jack. Have you seen your mother?"

Jack looked ill as he held up the note for Tess, who took it. "What's this?"

"Mom went to Helena."

"What?" Tess was completely confused; she opened the note and read it.

Darling Tess,

Forgive me. I cannot imagine putting your family through this, not after all you have done. I will leave the car at the train station. I have to go back to Helena and see about getting my old job back. It will be better this way.

In all my dreams, I never thought I could find such peace. Thank you for loving me.

> *Always,*
> *Claire*

"Why, Jack?" Tess asked in a dead voice.

"It's my father. I think if Telford finds out who he is, he'll cause trouble for you."

"Is your father that important?"

"I don't know. I just know he married into a rich family and he works for them. He's a lawyer. I think Mom figures if she leaves, Telford will back off. Maria found the note."

"Your mother is a silly woman."

"She loves us. She told me that. That's why she's doing it."

"I know, but she's still silly. She's taking the train. Damn that woman." She put her hand on Jack's shoulders. "I love your mother, and I'm bringing her back."

"She took the Jeep and the wagon won't start."

"Will you saddle Stella for me?"

Jack's grin spread across his face. "She's outside ready to go."

Tess laughed and pulled him into a fierce hug. "Don't worry. Everything will be fine." She ran to the bedroom and grabbed her boots. She was hopping on one foot as she struggled into them.

They both ran outside. "Go tell Dad, will you? Have him call the station and hold that train at Three Forks." Tess mounted Stella.

"Sure," Jack said and climbed up on Zeus.

Claire sat in a dejected heap by the window listening to the tourists. She glanced at her watch, wondering why they were pulling into the station and not going directly to Helena.

"This is what it must have been like," she heard a young woman say.

Claire looked over to see two women probably her age, smiling. Claire raised an eyebrow as she saw one woman reach over and hold the other's hand. Both smiled, and Claire saw the passion when their gazes met. She smiled sadly as she looked out the window.

"Folks, we're pulling into Three Forks, another little town from the Old West. Back in 1845..." Rick's voice called out, and all heads looked out the window. Filled with excitement, the tourists eagerly snapped photos.

"What in the world is that? A real cowboy?" a woman exclaimed.

Claire looked out the window and was shocked to see Tess galloping toward the train.

"Oh, God," she mumbled and slunk down in her seat.

"Uh, that's right. What would the Old West be without a real life cowboy?" Rick said and glared out the window.

The tourists snapped away with their cameras as Tess galloped alongside the chugging engine as it pulled into Three Forks.

"This is so exciting! Is this a train robbery?" an elderly lady asked as she watched.

As the train came to a stop, Tess pulled her hat low on her brow; Claire knew the stubborn pose. She nervously looked out the window as Tess peered through each pane. Spotting her, Tess narrowed her eyes and dismounted Stella.

"Rick, I believe you have someone in there that belongs to the Double R Ranch." Tess marched up the steps of the railcar.

The tourists applauded as Tess walked into the car. She was amazed and confused when Rick glared at her.

"You're gonna ruin this, Tess!" he hissed.

"I thought Dad called you."

"He did, but he didn't tell me you were charging in here like a bull," he whispered. He then gave his attention back to the tourists. "That's right folks, um, the Double R Ranch was once the biggest cattle ranch in southern Montana."

Tess looked down the aisle to see Claire hiding in the corner. "Claire Redmond, you're coming with me."

All heads turned as they watched the show.

Rick laughed nervously and cleared his throat. "Folks, that's Claire, the cook for the Double R Ranch. She won first place for her light and fluffy biscuits at the Fourth of July Rodeo in Silverhill. Held every year on the Fourth...of..." His voice trailed off, knowing he sounded like an idiot. He glared at Tess, who was laughing at his stumbling.

Tess marched to the seat where Claire was hiding. She glanced at the two women who were just staring at her in awe.

"Ladies," she said, touching the brim of her black Stetson.

"Oh, God." One young woman sighed.

"Claire, let's go. I'm taking you back."

"I do not belong to you, Tess Rawlins. I don't have to go anywhere."

"Um, there ya have it, folks. A good cook is almost as important as the cattle. All those hungry cowpokes..."

Tess turned her head and gave Rick a disturbed look.

"Cowpokes?" She turned back to Claire and grabbed her wrist.

"Let's go, Claire. I'm not kidding."

Claire struggled as Tess yanked her out of the seat.

"Oh, go, for godsakes!" the other young woman said eagerly. Both tourists were grinning wildly, snapping more photos.

The crowd laughed as Rick hid his eyes. Tess dragged Claire to the front of the railcar and gave Rick an apologetic look.

Rick glared at her with murder in his eyes as he cleared his throat. "Well, folks!" He continued sneering at his impetuous friend. "That's the show. Give a hand to Claire and Tess for giving us a bit of the Old West."

The tourists cheered and applauded. The two young women stood. "We're definitely coming back next year."

Tess grinned as she pulled Claire off the train. "Great, look us up." She tipped her hat once again. Claire then took a swing at her and knocked her Stetson sideways, much to the delight of the tourists.

Tess laughed in spite of the situation. She held Claire with one hand while she straightened her hat with the other. "The things I do for Claire's biscuits!"

"Those must be some biscuits," the young woman said.

"Okay, folks, that's just a little of what went on in the Old West. Now if you'll all settle back. We're headed for Helena..."

Tess heard Rick's voice fade off as the engine started to chug its way out of the station. Tess easily lifted Claire up on Stella and quickly mounted behind her, holding her around the waist.

"Sit still, Claire. We've got a ways to go, and I wouldn't want to drop you on your head," Tess whispered in her ear and pulled the reins on Stella. "And if I fall off this horse again, you're coming with me." The chestnut mare snorted and took off at a fast gallop across the grassland.

Jed paced back and forth waiting for Tess. Jack sat in silence at the kitchen table with Maria.

With that, they heard them riding up. Jed went to the kitchen door to see Tess gently helping Claire off Stella. She winced and rubbed her backside.

"I told you, me and animals don't get along!" she said angrily.

Tess hid her grin and reached for her. Claire wrenched her arm free and limped up the steps.

"You spooked her, Claire," Tess argued, trying not to laugh.

Claire ignored her as she walked passed Jed, who gave Tess a curious look. Tess waved her hand in dismissal and followed the sore woman.

Claire stood by the sink, filling a glass of water and rubbing her backside. Tess took off her hat and tossed it on the table. Both women glared at her, and she quickly hung it on the back of a chair.

"Okay, I want to know what's going on, why you were going to leave, and why in the hell you thought that was the only answer," Tess said, trying to control her anger.

"Jack's father is a very important man in Long Island. He married into a rich family. If Telford finds out about us, he could use that. Maybe he'll want Jack. I don't know." She helplessly sat back, wiping away the tears. "So you see why I must leave. They're already talking about us. If that Telford man will stop at nothing to get your land, then he may find out."

Tess walked over and knelt before Claire. She took her hand and held it tight. "The Rawlins family does not run from a fight. We're driving that herd to Colorado, and Jack's still coming with us. Even if Telford gets every other rancher in the whole goddamned state of Montana, we will finish this. You can't leave, Claire Redmond. We need you. I need you."

Claire hesitated for a moment, then buried her face in her hands and wept. Tess grinned slightly at Jack's horrified look. "Don't worry, Jack. She's just happy. Right?" Tess gently questioned. Claire only nodded, then threw her arms around Tess's neck in a fierce hug.

"S-so we're staying, right?" Jack asked hopefully as he looked around the room.

"Yes, son. You're all staying. We're a family, God help us," Jed said.

Maria smiled. "Emily and Stephen would be very happy and proud. It is good."

"Tess, did you check the route?" Jed asked.

Tess, Jack, and Jed rode the north pasture making the last-minute list of things to do before the morning drive. They all cantered along with Jack in the middle.

"Yes, Dad." Tess chewed on a piece of grass and winked at Jack.

"We have enough provisions, right? We'll be out for nearly three weeks."

"Yes, Dad."

"Now, Jack, you'll stay close to me for a while until you get used to riding the herd."

"Yes, sir." Now he winked at Tess.

"And Chuck will take the lead with Stan."

"Yes, Dad. Those chaps seem like they fit just fine, Jack."

"They do, thanks. I should wear them in the morning, too, right?" he asked, and Tess nodded as she chewed on the grass.

"Luke, Pedro, and Kyle will…"

Tess pulled the reins in on Stella and grinned. "Dad, you've been doing this every year. Relax."

"I know, I know. But this may be the last time we do this," he said thoughtfully as he looked around in the afternoon sun. "And I'd feel better if you were coming along."

"We discussed this. Claude's men will be there, too. You have plenty of men. I need to get the house in shape and check the Internet. Claire and I have a lot to do to get ready for our first guests. You'll be fine."

"So you turn the six bedrooms into a motel like for tourists."

"Right. They stay at the mansion. We offer meals, riding, fishing, hiking, and working the ranch. In the fall, we'll offer a real cattle drive for the more experienced riders. Folks will pay to do this, trust me. If you could have seen the people on the train yesterday, you'd believe me."

"So who's going to run this?" he asked seriously.

"Me and Claire," she said with equal seriousness. Neither saw the look of sadness on Jack's face. "We'll live in the mansion, if that's all right with you. Claire will take care of the cooking. Lord knows I can't."

"True."

"When do we leave?" Jack asked.

"Tomorrow, daybreak," he said. "Before everything starts and I don't get a chance, I just wanted to say how proud I am of you, son. After hearing what your life was like and not knowing your father, I'm impressed with the way you turned out. You're a fine young man."

Tess slapped Jack on the shoulder.

"What happens after this?" Jack asked.

"What do you mean?" Tess asked. She exchanged glances with Jed.

"I mean, what will I do? I want to stay on and work here, maybe try college."

"You and your mother are part of the family now," Tess said.

Jed now pulled the reins on his horse. "Tess is right. You're like a son, and no son of mine gets sent away. This is your home now."

Jack took a deep breath, and Tess knew he was trying not to cry.

"C'mon, brother. Let's ride."

Jed laughed as the two took off in a gallop. He pulled his hat down. "Wait for me!"

Claire and Maria were sitting in the kitchen idly talking. They heard the three of them ride up. Claire heard Tess's laughter and her heart beat wildly.

"Boy, it's hot!"

When Claire heard Jack's voice, she ran to the back door and flung it open. "Do not put your head in that trough!" she called out. Jack pulled a face. Tess laughed out loud. "You either, Tess Rawlins."

"I'll take care of the horses," Jack offered and led them to the stable.

"He looks so old. Goodness, are those Tess's chaps he's wearing?" Maria asked in amazement.

Claire nodded as Tess and Jed walked up the porch steps.

"You look like you're ready to drive the cattle now," Claire said as she looked at dusty father and daughter.

Tess took off her hat and hit it against her shirt and chaps. Dust flew everywhere.

A sharp rap on the screen door interrupted them. It was Ethan Drummond, sporting an evil grin.

Chapter 26

"Aren't you going to ask me in?" Ethan asked.

Tess sharply pushed open the screen door, nearly knocking his brown cowboy hat off his head.

"Good afternoon, Ethan," Claire said.

As Tess stepped back, Ethan walked in grinning.

"Hello, Claire. Thank you," he said. "I'd take off my hat, but Tess has already seen to it."

Tess clenched her teeth. "I'll be back. Nice seeing…"

"I think you may want to stay and hear this, Tess. You too, Mr. Rawlins."

"What can we do for you, Drummond?" Jed's voice was low and deliberate. "Have a seat."

"I'd rather stand. You may want to sit, however."

"What do you want?" Tess asked impatiently.

"I came here to tell you that you've been right all along to suspect Warren Telford's involvement regarding Steve's death."

"Explain," Jed said evenly.

"Quickly," Tess added for good measure.

"I know what you think of me, Tess. So just hear me out. It's true I went to work for Telford," he started, and Tess let out a sarcastic grunt, which Ethan ignored. "It's the reason I'm working for him that you don't know."

"I know, Ethan. Money, lousy money," Tess said angrily and took a step toward him.

Ethan sighed dramatically.

Jed stepped in as he watched Ethan. "Tess, let him finish. Then you can throw him through the screen door. Now go on, Drummond."

"Before Steve died, we were in Three Forks. He had just come from Sam Marks. The old guy told him some wild story, I guess. Steve believed him and was on his way to tell you, Mr. Rawlins, but he never got there," Ethan said.

A melancholy silence filled the kitchen. Tess fought the tears that caught in her throat as she saw the pained look on her father's face.

"He never told me what it was, only that everything was well documented."

"All this, then you went to work for Telford," Tess said as her anger mounted once again.

"I went to work for Telford last year after I went to the U.S. marshal's office again. The only way I could get them to come to Silverhill is if I had proof, concrete proof of his involvement," Ethan said, watching the reaction of everyone in the kitchen.

"And have you found this proof?" Jed asked in a low calm voice.

"Yes, sir, I believe I have, but I can't be sure."

Tess groaned suspiciously. "What's the proof?"

"There's a ledger in his bottom desk drawer. It's old and worn, and I believe that's what Sam was talking about to Steve. He also placed at least fifty thousand dollars in that pouch and locked it up. I thought that was odd, not to put it in the bank or at least in a vault. Telford then told me a particular story about this recent recession we're in. He told me about the small banks in this area that folded, but he didn't because he was smart and the bank was not. He had the money to buy the land and foreclose on the ranchers and farmers. Where would anyone get cash like that?"

Jed offered an explanation. "The same way my father did. He didn't trust banks. He kept all his money in his house in a safe. All of it. That's why we never lost the Double R during those years and the war years. My father didn't like Telford or his father for that matter."

"Telford had cash, so what?" Claire asked the obvious. "That didn't make him a criminal. A greedy old man, but not a criminal."

Tess chuckled as did the others.

"But where would he get that much money?" Ethan asked.

"I suppose that ledger would tell us," Tess said.

Ethan shot her a small smile. "So you believe me?"

She looked at Ethan and smiled grudgingly. "I suppose so. But if you're lying, I will still throw you through the nearest door," she said and meant every word.

Jed cleared his throat. "What does all this have to do with Stephen? I mean, the ledger is one thing, but proving he murdered Stephen is another."

"I hesitate telling you…"

"Bad choice of words," Tess interrupted as she clenched her fists.

"For just that reason, Tess. I can see being a college professor has done nothing for that hot-headed temper I remember from my youth."

"Get on with it, Drummond," Jed said firmly.

"Telford just about came out and told me he had Steve killed. He said I had one thing to learn. Always have someone in your back pocket…."

"Fucking Pat Hayward! I knew it!" Tess bellowed. Claire winced and tried to calm Tess.

Tess still fumed. "Let's go into town right now. I want to beat that little whelp…"

Jed kept silent and watched Ethan Drummond. "Gets it from her mama's side of the family. They're all high-strung," Jed said evenly, never taking his eyes off Ethan. "How did he get Pat?"

"It appears Pat got some underage girl pregnant. He needed money to take care of it, but the girl died," Ethan said in a quiet voice.

Tess nearly flipped the kitchen table over, and Claire had enough. She took Tess by the arm. "Tess, I understand your anger, everyone in the room understands it, but you need to keep a level head now, please. Think of what you're doing."

Tess said nothing as she stood there, red faced and breathing like a bull.

"Please," Claire amended softly. Tess blinked back her anger and nodded.

"Okay, Ethan. Finish up, then tell us how to get that ledger," Tess said.

"Well, that is about it. We can all surmise that Telford had Stephen killed and Pat was in on it from the beginning. Steve had told me that he went to Pat with this information from Sam. H-he knew all along. I suppose he went to Telford with it."

Jed took a deep sad breath as Maria put her arm around him. Tess clung to Claire's hand. Poor Jack stood by the door the entire time, mouth gaping and eyes bulging.

"I've already called the district attorney's office in Helena and explained the situation. He's sending a U.S. marshal in this afternoon at three. Telford and I are to see the two ranchers that have sided with him against you and your family at four o'clock. I believe your presence there is obvious, but not mandatory, according to the DA. They are coming only to question Pat Hayward and Telford."

"So we really don't have anything without that ledger or..." Jed stopped, then grinned. "Or someone who will testify to everything."

All eyes were on Jed. Tess watched him carefully. "Dad, I see that look. What are you thinking?"

Jed looked at Jack. "Saddle my horse, would you please?" he asked in a quiet voice, too quiet for Tess.

"Dad, you can't ride into town and—"

"Tess, you're my daughter and I love you. But I'm still your father and the head of this house."

Tess said nothing as Jed turned to Jack once again. "Saddle my horse, son."

"Yes, sir," Jack said.

As he made a dash for the door, Tess stopped him. "Saddle Stella, too."

Jack glanced at Claire, who nodded. "Okay," he said and ran out the door.

"Um, just what are you planning?" Ethan asked, looking back and forth from father to daughter.

"Tess and I are riding into town," he said simply. "To pay a visit on this fine day."

207

"Why not let me drive you?"

Tess nearly laughed at Ethan's terrified tone. She looked at the stubborn set jaw of her father. "We're riding," Tess said. "And my ass will never be the same," she mumbled.

"Oh, God," Ethan groaned. "You're not packin' any shootin' irons, are ya?" he asked sarcastically.

Claire bit her lip to avoid laughing.

A smile tugged at the corner of Jed's mouth. "You disturb me, young fella. I worry you're not taking Telford seriously. You'd better." Jed turned to Maria and Claire. "We'll be back by supper." He put his arm around Claire's shoulder and kissed her cheek.

Tess kissed her on the cheek, as well. "Don't worry."

"I'll worry if I want," Claire said.

Ethan walked up to Claire. "I'll be fine, Claire."

When he leaned in to kiss Claire on the cheek, Tess grabbed him by the back collar. "Let's go," she said sternly. "Young fella," she added sarcastically and pushed him out the door.

Ed Chambers stood in the stall, brushing down the black mare, whistling a happy tune. He heard the stable door open and casually looked up. He then dropped the brush. "Mr. Rawlins, Tess. Uh, how are you?"

Tess followed Jed as he slowly walked up to the stall. "Hey, Ed. Long time. How's business?" he asked as she picked up a bridle and examined it.

"Fine. Fine, sir. Business couldn't be better. I've got nearly ten horses now. My name's getting out there, so..." His voice trailed off as he swallowed, his gaze darting back and forth from the elder Rawlins, who was staring a hole right through him, to Tess, who was now examining the saddles.

"That's good. I'm glad to see you're doing so well. It would be a shame if something went wrong," Jed said evenly.

Ed looked terrified. So was Tess; she had no idea where her father was going with this.

"Wrong? Like what...?"

"Like a small stable fire," Jed said. "We had a bad one about a year ago. Ya gotta watch out for leaky lanterns."

Ed stood as tall as his shaking body would allow. "You Rawlinses can't come in here and threaten me."

"That's not a threat, son. A threat would be like... Oh, say, I'm gonna beat the living tar out of you and drag you behind my horse through the middle of town." Jed continued, his voice rising with each word. "That would be a threat."

Tess didn't know if she should laugh at Ed's expression or be scared shitless along with him.

"W-what do you want?" Ed asked as the sweat dripped down his neck.

Jed grinned happily. "See? That's all I wanted to hear. Would you like to help us?"

Ed nodded frantically.

"Well, thank you, Ed. That's very neighborly of you. I accept your offer." Jed sat on a bale of hay. "Now since you're so willing to help, this is what I want..."

Ethan parked his convertible by the bank. He stood by his car and checked his watch. 3:10. Just then, an unfamiliar car pulled into town. The driver parked by the sheriff's office. As the driver got out, he looked around and spotted Ethan, who gave him a short wave and nodded. The taller man acknowledged him and touched the brim of his white cowboy hat.

With that, Ethan looked up to see the Rawlinses. They sat tall in their saddles as they trotted down the wide town road with Ed Chambers riding in the middle, sporting a sick, pale look. Ethan shook his head.

"Geezus." He glanced at his watch once again. "Nope, not high noon." He looked around and wondered if Black Bart was lurking in the shadows.

He laughed quietly to himself. Though he scoffed at Jed Rawlins's old ways, inwardly, he admired him and Tess. He wished he had that security, that strength of purpose in his life. He hoped what he was doing here would give him that. He nodded slightly, acknowledging both Rawlinses, then headed down to the bank and Warren Telford. He would love to be in the sheriff's office, if for nothing else than to see Tess fly off in a rage and cram

Ed Chambers and Pat Hayward's collective heads through the cell bars. It might happen.

Tom walked out of the store just as Jed and Tess rode by with Ed. "Jed, what's the occasion? Business or pleasure?"

"Both, Tom," Jed said, and Tess chuckled. They stopped at the sheriff's office. The tall man in the white hat tipped his brim.

"Mr. Rawlins?"

Jed dismounted and nodded. "You're the U.S. marshal?"

Ed groaned pathetically as he dismounted.

"Yep. John McComb from Helena," he said and shook Jed's hand. He looked at Tess.

"This is my daughter, Tess."

"Miss Rawlins." McComb shook her offered hand.

"This is Ed Chambers. He can shed some light on the situation," Jed offered and patted Ed on the back. Ed smiled weakly and nodded.

McComb smiled slightly. "Ya look a little sick there, pal. Y'all all right?"

"Fine," Ed said in a dull voice.

McComb patted his breast pocket. "I've got a little something from the Circuit Court of Helena. Seems a concerned citizen offered some information on the death of your son, Mr. Rawlins. I'm here to find out what exactly happened."

Jed's jaw twitched as he nodded. "It's about time, Marshal."

"I'm sure it is, sir. Let's have a talk with Sheriff Hayward."

As they walked into the sheriff's office, Pat Hayward rocked in his desk hair, his hands clasped behind his head. Tess grinned. Life was good, eh, Pat? she thought. He sat forward quickly when the heavy door closed.

He looked from one to the other. His eyes widened when they stopped at the panic-stricken Ed Chambers.

"Jed, Tess," he said in a shaky voice.

"Pat," Jed said evenly. Tess said nothing.

"Sheriff Hayward, I'm John McComb, U.S marshal. I have a few questions for you," he said professionally. "May I sit down?"

"Oh, sure. Please," Pat fumbled and avoided Ed completely.

Tess was glad to see the fine sheen of perspiration forming on his weak upper lip.

"Thank you. I'd like to talk to you about Mr. Warren Telford and his involvement in the death of Stephen Rawlins."

Tess folded her arms across her chest and looked into his eyes. Jed didn't flinch. Pat Hayward looked as if he might faint.

McComb put on a pair of reading glasses. "Now, Mr. Chambers…"

"They threatened me!" Ed blurted out and pointed to Jed and Tess.

McComb looked up over his glasses. "They did?"

"Y-yes, they said they'd set my stable on fire if I didn't help them."

"That is just not true," Tess said, appalled at the idea.

"Be very careful, Mr. Chambers. What were their exact words?"

"I don't remember exactly. I…"

"I do," Jed said. "I told him I was glad his business was doing so well, and I'd hate to see anything happen."

"Right!" Ed accused and pointed a finger at Jed.

"Then he said last year we had a small stable fire and it'd be a shame if something happened like that when business is so good," Tess offered innocently.

"Right! That's what he said," Ed accused again and pointed at Jed.

McComb scratched his head. "Seems to me like they're just being concerned neighbors. Now, Mr. Chambers, why are you here?" He looked right at him.

For the next twenty minutes, Ed spilled his worthless guts. Pat Hayward nervously pulled at his eyebrow; Tess knew his time was up. When Ed finished, Tess stood close to her father, in case he wanted to carry out his threat.

"Sheriff Hayward, I'd like to know what you have to add to this," McComb said evenly. He, too, was trying to control his anger.

In the end, Pat Hayward sang like a canary.

Ethan sat in Warren Telford's office lounging in the chair by the window. He listened as Telford puffed anxiously on his cigar. Ethan smirked. He's actually nervous, Ethan thought happily.

"So, gentlemen, we agree. What goes on at the Double R Ranch is not how we want our community represented. We have a fine Christian community that does not tolerate decadence or perverted marriages. If we stand together, Jed Rawlins and his 'family' will have no other choice but to see this and go somewhere else... Like California." He laughed.

"Warren, I don't know. The Double R has been here from the beginning. Old Ned started it. My grandfather remembers him—"

"Enough with the Rawlins family!" Telford bellowed. "I'm sick to death of them! You're either with me on this or you're against me," he said as he leaned in. "And believe me, you don't want to be against me."

Both men shifted uncomfortably in their seats. Ethan was oddly amazed at the control this old man had over people. Well, not everyone. Speaking of which, he looked out the window to see Pat Hayward looking very ill walking ahead of the marshal. Taking up the rear were Tess and Jed. Ethan shook his head once again and smiled inwardly.

They looked like something straight out of a John Wayne movie. Both wearing chaps, they looked like they were ready for the last roundup, which they were. Ethan shook his head. The Rawlinses...

"You think about his, gentlemen. I'll be in touch with you." Both ranchers quickly stood and walked out. Telford puffed on his cigar, looking like the cat that ate the canary. Ethan preened inwardly. Your day is done, Telford, he thought happily.

"I'll see you in the morning, Drummond," he said, dismissing him abruptly as he walked out of his office.

Tess saw Warren Telford as he walked through the bank. She saw the confused glance when he looked at the U.S. marshal and Pat. His confused look turned nervous, and inwardly Tess couldn't be happier. They all met at the glass double doors.

"Good afternoon, Sheriff," Telford said evenly.

"Mr. Warren Telford?" McComb asked.

"Yes, and you are?" Telford asked as he puffed on his cigar.

"John McComb, U.S marshal. I have a court order here, Mr. Telford. It says the state of Montana thinks you might know something about the death of Stephen Rawlins. Sheriff Hayward, Ed Chambers, and I had a little talk, and it seems Stephen Rawlins's horse didn't throw him. If you'll come with me, sir."

Telford glanced behind McComb to see Jed and Tess watching him. Tess grinned and wriggled her fingers in a wave. Pat was squirming.

"I will not. I have nothing to say to you or anyone else. The sheriff and the coroner determined that the Rawlins boy was thrown from his horse. Just try to prove I was anywhere near that south pasture. I have dozens of witnesses who will testify as to my whereabouts that night."

"Sir, you'd best come with me. I'm bound by the state of Montana to bring you in, and since Sheriff Hayward here will be joining you…"

"You idiot! What did you tell them? Whatever it was, he's lying," Warren Telford bellowed as he pushed by McComb and headed out the doors.

Jed was quicker than McComb was. He grabbed his old nemesis by the back of the collar and yanked him back. Telford reared around and took a healthy swing, catching Jed in the jaw.

All at once, mayhem broke out in the Silverhill Bank.

Chapter 27

"I can't wait any longer, Maria, I'm going into town. I have a bad feeling here." Claire grabbed for the keys to the Jeep.

"Chuck has the Jeep, Mom, and the old car won't start."

"Damn it!" Claire exclaimed.

"We'll have to ride, Claire," Maria said. Jack jumped up and dashed to the stable to saddle the horses.

"Maria, I-I can't ride a horse," Claire said seriously.

Maria rolled her eyes.

"It'll be fine. It's only a short distance. Come quickly."

Jack led three saddled horses from the stable. "I'll help you up, Mom."

Claire tentatively walked up to the horse. "Nice horse," Claire whispered stupidly. Smelling her fear, the horse snorted and backed up. "Ah!" Claire screamed and backed up, as well.

Jack tried not to laugh. "C'mon, Mom." He held the horse.

Maria gently took Claire by the arm and held the stirrup for her. "Up you go. For heaven's sake, Claire, you're going to spend the rest of your life on a ranch." She grunted as Claire tried to mount the snorting beast.

She got halfway up poor Daphne while Jack steadied the petrified horse.

"Oh…" she whined as Maria threw Claire's leg over.

"Now just hold on to the reins and clench your legs to the horse's side. Don't you dare fall off," Maria threatened as she expertly swung up on the mare.

Claire held the reins as if she was holding a soiled diaper. Maria rolled her eyes and slapped Daphne on the flank. As the horse took off, Jack and Maria watched for a second as Claire screamed and bounced horribly in the saddle.

"She looks ridiculous. Come, Jack, before she kills herself."

Jack laughed as they took off, easily catching up to Claire, who was still bouncing and screaming and bouncing and...

By the time they rode into Silverhill, Claire had stopped screaming but was still bouncing. As they trotted down the middle of the street, they heard a horrendous crash.

Warren Telford had just flown through the glass doors of the Silverhill Bank. Right behind him was Jed. He angrily reached down and picked up the groaning man as the glass crunched beneath his boots.

"C'mon, get up," Jed encouraged with a grunt, then lifted Telford to his feet. He punched him again.

"Oh, my God," Claire exclaimed.

Maria shook her head. "Fighting like two school boys."

"A real live cowboy fight," Jack said with enthusiasm.

With that, McComb, Pat, and Tess ran out. "Dad!" Tess called as he was about to hit Telford again.

"You and your family," Pat spat out, and Tess whirled to face him. "Why did you have to come back from California? You should have stayed out there, fucking the female population. Claire Redmond's no better, her and her bastard son..."

That was it.

Tess reared back, and with a low growl that seemed to come from her soul, she punched Pat square in the face. His eyes crossed and he folded like a bad poker hand. He slid as if he had no backbone at all, which he didn't, unconscious before he hit the ground.

"Shit! Damn! Shit!" Tess cursed as she wrung and flexed her bruised hand.

Jed had stopped beating Telford, who was slumped against the building. McComb held him up.

"I want to press charges," Telford said angrily as he spat out a tooth.

"Didn't see a thing," McComb said and hauled him toward the sheriff's office. He easily picked up Pat by the back of the neck, dragging both men. "Mr. Rawlins, I'm not sure when the hearing will be…"

"Marshal, I'm driving my cattle to Colorado tomorrow." He looked to see the rest of his family. "I'll be back in three weeks…" He then looked at a few of his neighbors who were standing there watching the two ranch owners who sided with Telford. Tess came up to him and handed him his hat. Setting it firmly on his head, he put his arm around Tess's shoulder.

"You know where to find me. On *my ranch* with *my family,*" he finished emphatically, then flexed his bruised jaw.

"Let's go home, Dad," Tess said.

Jed gave her a sturdy hug and let her go.

Ethan Drummond leaned against his convertible. Tess saw him and hesitated for a moment before walking over with Jed.

"Drummond, I'm indebted to you, son." Jed held out his hand.

Ethan took the offering, then looked at Tess.

"I'm sorry, Ethan. Thank you. I mean that sincerely." She pulled him into a strong embrace.

"I miss Stephen, Tess, and I'm glad it's over," he whispered in her ear and hugged her once more.

Tess pulled back and nodded. She then turned and grinned happily at the three riders. She gave Claire a disturbed look. "What are you doing up there?"

"Don't be so smug. I'm in pain. I think I may have broken something of great value," Claire complained.

Tess laughed and easily swung up behind her. With a whistle, Stella came trotting over to them.

Claire glared at the cocky grin. "Okay, okay. I don't have a way with animals. I told you."

Tess reached around her and grabbed the reins. "But you do have a way with me, Claire Redmond. And that's all that matters," she whispered in her ear. Claire shivered as she held onto the pommel. "Let's go home."

"We couldn't have scripted this better, Dad," Tess said and motioned to the setting sun.

Jed laughed as the Rawlins family rode out of Silverhill at sunset.

"This is just too cool," Jack said as he rode next to Claire and Tess.

As they passed by, Jack noticed Rebecca Riley standing outside her father's hardware store. She grinned and waved. Jack completely avoided Tess and Claire. He couldn't hide his blushing smile as he touched the brim of his Stetson in her direction.

"Seems like a nice girl," Claire said. Tess tightened her arm around her waist.

Jack shrugged as he looked straight ahead. "I guess."

Tess looked back, then leaned closer. "She's still standing there watching you."

"She is?" Jack asked, the grin spreading across his tanned face. He sat taller in the saddle as they rode out of town.

"I missed it?" Chuck sat in a dejected heap.

Tess laughed. "Yep. And you missed Claire on a horse."

Claire closed her eyes and said nothing.

"That must have been better than a sock on the jaw," Chuck admitted. "Seriously, we always thought Telford had something to do with Steve's death, and I'm glad it's over. What a horrible man."

Jed reached over and took Tess's hand. She couldn't get over how strong it felt, even though it was trembling slightly. "It's over, Tess. I think Steve can rest now with your mother. I know I can rest." Tears welled in his eyes as Tess held on tight.

"It's a relief to know the truth. Now, Chuck, is everything ready for tomorrow?"

"Yep. Claude's men are watching the herd."

There was silence around the table until Jed spoke. "This might be the last time we do this. Let's make sure everything goes smoothly."

"It will. It always does. Claire and I will be waiting here for you. By the time you get back, we'll have the house ready and the Double R Guesthouse and Ranch will be raring to go."

Jed smiled and patted her hand. "I know it will, sweetie."

"But for now, I have a few papers to go over." Tess stood and kissed the top of his head.

It was quite a domesticated scene laid out before Tess later that evening as she sat at the desk going over the bills. Jack lay sprawled out in front of the fire; Claire was reading, absently twirling her hair between her fingers. Tess smiled at her deep concentration as she flipped the page and marveled at how content they both seemed. What was more revealing was how comfortable Tess felt watching them.

In a few short months, she had come to care for Claire in a way she never thought she would. The idea of falling in love was not averse to her, just falling in love at this time in her life. On the verge of being fifty, Tess thought the days of romance were long gone. And now, sitting there deep in thought was Claire Redmond. She couldn't help the smile that spread across her face as she sat back and gazed at Claire while she read. What a gift, she thought. How she deserved Claire, Tess would never know, but there it was—her life a few feet away from her.

As if reading her mind, Claire looked up and cocked her head. Tess grinned, and like a dope, she waved. Claire chuckled and waved in return, then winked. With that one seemingly innocuous gesture, Tess's heart fluttered, so much so, she had to catch her breath.

Claire started to say something when Jed walked down the hall and into the living room.

"Look what I found," he said.

He was holding a leather-bound book. To Tess, it looked to be the size of a paperback book. It was then she realized what it was. "I thought you went to bed. Uncle Jeremiah's book?"

Jed sat by the fire and nodded. "Yep." He looked at Jack, who was now kneeling by his side. "This was written by my uncle, Tess's great-uncle. He's the one responsible for the south pasture. He developed the seed for the grass and the alfalfa that's growing there now."

Tess stood behind him and looked over his shoulder at the handwritten pages. As if she were ten years old, she remembered how her uncle would read from his memoir about how the ranch was started by his father Ned Rawlins in 1886 when he went to Missoula and gambled the money he earned as a ranch hand and won enough to purchase the land and turn it into one of the wealthiest cattle ranches in Montana.

Jack was enthralled as he listened to Jed read aloud. Claire and Tess sat on the hearth and listened, as well. At one point, Jed stopped and gazed into space. Tess exchanged a worried glance with Claire, but Jack didn't notice Jed's confused look.

"What a great story, go on," Jack said, still kneeling by his side. "What's wrong?"

Tess could see the tears sparkle in her father's eyes when he looked at Jack. The sad smile had her near tears, as well. "Nothing, son. Why don't you read for a while?"

"Are you sure?" Jack reverently took the book when Jed handed it to him.

Jed put his head back and stared at the log-beamed ceiling, a ghost of a smile flashed across his face.

Jack cleared this throat and started reading, "I remember Dad telling us how he won the Double R on a hand of poker in a saloon in Missoula." Jack laughed. "This is so cool." He turned the page and continued. "He had enough to buy a thousand acres, including the south pasture. And now, he could marry Lucy Rogers. In time, he purchased another four thousand acres and built the big house for my mother and the five children she bore."

As he continued, Tess felt Claire's hand in hers, giving it an affectionate squeeze. Jed closed his eyes and was asleep within minutes.

"Jack," Claire whispered.

Jack stopped and followed Claire's look. Jed was softly snoring, so Jack closed the book and placed it on the table. He gathered the afghan and placed it over Jed, who stirred and opened his eyes. "Steve?" he whispered.

The look on Jack's face broke Tess's heart.

"Yes, sir," he whispered. "C'mon, we have a big day tomorrow. We gotta get the herd to Colorado. You need to get to bed."

Jed groaned and stood. "You need to get some sleep, too, Jack. G'night."

"Do you think it would be okay if I read this some more?"

Jack asked.

"Sure, son."

"I'll be very careful with it. I'm going to bed."

He kissed Claire on the cheek, and to Tess's surprise, he kissed her, as well. "G'night."

Tess was stunned as she watched him walk away. She turned to Claire, who was wiping her eyes. "If he doesn't stop making me cry."

Tess put her arm around Claire's shoulders. "He's a good kid."

"I could use a cup of coffee, c'mon." Claire pulled at Tess's hand.

"And I'm sure there's some pie left, as well."

"What do you think is going on with Jed?" Claire asked as she cut the pie, placing it on a plate.

Tess took the offering. "It's been happening for the past few weeks. He gets that faraway look, almost like he's confused. He's called me by my mother's name more than once."

"You know he's called Jack by your brother's name, as well." Claire sat opposite Tess and drank her coffee. "I'm sure I know what you're thinking."

"I'm sure you do. And I hate to think about it."

"Maybe he's just tired and needs to rest and not worry about anything."

Tess heard the hopeful tone and tried to believe it. She took a deep breath and let it out slowly. "Maybe. But I have to be realistic about it. He's had a heart attack and he's nearly seventy. I know that's not that old…" She drank her coffee and changed the topic. "Well, Jack seemed interested in my uncle's memoirs."

"Yes. He loves this place, Tess."

"Do you?"

Claire smiled; she reached over and took Tess's hand. "Yes, I love this place, and I love you."

"I'm not interrupting, am I?"

Both women looked up to see Jed standing in the doorway.

"Of course not. Sit down. I think there's one piece of pie left that your daughter hasn't eaten."

"Surprise, surprise," Jed said, sitting at the head of the table.

"You two are hysterical." Tess saw how tired he looked but said nothing. "I thought you went to bed again."

"I need to talk to you." Jed smiled at Claire when she placed the pie in front of him.

"I think I'll go to bed. You two don't stay up too late," Claire said.

"No, Claire, please stay. I didn't mean to exclude you because this involves you, as well."

Claire sat and glanced at Tess, who was frowning as she watched her father.

"Lately, I've been noticing certain things happening to me." He looked at Tess and held up his hand. "Let me finish, Tess. I'm forgetting things, and I'm getting tired so quickly. I know I gotta go see Doc, and I'm not looking forward to it. But I'm no fool, either." He stopped and took a bite of pie. "This is good, Claire. You're a fantastic cook. We'd be lost without you. Wouldn't we, Tess?"

Tess smiled and agreed. "Completely."

Claire blushed and drank her coffee. Jed looked at both women and nodded. "And Jack is an enormous help on the ranch. He's learned so quickly, he's a smart boy. Reminds me so much of Stephen."

The last sentence hung in the air around them until Jed continued. "I want you and Jack to stay on here at the ranch. It's good for Jack. He can finish school, then we'll talk about college. He says he loves to write, and I'd hate to see that go to waste. He says he also loves ranching. Tess found she could do both, college and the ranch, maybe someday Jack will feel the same."

Claire placed her hand on Jed's arm. "Jed, I appreciate what you're saying. To be honest, Jack loves it here, and so do I." She avoided Tess's grin and continued, "But Maria…"

Jed smiled and patted her hand. "Maria is part of the family. There's no worrying about her. You and Jack are part of the family now, too, Claire. I know how you two feel or how you're beginning to feel about each other." He looked at Tess and Claire. "So we stay together and work this out."

He stood and picked up his plate. "I'm taking my pie and going to bed. G'night, ladies."

"Good night, Jed. And thank you," Claire said.

"G'night, Dad," Tess said. He patted Tess on the shoulder as he walked away.

As they sat in silence, Jack walked in the back door. "Hi."

Claire smiled. "Hi, sweetie. Can't sleep?"

Jack shrugged. "No. I...I just wanted to say thanks for letting me do this, Mom." He had his hands in his pockets as he leaned against the kitchen counter.

"It's time for you. Just please be careful."

Tess laughed along with Jack. "I will. I promise."

"Thanks for being my mom and taking care of me," he said.

Claire stood and opened her arms. Jack flew into them. Tess wiped her eyes, saying nothing. "Don't ever thank me for loving you, Jack. You're my son." She pulled back. "Now you get some sleep." She reached up and touched his cheek.

"Okay. See ya in three weeks. Take care of her, Tess."

"I will. Have fun."

Jack quickly walked out; Claire took a few steps toward the door, then she stopped. "He's no longer my boy."

Tess walked up behind her and put her hands on her shoulders. Claire turned around, threw her arms around Tess's neck, and sobbed. Tess encircled her waist and held on, murmuring soft words of love into her silky hair.

"He'll always be your boy, sweetheart," Tess said.

The moonlight bathed the bedroom, casting a shadowy light on Tess's face as she slept. Claire lay on her side watching her. She reached over and brushed the blond hair away from her face. Tess stirred in her sleep, letting out a gentle snore, and Claire ignored the urge to lean over and kiss her. Instead, she slipped out of bed and into her robe.

She took a deep breath of pristine Montana air as she stood on the porch. It was late August, and the night was humid, but the breeze that blew over the grassland seemed to cool her overheated body. Claire laughed and rolled her eyes thinking of their lovemaking just a short time ago. Tess was an ardent lover, and Claire reveled in her romantic touch.

"How lucky am I?" she whispered into the night, pulling her robe around her.

With Jack and the rest of them driving the herd to Colorado, it seemed too quiet, but she welcomed the time alone with Tess. The crickets chirped and the night birds called. In the moonlight, she could see the snow-capped Bitterroots and hear the water rippling in the stream behind the house.

These things haven't changed in decades, she thought. How many women have stood on this porch, with their partners sleeping inside, contemplating how lucky they were to be part of the Rawlins family and how they loved their men and this prairie? During her summer here, Claire had grown as much as her son. She found love, true and abiding love in Tess Rawlins. Jack suddenly became a man, who also loved this family and the land. Claire had left her old life behind and stepped into a world of honest, compassionate love. Tess did this for her; she awakened feelings Claire had no idea existed.

She gazed at the grassland shimmering in the moonlight. She smiled when Jack told her how Tess recalled her childhood and how she would lie in the tall grass watching the clouds drift by, feeling as though she was swimming in a sea of grass.

Claire grinned when she heard the screen door creak. She gasped when she felt Tess's warm arms wrap around her waist. "Did I wake you?"

"Nope," Tess whispered against her ear. "I rolled over and got nothing but pillow."

Claire laughed and leaned back into her body, resting her head against Tess's shoulder.

"Whatcha thinkin'?"

"How lucky I am to be part of all this."

"You may not feel like that when we have a house full of guests waiting on dinner."

Claire tightened the arms around her. "That day will come, Tess. This is a good idea." She turned in Tess's arms, snaking her hands behind her neck. "You saved everyone."

Tess shook her head. "No, darlin'. You saved me from a life of loneliness, and Jack saved me from saddle sores."

Claire laughed and pulled her down for a tender kiss. Claire nodded and pulled away. "Will this be the end of it?" Claire asked, thinking of the cattle drive.

Tess turned to her. She searched the pretty face she loved, then kissed her lightly on the lips. "It's just the beginning, Claire Redmond. Rawlins and Redmond, the Double R Ranch. We're next. It's our time and we'll make it work. Then it'll be Jack's turn, and it'll go on and on forever."

Epilogue

"You have to stop crying at some point, honey," Tess said, holding Claire's hand tightly.

Claire nodded and wiped her eyes as she looked at the stage. It was a beautiful Montana summer afternoon with not a cloud in the sky. The sunlight filtered through the trees, shading them from the heat, although Chuck and Pedro fanned themselves with the program handout.

Jed turned to Pedro. "This is a wonderful day for you."

Pedro nodded, and Claire could tell he was fighting to keep his emotions in check. Jed leaned over Tess and placed his shaky hand on Claire's arm. "I'm so proud right now, Claire."

Again Claire nodded, clinging to Tess's strong hand. "I am too, Jed." She looked at Tess through her tears, watching the summer wind blow through her blond hair, now shimmering with a few strands of silver. In this unguarded moment, Tess smiled, her tears welling in her blue eyes as she kept her gaze on the stage.

"I love you, Tess Rawlins," Claire whispered.

Tess looked at her then and winked. "You have absolutely no choice in the matter, sweetheart. You're stuck."

"Thank God for that."

Tess leaned over and kissed her cheek. "Thank God for you."

The dean of Milburn College addressed the audience, beginning the commencement ceremony. While everyone listened to his speech, Claire had eyes for only one person. In the front row, sitting tall and looking far too grownup, was Jack. On his right was Rebecca, and on his other side, Pedro's son, Manny. Claire smiled as she remembered how they became friends through these years—good friends that would last a lifetime.

When Jack's gaze locked with hers, Claire smiled. The flood of memories that flashed before her eyes were so thick she could barely see Jack. What she saw was the happy baby he was and the gentle yet strong man he had become while living on the ranch. She remembered how Tess and her family changed their lives that April morning years ago when she first laid eyes on Tess Rawlins at the bus depot and fell in love. She could say that with absolute surety now after all these years. For Tess had found the way to Claire's heart, and from that day forward, there were daisies on the kitchen table for Claire; there was no doubt they would love each other the rest of their lives.

She glanced over at Jed, his eyes glistening as Jack, who he regarded as his own son, received his diploma. Along with the rest of the family, Claire knew Jed's mind had been slowly slipping these past few years, and someday he would be reduced to remembering nothing at all. But, God bless Jack, who would take the leather-bound memoirs of Jeremiah Rawlins, and retell the beginning of the Double R Ranch. He would sit by the fire and read it over and over, willing Jed not to forget. It was, at times, heartbreaking for her and Tess to watch.

"That's my boy," Jed whispered now as he watched.

Yes, Claire thought, that's our boy.

With the diplomas handed out, Jack, Rebecca, and Manny made their way through the crowd of graduates and family to where they stood. Claire hugged him so fierce around the neck Jack made a laughing strangling noise and tried to keep his graduation cap on his head. Tess laughed along and gently pulled Claire away.

Jack leaned down and kissed her on the cheek. He turned to Tess, and as he kissed her, he whispered, "Thank you for loving my mother."

Tess pulled back and swallowed. "My honor by far, Jack."

It was then Claire noticed the book Jack was holding. "What is that?" Claire asked, wiping her eyes.

Jack held the book reverently in his hand and stood in front of Jed. "This is for you, Jed."

Jed looked confused as he took the book. He put on his glasses and read the cover. He was speechless as he looked from the book to Jack. "Sea of Grass," he whispered. "By Jack Redmond?"

Claire was stunned. "Jack, how in the world did you find the time to write a book?"

"Much less get it published," Tess added, completely in awe as she looked on with the rest of them.

"I've been working on it for three years. With Manny and Rebecca's help, we took the memoirs from your Uncle Jeremiah. It wasn't too hard. He did all the work. The college agreed to publish it and keep it in the library. It'll never be forgotten."

Claire's heart ached when she heard Jack's voice tremble.

"I cannot believe you did this, son," Jed said; he took off his glasses and cleaned them on his shirt. "Damned glasses."

Everyone turned around when Chuck sniffed loudly and blew his nose in his handkerchief.

"Read the dedication, Jack." Rebecca slipped her arm through his.

Claire saw the look of pure devotion in Rebecca's eyes as she looked at Jack. This is good, she thought, and looked at Tess who must have seen the look, as well. She smiled and wrapped her arm around Claire's shoulders.

Jack opened the book, but when he read, he looked at Jed. "To Jed Rawlins, who I've loved as the father I never knew and who graciously loved me as the son he had lost. I will remember how he taught me to fight for family and what you believe in, how he told me of generations before him who out of a simple act of faith and love started a cattle ranch and fed a starving nation through two world wars and who took five thousand acres of lonesome Montana prairie and nurtured it into a sea of grass."

About the author

Kate Sweeney, a 2010 Alice B. Medal winner, was the 2007 recipient of the Golden Crown Literary Society award for Debut Author for *She Waits*, the first in the *Kate Ryan Mystery* series. The series also includes *A Nice Clean Murder, The Trouble with Murder,* a 2008 Golden Crown Award Winner for Mystery, *Who'll Be Dead for Christmas?* and *Of Course It's Murder*.

Other novels include *Away from the Dawn, Survive the Dawn, Residual Moon,* a 2008 Golden Crown Award Winner for Speculative Fiction, *The O'Malley Legacy* and *Winds Of Heaven*. She is also a contributing author for the anthology *Wild Nights: (Mostly) True Stories of Women Loving Women*, published by Bella Books.

Born in Chicago, Kate resides in Villa Park, Illinois, where she works as an office manager—no glamour here, folks; it pays the bills. Humor is deeply embedded in Kate's DNA. She sincerely hopes you will see this when you read her novels, short stories, and other works by visiting her Web site at www.katesweeneyonline.com. E-mail Kate at ksweeney22@aol.com.

You may also enjoy:

Winds of Heaven
by Kate Sweeney
Price: $16.95

After the untimely death of a former lover, Casey Bennet receives a letter from Julie's lawyer, begging Casey to help Julie's partner, Liz Kennedy, and their adorable, yet precocious three-year old, Skye, who are now alone.

An avowed bachelorette, Casey has no idea what's in store when she grudgingly agrees to help Liz, who, by the way, is also pregnant and due in four months.

Casey, Liz, and little Skye find themselves in for a hilarious, tender ride that will change their lives forever.